PRAISE FOR WHAT WAITS BELOW

"I read *What Waits Below* in one bleary-eyed sitting, and I swear by the end the words were wriggling right off the page. I thought I was devouring it, but nope, this book devoured me. First, it burrows. Then it erupts, taking what's left of your brain right with it." – **Clay McLeod Chapman, author of *Ghost Eaters***

"A thunder beneath your feet, a power you haven't felt before gathering in the broken earth...in *What Waits Below*, Caleb Stephens is ready to tear out your willing heart with both hands." – **Andrew F. Sullivan, author of *The Marigold* and *The Handyman Method***

"*What Waits Below* is an apocalyptic road novel with a foot slammed squarely on the accelerator. Stephens crafts his story as an ode to the horror paperbacks of yore, where reading is akin to being swallowed whole, devoured by the power of unreality. But for every torn-up carcass, every tense square off, every horrifying revelation—there's an underlying notion that people are good and worth fighting for. *What Waits Below* is a squint-through-your-fingers creature feature that never loses track of the people you hold when the monster comes for blood." – **Carson Winter, author of *Soft Targets***

"If you're looking for a book that's going to make you feel safe and warm, *What Waits Below* is not the book for you. Stephens doesn't pull any punches as he takes you on a journey that's visceral, raw, and absolutely brutal. This book is a cult classic in the making." **– Caitlin Marceau, award-winning author of *This is Where We Talk Things Out***

"Caleb Stephens' *What Waits Below* has all the thrills and epic scope of a long-running, post-apocalyptic TV series with none of the downside. There are no filler episodes or subpar seasons here as Stephens has crafted an exhilarating binge that will leave you satisfied." **– CB Jones, *The Rules of the Road***

"Caleb Stephens has one speed: GO. *What Waits Below* devoured me in twenty-four hours, the drill bit of propulsive prose digging into my spine with the one-two punch of tender brutality that infuses every story Stephens births. He mines the beauty—and dysfunction—of family with a realism that makes me want to apologize to certain relatives and flip off others." **– Christopher O'Halloran, author of *Pushing Daisy***

"In *What Waits Below*, Caleb Stephens has managed to create a triple threat. One that is not only world-ending and road-trip taking, but thrives as a creature feature from a bygone era as well. Go on, take that ride. Thank me later." **– Beau Johnson, author of *Brand New Dark***

ALSO BY CALEB STEPHENS

You'll Never Know

If You Lie

The Girls in the Cabin

If Only a Heart and Other Tales of Terror

CALEB N. STEPHENS

THRILLERSCAPE PRESS

For my parents, who taught me to dream big.

CHAPTER ONE
THE SHIRT

It's raining as I step outside and lock the door to the Ink Tank. October rain. Texas rain. Dark and black. A nasty, piss-warm spray smelling of ozone and motor oil and slaughterhouse shit. I drive past the place every day on the way to work: dusty parking lots and semis bloated with cattle, a jungle of corrugated steel and rusted iron. Sometimes I play out the horrors in my head. Dull-eyed cows trudging slack-jawed through a maze of concrete chutes. Men in flannel shirts waiting impatiently to kill them, bolt pistols in hand, lips stuffed with chew. Fat men. Men who drink too much and go home to their high school sweethearts at night. The Tammys and Brendas and Tinas of the world. Ancient Texas prom queens with chemically damaged hair and axes to grind.

Angry women not so different than myself.

Tank pulls up beside me in his gun-metal black El Camino, a cigarette blossoming red between his lips as he rolls down the window and squints against the drizzle. "Looks like this one might get bad. You want a ride?"

"Nah, I'm fine," I reply. "I like the rain."

I hate the rain. But not as much as I hate smelling like an ashtray.

The smell brings back bad, shag-carpet memories drenched in smoke and despair; my clothes ever-tinged with nicotine. All those years spent avoiding my aunt Vivian's pack-a-day habit and her barely concealed contempt at having to raise Mac and me. I used to steal her dryer sheets and rub them over my clothes on the way to school. Poor kid perfume—trailer park chic.

"Oh, come on. You really gonna do this?" Tank asks. "Make me sit here and beg like an asshole? Even after I gave you that sweet necklace?"

I absentmindedly brush a finger against the onyx spider pendant. "No worries. I'm good. Really."

"Suit yourself," he says, rolling his window back up, pausing halfway. "Hey, Brynn..."

"Yeah?"

"You should tone it down on the Blues some. Let your body recalibrate a bit, know what I mean?"

"Whatever," I mumble, staring down at the black and white swallow lacing up my forearm, the feathers so real, I sometimes wonder if it will fly away. The tattoo Tank gave me three years ago when I'd first conned my way into a job at the Ink Tank with a short skirt and a hastily drawn skull. It wasn't my best work, but good enough.

"Seriously," he continues, "that shit'll mess you up. You remember Cathy's dip-shit kid, what's his name, Andy or whatever? The one who got that stupid Nike tattoo a few months back."

I nod.

"Well, I hear he's in the ICU down in San Antonio." He shakes his head and mutters something. "Kid OD'd the other day. Mixed a few Bars with some Vikes. Bad news that. From what I hear, he was jumping off the walls one minute, completely brain-dead the next. Guess he just keeled over and stopped breathing."

I give him a blank stare. I've heard this story a million times. Well, not *this* story, exactly, but ones just like it. The tragic cases. All the kids turned to vegetables. The teenagers strapped to life support machines. The devastated families. The tearful obituaries blaming the opioid epidemic, like it's this evil *thing* running around, shoving pills in peoples' mouths like they don't have a choice, which is bullshit, really. Everyone has a choice. I made mine. I know what can happen. I don't need the daily reminder, thank you very much.

"Never mind," Tank says. "Look, I'm just saying take it easy is all. Believe it or not, I kind of like having you around."

The irony of this coming from the pill king of Texas is ridiculous. Tank's as bad as me, probably worse. Even though he tries to hide it, the guy's balls-deep high most shifts, his eyes all irises, his pupils pinprick stains. I think about the fresh bottle of Roxicodone in my jacket pocket, the one he just sold me ten minutes ago, and stifle a laugh. "Maybe you should stop dealing to me, then."

A grin splits his stubbled jaw, his eyes glittering beneath carefully spiked rows of peroxide hair that look sharp enough to cut. "Nah, I know you. You'll just get it somewhere else. Probably buy some of that gray death shit or something."

"Yeah, probably. You remember that."

He rolls his eyes. "You're impossible. So, see you tomorrow or what?"

"Where else would I go?"

"All right then. Get a move on before this storm lets loose."

I straighten and give him a mock salute. "Sir, yes sir."

He expels a cloud of smoke and shakes his head. "I don't know why I put up with you sometimes."

"Beats me," I say with a shrug. "Night, Tank."

"Night, B."

With that he's gone, the El Camino muffler-less and growling as he tears out of the parking lot. I watch him go with a smile. Truth is, I love the guy and I'll work as many shifts as he'll let me. Yeah, the money's okay. And it doesn't hurt that he's decent looking, but that's just a perk. The real reason I drag my ass to work every day is simple. Tattooing is the only thing that stops the thoughts. The sticky-wet ones that creep up on me when things get too quiet. The ones always simmering in my brain, waiting to boil over if I let them.

With a deep breath, I step from the safety of the awning and into the night. The pills clink their sweet song as I cross the parking lot and make my way across Wilson Avenue toward Tony's Chicken 'N Ribs and my shit-bag car parked somewhere in the back. Tank doesn't let me park in front of his shop, says he needs the spots for his "customers." The other pill heads. Translation: *Don't fuck with my income stream, B. You know the druggies are too lazy to walk.*

Sad thing is, he's right.

I pause at the shack steps and breathe in the pecan smoke wafting through the door. It's nearly enough to pull me inside for some brisket. Maybe a beer or two. But that means seeing Tony, and I'm not up for any of his bullshit stories tonight, listening to him blab on and on about whoever he's banging or whatever motorcycle he's into this week. That, or his old army-hero medic tales about him and Tank in Iraq. I don't get why Tank loves the guy so much. All he wants to talk about is himself, but he makes one hell of a barbecue brisket sandwich and kicks me an extra parking spot in the back, so I tolerate him.

Stomach protesting, I head for the sidewalk and seize to a stop as a bolt of electricity rips through my quad. I gasp and clutch the muscle, feel it twitch like crazy beneath my fingers. It's been happening more often, these spasms. This strange muscle paralysis. A bicep here, a quad there. Sometimes a lame foot. I know I need to get it checked out, but not now. Not tonight. I have other, more pressing plans to attend to. Namely getting good and fucked-up. Just the thought of plugging a few Dillies has my skin tingling, and my Roxies, my get-me-through-the-day pills, are wearing off. I need to re-up and fast before I crash.

I reach the alley and spot my car: a late-nineties Honda Accord with the H on the front long since sacrificed to a pothole and an abundance of Moscow Mules. I vaguely remember the night: sloppy sex with some college kid, the preppy-rich type with his collar flipped up like he was fresh from the eighties. A real, *Hey, Bro,* frat type. I didn't care. I'd wanted someone to fuck, to use, which I did. Then I stole his Rolex and pawned it for two grand the next day. *Yay,* free pills for a month—lucky me.

The sky cracks open, and I slide into my car just as the rain starts to hammer down. I grab a dirty towel and run it over my arms, my face, careful to avoid the mirror. There's no reason to look. I know what I'll see: mascara trailing down the sides of my snub nose. A baby's nose. I hate it. It's like I haven't quite grown up, like I'm still waiting for puberty to strike.

And my hair? Short and black—matted above a set of too-small, round kitten eyes. Your basic brown, nothing special. I have delicate cheekbones and rosebud lips that give me the appearance of something fragile, something to be coddled, one of those starlets from the fifties who prance around town uttering breathy quotes while smoothing her dress: *Oh, golly gee. If I could just meet the right boy, things would sure be peachy.*

I don't mind. I let people think what they want. It's good camouflage. Piss me off enough, and I'll rip your heart out through your throat.

I fumble the keys from my pocket and fire up the engine, the rain promising a first-class, white-knuckle joyride back to my boxed-in apartment: Pineview Suites. No pine. No suites. Just a hastily thrown-up piece of suburbia with a nice view of the dumpster and the empty lot behind it. Oh, and lots of plastic grocery sacks. I have no idea how they got there in the bushes, in the trees, strewn all over the rusted chain-link fence like broken white birds. It makes no sense; there isn't even a grocery store nearby.

I flip on the headlights, the wipers... and stop. Something—*A shirt? A towel?*—is wrapped around the far blade. It thumps a monotonous *whump-click, whump-click* over the windshield. I squint at it. It's a hoodie, and a dirty one at that—all grease-stained and torn. It smears a rainbow of oily film over the windshield with each pass, one that the rain fights, and fails, to clear. Probably the work of some drunk fuck inside of Tony's with nothing better to do than screw up my night.

With a groan, I shove my way back out into the downpour and am instantly drenched, the drops fat and heavy as I round the hood and take hold of the shirt, giving it a sharp yank. The blade comes with it, slapping back to the glass an instant later. That's when I notice the knots. They're thick and full of purpose. The work of a special kind of asshole. I run my hands over my jeans and try to wick off some of the moisture. Fail.

"Shit!" I mutter to myself as I try again.

A hot sting pierces my neck.

I hiss and jerk forward, try to scream. A massive palm clamps over my mouth before I can. I thrash and bite down. Hard. Taste dirty-salt skin. A growl erupts from behind me. A man's growl. A *large* one.

Oh, God.

The grip weakens enough for me to rip free and scramble around the hood, a thought flaring—*Tony's! I've got to get inside!* Suddenly, it's the only thing that matters. *The* most important thing I've ever done.

I bolt for the red steel door I've stumbled through drunk as shit a thousand times. I don't bother to look back. I know the man is there. I can hear him smacking through the puddles after me.

Get inside, Brynn! Do it or you're dead!

I know it's true. I've seen way too much TV murder porn about women who were taken. Women who never fought back. Women who became corpses.

Reach the door!

My legs slosh left... right. I order them to behave, to move faster, but something is wrong. They aren't working right. Nothing is. A sick slug of adrenaline greases my stomach, and I paw at my eyes. I can barely see the door. It looks like it's melting, the paint running down in gluey waves. And my lungs—I can't breathe.

The steps draw closer.

I push forward. Eight feet to the door.

My left foot goes numb.

Six feet.

Everything spinning.

Four.

I slam to the mud.

Panic shreds my chest, and I try to scramble up again. A hand grabs at my shoulder, my arm. I kick out and claw forward, my fingers digging desperate trenches through the muck. I can't move. *Why is it so hard to move?* The rain hisses down around me like gunfire, everything so loud. Too loud.

I'm burning up.

Fingers search and prod. A steel band of pressure wraps around my waist. I cry out and kick back again, and this time my foot connects with something, but it's a baby kick, the fingers only loosening for a moment before tightening once more.

My vision glosses over. "Please... no," I whisper. A thin stream of halogen bleeds down at me through the rain as I float upward—up, up, up—impossibly high, before I'm slung over a broad shoulder.

"Stop... don't... do... th-this... please..." My tongue works over my gums, cavity thick.

No response comes but that of a throaty grunt as I'm carried away from the door, a final thought blazing up at me as I black out.

I am *so* fucked.

CHAPTER TWO
THE VAN

I wake slow and sticky.

Wax coats my tongue and a nasty headache buzzes at the base of my skull. The air is acrid with cigarette smoke. I try to open my eyelids and fail, try again. Everything is a blur, like my eyes are smeared with Vaseline. I can't focus. I blink once. Twice. Try to clear the haze. A ceiling appears through the fog—the dim glow of dashboard lights.

Moving.

I am moving. I roll my head toward a window where a fly bangs senselessly off the glass. The hiss of wet rubber on pavement stings my ears. In the distance, I catch a flicker of downtown Austin hulking beneath a sky of fine, gray mist.

I need to wake up. I need to—

———

My eyes snap open.

Outside, the sun roars down over the road in glittering fragments. The clouds have migrated south, replaced by gritty, dry plains for as far as I can see. Vast fields of empty dust and rock speckled with wind turbines. A memory fires.

The alley.

The sharp sting in my neck.

A needle. *Oh, God.* A needle filled with...*something.*

Crawling through the mud and slop.

Thick sausage fingers around my mouth, my throat.

I raise my arm and stare stupidly at the ring of metal biting into my wrist. A... handcuff.

Ohfuckohfuckohfuck.

Oh, Jesus.

I try to make a fist, and my fingers barely twitch. I swallow... hard. A grunt draws my gaze toward the driver's seat, toward a hulking form planted behind the wheel. The man is big. No, that's the wrong word for him. More like huge, *massive,* wearing a short-sleeve checkered shirt and a faded green ball cap. All I can see are his shoulders and a sun-leathered neck capped in a black fringe of hair.

My blood hardens to ice. I start to hyperventilate. *I'm dead. I'm so dead.* My thoughts splinter into a million shards.

How the hell did I get here?

Who did this to me?

Someone saw. *Surely* someone saw.

Maybe Tank stuck around. *Yeah, right.*

My phone. Mac. I was supposed to call him back. He'll notice. He *has* to.

But he won't. It's nothing new. I never return his calls.

I'm such a shitty big sister.

I need to get out of this. Whatever *this* is...

What if I can't?

The man's eyes catch mine in the rear-view mirror, flick back to the road. They're hard... familiar. Why do they look so familiar?

"Bout time you woke up."

The voice is graveled and rough. It reminds me of something...
of some*one*.

It clicks, but it can't be. *Please no, don't let it be.* He's locked up
halfway across the country, imprisoned for the next fifteen years, *at
least*. Or is it twenty? It's been so long, I can't remember.

"*Alan?*" I venture, my voice weak.

He says nothing. It's enough.

I clamp my mouth shut. *Holy shit.* It *is* him. My psycho father,
the needle man back to stick me again.

"H—how did you find me?" I ask, my voice wavering. "How did
you get—"

"Out? Don't worry about that. It's not important."

"Where... where are you taking me?"

"You know where."

The shelter. The one he obsessed over when I was a kid. The one
he blew his retirement on to protect us from the imaginary monsters
living in the ground... in his head. The feeders he'd called them. It
always came back to the feeders.

Beads of sweat erupt across my forehead. This is so much worse
than if I'd been abducted by some random whack-job.

I stiffen, cold panic bubbling up my throat. "*Please*, you have to
let me go. You *have* to, Alan. Pull over, okay? I won't tell anyone I saw
you. I don't care how you got out or what you did. I promise. Just
uncuff me and—"

He raises a hand and gives it a shake. Something rattles. *My*
bottle. His eyes are black chips of ice in the mirror. "How long you
been on this shit?"

"I don't know what you're—"

"How long?"

"A while."

My vision blurs again, my head wobbling. I *need* that bottle—need what's inside it. How long has it been? A few hours? A day? More?

"You're too thin," he says, rolling down the window. "This shit's poison. It's gone."

I flap against the cuff, frantic, my arm finally moving, my body slowly waking up. "No! Wait! Stop. Don't do that. I'll do whatever you want. Just don't toss those. *Please.*"

He pauses, glances over his shoulder. "No? Why not?"

"Because... I need them, okay? I can't go cold turkey. It'll screw me up."

"All the more reason."

"No, you don't understand," I plead. "I need to ease off them. If I don't, it could kill me."

He starts tapping his foot, a reflex I remember well. A tic proportional to his disintegration. Herky-jerky movements that match the rhythm in his skull; the one only he can hear. If it isn't his foot, it's a finger, or a knee, or a slight bob of the head followed by an angry pulse of the jaw.

He blinks and then flips the bottle into the passenger seat. "You need to eat something."

"I'm not hungry."

"Here," he says, grabbing an overripe banana from the dashboard and passing it back to me.

"I said I'm not—"

"Eat it." His voice is low. Cold. An order. Arm shaking, I grab the banana and peel it with my teeth, choke down a few sloppy bites as he watches, my stomach swelling in protest. When he looks away, I toss what remains to the floor.

He raps a finger on the steering wheel. "Look. I had no choice. I had to black you out last night. You wouldn't have come, otherwise."

It's true. I would have run. Far, far away. And I still will. The first chance I get.

"They're coming this time," he continues. "I can feel it. There's too many of them in the ground down here, too much oil."

"They're not real," I mumble, my voice so quiet, I can barely hear myself.

He pauses. "What was that?"

"You heard me," I spit, suddenly desperate. I can't go back again. Not there. Not with him. It will break me this time. "They're. Not. Real. They never have been, and they never will be. Mom's dead because of this shit, Alan. Because of *you*. They're only in your head. You're sick. You need help."

His jaw flexes, the back of his neck darkening to the dangerous shade of purple I remember so well as a kid. He eyes me in the mirror. "So, you still think I made it all up, do you? After all this time? After what I've done to get you?" He shakes his head. "You have no idea what's waiting below. No idea. They're real, all right. Real as the sun is hot."

"No. They're not."

"Yes they are, goddammit!" he says, spinning around, his teeth slick with tobacco juice. "They are! You best believe that. And you're coming with me no matter what I have—"

A horn blares, and my eyes dart to the windshield.

"Alan, watch out!"

He twists around, swerving out of the path of an oncoming semi that blows by so close, the rush of wind from its passing rattles the van.

We should be dead.

My heart hammers in my chest as I slide back against the seat.

A few more inches and we would have been.

I wipe the sweat from my face and realize my hand is shaking. I stare at it stupidly.

"That one's on you," Alan says, wagging a finger. "On you."

My stomach gives a sudden, painful jerk. I try to hold back the sour wave rising up my throat.

It's useless.

A warm slick of spew erupts from my mouth and sprays over my shirt, my jeans, the temperature of gently heated soup. Another clench hits, and I heave chunks of banana and stomach acid all over the floorboard. My stomach boils at the smell. Saliva clings to my lips in strings.

The van is suddenly hot. So, so hot. Boiling hot.

"Jesus," Alan mutters, his eyes dim-brown marbles back in the mirror. *"Jesus."*

CHAPTER THREE
TRUCK STOP

The truck stop is garish, the kind of place that appeals to leathered truckers looking for a cup of coffee and a quick blowjob. But—*Hey!*—it's apparently got *The B-st Cinnamon Rolls in Tex-s!* according to the billboard out front.

Alan drives to the northernmost edge of the lot, a couple of football fields away from the gas pumps, and parks next to a dusty expanse of sagebrush and oak, miles of it, not a drop of civilization in sight.

"I have to pee," I mutter.

Alan ignores me and dislodges himself from the van, adjusts his ball cap. John Deere. He squints toward the building and stuffs a wad of chew in his lip. It's my first good look at him in over eight years. Deep cracks split his weathered face, which is harder than I remember, and his once jet-black hair is now peppered with gray. He's still large, but not in the I've-given-up-on-life-gonna-drink-my-ass-off way he used to be. Instead, he's all muscle, his arms roped with it, his legs. I know the left one ends at the kneecap.

I lean forward and try again. "Seriously, my bladder's about to explode."

He lobs a rope of tobacco to the side and glances back. "Nope. You're staying put. Here"—he leans in and scavenges something from the floorboard, an empty Gatorade bottle, his spitter, and tosses it back—"use this."

I kick it away. "You can't be serious."

"Suit yourself." He slams the door and rounds the hood toward mine, jerking it open with a grunt. I pick up flecks of movement in my peripheral vision. Cars idling next to gas pumps. People milling about, chatting in groups.

I scream.

He's on me before I can take another breath, jamming a handkerchief in my mouth as I buck against him. The taste of old sweat and dirt mixes with my saliva. I gag and try to spit it out—nearly vomit again.

"Shut up," he hisses in my ear. "Not another sound. I'll put you to sleep if I have to."

I arch my hips and try to kick him, but he holds the cloth in place with one hand and grabs my throat with the other, squeezing until my vision blackens. "I said. Shut. Up. If anyone heard that, you know what I'll do to them." His jaw is clenched and twitching. I can't breathe, my nose running, tears clouding my eyes.

He snatches a roll of duct tape from the floor and winds a length of it around my mouth, the back of my head, my mouth again, then shoves me back against the seat, his eyes slits as he slams the door.

I suck a sliver of cheek between my teeth and bite down. I can still feel his fingers wrapped around my neck, taste their grease in my mouth. I'm suddenly eight again and waking to a syringe in my arm, him injecting me with whatever that shit was that had me throwing up in the bathroom an hour later. His "vaccinations" he'd called them, the only way to save me from the coming apocalypse.

He'll kill me this time, I think. *One way or another he will.*

I whip my head back against the seat. *Why, why, why, didn't I take Tank up on that ride? Why?*

I like the rain. God, I'm so stupid.

My eyes roam the van, take in the dark, tinted windows and the clump of yellow foam oozing from the crack in the seat next to me. The vehicle is old and busted. Stolen no doubt, something the cops won't be hot to locate, which means it's up to me to find a way out, and I have to find it *now.*

I twist left and examine the cuff, pull on the chain. Nothing happens. I jerk harder, too hard, and my wrist erupts in a bright wave of agony. I squeal and rub it, fighting for oxygen through my nose. Then I'm back to hyperventilating. Panicking.

There *has* to be another way.

I jam my free hand into the seat and follow the cuffs to where they attach to a metal rod that runs through a maze of coiled springs. One that instantly razes my skin. I hiss and yank my hand free, stare dimly at the inch-long cut below my wrist as it turns from white to pink to red.

Shit!

SHIT! SHIT! SHIT!

I shriek into the handkerchief and pound my fist into the seat. *Fucking Alan! Fuck!*

Blood sprays all over the vinyl, my jeans. I'll never be able to—

My eyes light on something in the front seat. A duffel bag.

Maybe?

I stretch for it and manage to work my fingertips over the shoulder strap, straining until—*Yes!*—it moves an inch, two, then thumps to the floor. I cast an anxious glance back at the truck stop with my heart racing—still no sign of him—before reaching down to fumble the zipper open.

The bag is stuffed with clothes: plaid work shirts and jeans and boxers, mismatched pairs of socks. I rip them out and dig deeper. *Dammit!* A toiletry bag. An old bible with the cover torn off. Some stray earplugs and a blue windbreaker. A leather-bound binder. No handcuff key. No hidden zippers or pouches. No gun. Nothing I can use.

I thump back against my seat and grind my teeth. There's no way—

The binder. I didn't check the binder.

I jerk forward and dig it out, wrestle it awkwardly onto my lap. It's thick and heavy, stuffed with all kinds of crap. I tear through it in search of a hidden pocket, an envelope, *anything* that might contain a key, or better, something sharp to stab Alan with. There's nothing, just a bunch of old newspaper clippings and laminated photos. I give it a frustrated shake, and something falls onto my lap. A yellowed map of the U.S., which I unfold.

**Energy Information Administration.
Lower 48 Shale Plays**

Red X's cut through names I don't recognize: Eagle Ford, Haynesville-Bossier, Marcellus, Uinta. And a few I do: Bakken, Permian, Denver-Julesburg. Names that would spill out of Alan's mouth from time to time when I was younger. Names that had something to do with the oil and gas business. They were worthless to me then, and they're just as worthless to me now.

I toss it aside and open the binder to a newspaper clipping from

The Oklahoman. The headline reads *Unexplained Earthquake Rocks Enid. Two Residents Missing.* There's a photo of a couple—a girl with big, Aqua Net bangs, wearing an eighties blouse, pressed against a man in Coke-bottle glasses. Blood drips from my hand and pools annoyingly on the plastic. I wipe it off and turn the page.

Another clipping, this one about some earthquake in California with a few grainy photos of an oil well fire and a smoldering tank battery. More people vanished.

I keep flipping, stop on a tow-headed kid clutching a basketball, a dim grin smeared over his face. *Tulsa Child Missing Since October.* More of the same follows. An elderly Pennsylvania woman gone, and two vanished brothers from Wyoming dressed in hunting gear, sporting shit-eating grins.

A chill burns down my spine. *Did Alan have something to do with this?*

I skim through a few more pages and pause on a picture of Alan—a much younger Alan—clad in brown overalls with his hair parted neatly to the side. He stands next to a sun-cracked Native American with his shirt unbuttoned to mid-chest. Neither of them are looking at the camera. Instead, they're both staring down at this... *thing.* A spider lying dead on the ground. But not a spider. Something I can't—

The door bangs open.

I drop the binder and kick it beneath the pile of clothes. Alan appears clutching a plastic sack bulging with junk food and water bottles along with a carton of Kool menthols. In his other hand, a new tee-shirt for me. Even from where I sit, I can tell it's several sizes too big.

He moves to get in and stops, his gaze falling on the blood spattered everywhere.

"What the hell? What happened in here?"

I make a few muffled sounds and point at the gag.

He fingers the tape. "Not a word, understand? You scream, and I'll keep it on the rest of the way."

I nod.

He rips it off, eyeing me as I rub my cheeks.

"Well?" he asks.

"I cut myself."

His mouth twists. "Yeah, I can see that." He slides in and rummages through the glove box, grabs a Band-Aid, and tosses it back. "Here. Clean yourself up."

I just stare at it for a moment and then lean back and close my eyes. The blood suddenly feels cool on my hand. Cold.

Let it run, I think. *I've got no place to be. Nowhere to go.*

Let it run.

CHAPTER FOUR
MEMORY LANE

Before...

I stare at him through my bedroom window, watch his black curls tick up and down in time with the truck's air conditioner. He's talking to himself again, mumbling something I can't understand. And his eyes... they're clouded. Distant. Like maybe no one's home. I lean forward and try to follow his lips, but they're moving too fast. *Way* too fast. It's impossible from up here, anyway. I should know. I've tried. All week, in fact, because this keeps happening. Him sitting out there mumbling to himself. Me inside watching.

He suddenly laughs and smacks the dash. Looks up.

At me.

I jerk back from the window and nearly tip off my chair. *Dad, what's wrong with you?*

Doesn't matter. Well, tonight, at least. Tonight, I'm taking cover at Cass's house, away from another *Hey-let's-pretend-everything's-fine!* family dinner. I can picture it: Mom serving up her fake plastic smiles while Mac forks a pile of broccoli around his plate and complains about his stomach. *Mommy, my tummy hurts. No, really! It does.* Mom rolling her eyes and telling him no dessert if it hurts. And if it's one of those nights (which seem to happen more and more often of late), the crazy *tap, tap, tap,* of Dad's fork dancing on the table, tapping faster...and faster, until he can't hold the words in any longer.

The feeders. They're coming. Any day now, they're coming.

Mom hollers it's time to go, so I shake the thought from my head and grab my backpack, then tramp downstairs to her swirling about, snatching her purse and shouting at Mac to get his shoes on. "Turn off the video game, Mac," she says, flicking him on the head with a fingernail. "Now."

I'm not sure exactly when it happened, but she's stopped leaving him alone with Dad.

"A few more minutes," Mac says without turning around. I know from experience *a few more minutes* will never end, so I decide for him and jab the power button with my toe.

He hurls the controller at me. "Ahh, c'mon! I just got past level four!"

"Too bad. You're not making me late again."

"Shoes. Now, Mac," Mom adds.

"*Fiiinne.*" He blows the bangs from his eyes. They're crazy blue. Like Mom's. I wish I had them instead of Dad's boring brown. Whatever, at least I didn't get his lips.

I spin around to grab my jacket from the closet... and freeze.

It's Dad, but not the *Hey, Honey, I'm home!* version. This version is a train-wreck: shirt untucked and spotted with mustard, Carhartt's completely caked with mud. His eyes narrow. "Where do you think you're going?"

"Cass's. Her parents are taking us to dinner."

Mom eases to my side and stiffens, her hand floating to the silver swallow necklace around her neck. I don't know what it is about her and swallows. She's always loved them, their songs and tail feathers and how graceful they are in flight. She says if she could be anything, it would be a swallow so she could fly away. I can tell it's what she wants to do right now. Fly away.

So do I.

Dad's eyes tick toward Mom. "It's time."

She frowns. "Let's not do this tonight, okay? Listen, I left you some casserole. It's in the fridge. Why don't you go heat some up? Mac and I will be back in half an—"

"Sit down," he says, motioning toward the couch. "All of you. We need to talk."

Talk? Noooo. It's happening. I can feel it. The crazy circus is about to come to town. A flare of panic burns through my chest. "Daddy, please. Can we talk later? Cass is waiting for me."

He crosses his arms and gives me his *I mean business* look—eyebrows slanted, the bridge of his nose creased. "Brynn, sit. I'm not going to ask again. You too, Mac."

Jerk! I think. But his tone is enough to send me flopping onto the couch next to Mac, who already looks like he's about to cry. Mom sits with a huff and waves an arm. "What is it, Alan?" She's all cheekbones and full lips, her eyes a clear blue-green. The way she perches on the couch, with her hands folded neatly in her lap, makes her look like she was copied straight from some little girl's princess coloring book. I have no clue how Dad snagged her.

He pulls his cracked-leather recliner across from us, collapses into it, and then leans forward, his forehead bright with sweat. "All of you need to go pack. We leave tonight."

"Uh-uh, nope," Mom says, standing and snatching up her purse. "We're leaving."

I don't need the prompt. I'm already on my feet and pulling Mac up. Dad rises with us.

"No one's going anywhere."

Mom whirls on him. "Yes, we are. I'm not doing this with you rig—"

"Sit down," he snarls. "NOW!"

Her face pales and she steps back, but then her features tighten, and I know shit is about to explode. "Don't you *dare* talk to me that way, Alan" she snaps back, the whites of her eyes flashing. "We are *not* doing this in front of the kids again. You *promised*." Mac tugs on my sleeve and I look down. His lip is trembling. I pull him close and mouth *I'm sorry*. He shouldn't have to deal with this. Not at his age.

"Wait. Just wait, okay?" Dad says, raising his hands, his voice suddenly soft. "I'm sorry. You're right. I shouldn't have yelled. But look, Laura, this is happening." They're coming. Nothing can change that. And we're not safe here."

She reaches over and grabs my hand and tugs me toward the door. "Get out of our way, Alan."

"No."

She stops with a hiss. My eyes widen at the dark, angry metal in Dad's hand. A trigger. A barrel. A gun. *Oh, God.* A real live gun. My brain scrambles to keep up. I didn't even know he had one. He's crazy, but he's never been *this* crazy before. Even him stumbling into my room at night to jab me with his needles when I was a kid pale in comparison to this. Butterflies wing through my chest.

"Wh—what...are you doing?" Mom asks. Her voice is hollow. She's scared, like me, and for some reason that frightens me even more. "Where did you get that?"

He glances down at the gun like he can't believe he's holding it either, looks up again with sweat beading on his nose like he's about to have a heart attack. "I—I've built us a place," he says. "In the mountains. Somewhere safe."

"What do you mean...you've 'built a place?'"

He brightens at the question, like he forgot he just pulled a gun on his family, and the words all spill out at once. "It took a couple of years, but it's perfect. No one knows it exists except for Tasker. And even he doesn't know where it is. It's hidden. Soundproofed. The feeders won't be able to hear us in there. Or get to us if they do. I've made sure of that."

My mind struggles to make sense of what he's saying. He's been gone every other week for work for as long as I can remember. Suddenly, I wonder if he even has a job.

Mom lifts a hand, and I notice it's shaking. Bad. "Give me the gun, Alan."

The corners of his mouth tick in and out as if he's thinking about it, but then some terrible light flashes through his eyes, and he tightens his grip. "No. No...they're my kids, too, Laura." He waves a finger toward the door. "And those things are coming. *Any* day now. For you. For me. For all of us. The kids included." He hitches up the right leg of his jeans and wags the gun at his prosthetic. "Do you want them killed? Do you want them to be devoured like *this*?"

She shakes her head. "No, Alan, no. Of course not." Her voice is quaking, thick with fear. Dad has never so much as raised a hand to her, or to any of us for that matter, but in this moment, I know he'll kill us if we don't stop him.

If I don't stop him.

I wipe at tears I didn't know were there and make the decision. I know what I need to do. *He won't hurt you,* I tell myself. *You're his little girl. His Bear. No way he'll hurt you.*

I lurch forward. Mom's hand skims my arm. "Brynn, *no*…"

I brush her off, wonder if I'll even reach him before I topple over, his eyes clear as I near. "Brynn, get your brother and get in the truck."

"Okay, Daddy. Okay. But put down the gun first. *Please.*" My voice sounds distant and lonely, like I'm standing in the middle of a long, empty tunnel talking to myself.

He glances down at it and the weapon wobbles, dropping an inch as I move closer.

"Alan, stop this," Mom says behind me. "Dear God, please stop this. This isn't you."

His gaze hardens. "I love you, Laura. You know I do. But the kids, they're not safe here. I don't care what you think. I'm taking them. I won't let those things—"

I swing my arm down. Hard. He jerks the gun back, but not before I smack the barrel. It all happens so fast: The crack of the bullet. Mac's screams. And someone else's…

Mom.

Dad shoves past me, and I twist around. Mom is on her knees clutching her stomach. Dad crouches next to her and pulls her into his lap. "No, no, no," he cries. "Laura, no!" His eyes are hot with panic. And the blood…there's so much of it. Blood everywhere— pooling between his fingers. Spilling to the floor. She looks at me and gurgles something, points. That's when I feel the burning in *my* side, sudden and hot, like someone jammed a knife between my ribs. I clutch it and my hand comes away red. I'm bleeding, too. Why am I—

I collapse to the floor.

Oh, God, it hurts so much.

I can't breathe.

I.

Can't.

Breathe...

I can only lie there, gulping wet breaths as my vision turns black.

CHAPTER FIVE
ROAD TRIP

Here's the thing about reality. It sucks. It's too *real*. Too much emotion. Too much pain. I prefer my edges dulled, everything cotton candy, nothing too bright or too loud. A few pills and I'm there, floating helium-happy through the day, oblivious to life's little land mines. And now that I think about it, *prefer* is really too weak a word. It's more like *need*. Yeah, that feels about right. *I need it.* I *need* it like I need oxygen, and right now, the air is getting thin.

"I need a couple pills," I blurt.

Alan glares at me in the mirror, eyes tinged with some emotion I can't quite decipher. Pity? Anger? No, that's not it. It's disgust. Definitely disgust. I can barely hold his gaze as he grunts and reaches over to the passenger seat for the bottle, taps a Blue into his hand, and bites it.

I jerk forward. "*Hey*, what are you doing?"

"You get half," he says, spitting the wasted sliver out the window. He passes the remainder back to me, which, despite my rage, I gulp down greedily. Not enough. Not by a long shot. But I'll take it. I need a hundred milligrams of Roxy a day just to operate. Sixty minimum. This puts me at forty. Maybe.

"I need another," I mumble.

His eyes remain in the mirror, burn over me until I can no longer stand it.

"What?"

"When did this start? The pills."

"You don't get to ask that," I snap back.

He sighs, taps the steering wheel. "Look. We need to talk. Get on the same page here."

I massage the wrist of my cuffed hand and spin a few circles over it with my thumb. "So give me another pill, then."

He falls silent, and I stare out the windshield at a clump of rusted pump jacks bobbing mindlessly up and down, ever thirsty for oil. Here and there a spray of bluebonnets. Jags of buffalo grass and dirt. Hills dressed up in skirts of lifeless rock. The washed-out, pale-blue sky above, the sun burning down from it like an angry eye: *I see you, little girl. Oh yes, I see you...*

"Here. Take it before I change my mind."

I look down and realize he's got a Blue in his hand. An *entire* pill. I snap it up and push it under my tongue, exhaling in relief as it dissolves into my bloodstream.

"We need to stop for a few things," he says. "Some water in case I have problems with the well or the generator. But once it's started, we're good. Food's not a problem, either. I've got enough to keep us out of trouble until we start to grow our own, which shouldn't be too hard. I've got seeds. Lots of them. We'll make do."

I try to quell the panic bleeding through my chest at the thought of reaching the shelter. With *him.* I've got to find some way to escape before we get there. I *have* to. And there's something else that's been bothering me, a question I've been too scared to ask since the moment I woke up. But it's a question I need to ask, even if I'm afraid of the answer.

"So, how'd you get out of prison, Alan? Did you hurt someone?"

Silence. His fingers march across the steering wheel like anxious spiders. A tendon ripples in his neck.

"*Shit,*" I mutter under my breath. He did. Twenty years in Florence Correctional for manslaughter without the possibility of early parole. So much for that.

He clears his throat. "*Like* I was saying, I have enough food. Medical supplies, too. We'll have access to all of the basics. Hot water. AC. Plenty of electricity. I've..."

I tune him out. All I want is to go back to my shitty apartment and close the blinds, sleep for a week straight. Maybe longer. I want to stare at the television and get faded on a cheap box of wine. I want to forget. *Everything.* Pour myself a hot bath and slide beneath the water and never come up again. Just watch it all blur away through a sheen of soapy film.

I blink, realize he's still rattling on. "...those people, they aren't ready for it. None of 'em, buncha sheep. The whole lot. And the government. They know what's going on. They always have. We vote these scumbags into office and what do they do? A whole lot of nothing is what. 'Cept burn through our money. And they do a damn fine job of that. The prisons are practically country retreats these days. Trust me, I know. I've been..."

Whatthefuck. What. The. Fuck.

I can't handle this nonsense. This insanity. My own father, the crazy nut. The psychopath fugitive conspiracy theorist. Not like Tasker, Alan's only real friend when he began to tailspin. Someone normal. And funny. Was actually *there* for me and Mac when we needed him, even after Alan got locked up. Would check in on us from time to time. Bring Mac video games and me books to read. Cheesy teen romance novels I hated. But still. I think of his clear blue eyes and suddenly miss him, think of the way the corners wrinkled when he smiled after one of his stupid knock-knock jokes. His dumb cowboy hats.

Why couldn't he have been my father? He wouldn't have screwed me up like Alan did.

He wouldn't have shot me.

I dig my nails into my forearm and drag them over the skin. Outside, the wind whips bits of sand against the van and scatters tracks of it across the windshield; tracks like the red ones bubbling up beneath my fingernails.

Alan eyes me in the mirror. "Do you know how I lost my leg?"

A wellsite explosion right before I was born: four men killed, Alan the only survivor. It was drilled into my early childhood with the intensity of Santa Claus, countlessly rehashed over the family dinners and summertime campfires of my youth. I'd sit there listening wide-eyed, pumping him full of questions as I traced my fingers over the pitted plastic of his prosthetic.

I rub my temples and mutter a yes.

"No. You don't." He shakes out a menthol, lights it. "It was them. We'd just rigged down, just a couple of us still at the well site. It was pretty late, nearly dark. I was by the trucks getting some tools when it happened. Pete Wozniak, you remember his kid, right? I think she played tee-ball with you."

I do. A thrift-store girl with lanky arms and red-frizz hair. I often caught her scowling at me in class. *Why you? Why'd you get to keep your Daddy?* I wanted to tell her she could have mine.

"Anyway, Pete was working the wellhead with the others when I felt it. This weird vibration in the earth. Then there was this crunching sound like an ocean of glass being chewed right beneath my feet. I'll never forget that sound. It was...indescribable." He shakes his head. "I'm not sure what happened next. All I know is I cracked my head pretty good on the truck when the well exploded. When I came to, they were swarming over my foot." His eyes flick to mine. "They'd already taken it to the bone. And the other guys...there wasn't much left of them. Just bits and pieces."

Something about the way he says it, the intensity of it, bothers me. He takes another pull on the cigarette and exhales a blue stream of smoke. I struggle to reconcile this new information with the tidy, gas-leak version of my childhood. The pile of casing collapsed on his leg, the firefighters dragging him from the flames.

"Didn't have much choice after that," he continues. "Everything was covered in oil, even them, so I did the only thing I could. I torched the bastards. Turned them to ash, including my leg."

It's true Alan was burned. I've seen the scars. Little flickers of them through open bathroom doors as a kid. At night in his room when he thought no one was watching. Mottled skin. Little piles of pink flesh. Shiny red valleys.

Something twists in my stomach. This story, these *things* crawling out of the earth and devouring his foot, it's too much. I need a drink. Something mostly vodka.

He clears his throat. "There's something I been meaning to ask you. Have you...felt them? Had any headaches or bloody noses lately? Any arm pain or your legs locking up? Any nightmares?"

Headaches. Check. Bloody noses. Plenty. Both come hand-in-hand with pharming. Nothing to worry about. Anyone who takes pills has them from time to time. No big deal. But the limb pain and the dreams... Acid inches up my esophagus. *Stop it. Don't go there.* Surely there's no connection. *Surely.* Throw enough spitballs at the wall and some will stick. There *are* no monsters. No feeders. Just like there weren't all those years ago when he said we had to run. The day my entire life evaporated.

But what was that thing in the picture?

He squints. "You *have*, haven't you?" His tone climbs a notch like we're both in on the dirty family secret. "Don't worry, they got inside me too. Beneath my skin. Down into my bone. Ever since that day I've felt them. Why do you think I was so panicked to get to the shelter that night when you were a kid? It's because I could feel them. I knew they were coming."

Yeah, and nothing happened except for Mom dying.

He drones on. "When they get closer, it gets worse. And it's been getting worse lately. *Way* worse than before. This time it's for real. I know it. All these years I've wondered if it spread to you or to Mac. I'll have to ask him. Maybe it hit him, too."

"Uh-huh." I close my eyes. I'm teetering on the verge of consciousness, the Roxy finally doing its job, but something he said bothers me. I crack my eyes open. "Wait, what'd you say?"

"I said I'm looking out for you. Really, I—"

"No. About Mac." But I already know his answer. Of course, he's going to abduct Mac, too. *Of course*, he is. I should have seen it coming. I jerk upright. "No, Alan. You leave him out of this. He can't see you. It will ruin him."

"What are you talking about?"

"Do you have any idea what that will do to him? It took him years to get over what happened. *Years.* Do you know how much shit he took from the other kids at school when you got put away? They said you were crazy. They called you a psychopath. And the worst part is, he always defended you. He got into so many fights. He idolized you, Alan. You were his hero. When he finally came to grips with what you did, it broke him. You *can't* put him through that again."

His fingers start to dance on the steering wheel, faster and faster. "I'm not leaving him behind. He's my son. And he's your brother. He's coming with us. He's gonna survive, goddammit. And I don't want to hear another word about it, or I swear I'll—"

"You'll do what? Shoot me again?"

His craggy features harden in the mirror. For a moment, I expect him to reach back and choke me, but instead, he tightens his grip on the wheel and says nothing at all. I slide back against the seat and watch him stare through the windshield at the glittering black asphalt and miles of hardpan rock—his silence suffocating, his labored breathing more terrifying than anything he could have said.

CHAPTER SIX
HELLO OFFICER

The van jolts and I snap awake with a headache pulsing at the base of my skull. An army of pinpricks chews through my cuffed arm as I push upright and rub it back to life. It's grown dark outside, nearly black. I squint as the brights of a passing car halogen-sear my retinas.

"Where are we?" I ask.

"About an hour south of Trinidad," Alan replies.

"So, are we going to stop soon, or do you plan on driving until you pass out?"

"No time to stop. We've still got a long way to go."

"How about some food, then? Some real food. No more of that gas station crap."

"Sorry, too late," he says, holding up a crinkling plastic bag. "Gassed up while you were out."

My stomach heaves. *Great.*

He passes back a water and I gulp down half the bottle. Pills always make me crazy thirsty, and speaking of pills...

"Listen, I um, I need a few more... you know."

A queasy silence. I can imagine Alan's lips twisting down in disgust. Whatever. At least I don't have to see it. Finally, he fumbles for the bottle and shakes out a pill, does the Daddy-play-doctor-bite-the-pill-in-half-thing again, and then tucks the bottle back into my jacket pocket before tossing it in the passenger seat. He hands the sliver back and I tense.

Half a pill. Again. Jesus.

I know how much abuse my body can take, and this isn't it—not even close, not by a mile. I scoop it up and then sink my fingernails into his palm and rake back as hard as I can.

"Christ, Brynn!" he hisses, jerking free.

The van swerves left. Right. Tires squeal. A horn blares.

He straightens out and brings his palm to his mouth, sucks at what I hope is a decent amount of blood. When he speaks, his voice is coated in poison. "I've had about enough of your shit. You'd better get a fucking grip on the new state of things, Brynn. I'm in charge here. Me. Not you. And if you don't get that through your head right now, I'm going to have to—"

The van's interior detonates into a storm of blue and red.

Alan hammers the steering wheel. "Goddammit! *Fuck!*"

My heart leaps. It's over, it's *finally, over!* I can see it all so clearly. Alan will be arrested and sent back to prison with an extra decade or two tacked onto his sentence depending on who he hurt and what he did to break out. I'll get back to work. Tank will be pissed at first. Act all mad about me disappearing on him for a few days. But then he'll lighten up when I tell him what happened.

Wait. Your old man did what? Kidnapped you? You gotta be kidding me. Goddamn, you got some shitty luck, B!

And I do because we aren't slowing.

My headache clicks up a notch. I reach forward and yank on Alan's headrest. "Hey, what are you doing? Pull over."

He doesn't respond so I shake harder. "Did you hear me? I said pull—"

He snatches my wrist and sinks his fingers into my skin until pain rockets up my arm. "Knock it off."

He's not going to stop.

He *has* to stop.

"Alan, please pull over," I beg. "You can't outrun him. There's no way."

"Not here," he says with a nod toward a green exit sign up the road. "There. And here's what's going to happen. You're gonna keep your mouth shut and let me do the talking. All of it. You don't say *any*thing. Not a single word. You do that, and everything will work out just fine. You don't, and things won't end up so good for him... or for you." He tosses my jacket back. "Now cover up those cuffs."

I fling it to the floor. "No! Pull over!"

Alan ignores me as we coast down the exit, bang onto a washboard-rutted road, and rattle to a stop. It's dark down here. Nothing but clouds of dust fogging the headlights. He leans over and hammers the glove box with his fist, digs something out. "You see this?"

My side flares at the sight of the gun—a Glock like Tank's. Images rush through my brain. Mom lying in a pool of blood. Me lying in a pool of my own. My vision flickering and fading away. The hope I felt a second ago dissolves. He's not going to let me go. He'll never let me go.

Ever.

I nod.

"Good. Then don't make me use it." He picks up my jacket and shoves it back in my lap. "Now, like I said, cover up those damn cuffs."

I do, my thoughts racing: Maybe the cop will recognize me?

Maybe he'll recognize Alan? There has to be an APB out on him or something like that, right? Or the van. It's stolen, no doubt. But has anyone reported it missing? Does anyone even know it's gone?

There's a harsh rap on the driver's side door, and I look up as a flashlight carves through the window. Alan rolls it down. "Evening, officer. How can I help you?"

"Mind telling me why you brought us way down here?" the cop replies.

A brief pause. "Didn't want you to have to stop in traffic is all."

"Next time pull over at the exit. No need to go any further." The man's accent is pure, don't-fuck-with-me, Texas tin. A sliver of hope flutters to life in my chest. I just need to get his attention, just need to warn him somehow.

"You know why I stopped you tonight?" the man asks.

"No, sir," Alan replies.

"You were swerving back there. That, and you got a busted taillight."

"I wasn't aware. Thanks for letting me know, officer. I'll be sure to get that fixed."

Scream, Brynn, I tell myself. *Do it now, or you'll never escape.*

My lips peel apart, but my throat is so swollen, all I can do is croak.

The cop drawls on. "Be sure you do. License, registration, and insurance, please."

"Sure thing," Alan says, leaning over and making a show of rummaging through the glove box. I shift to the side, and the movement brings the cop's flashlight arcing for my eyes. He lowers it enough for me to make out the smudgy outline of a campaign hat and a weak jaw. "Evening, Miss. Didn't see you back there. You all right?"

I glance nervously at Alan, and he gives me a subtle shake of his head.

"Ma'am," the cop repeats. "Are you okay? You look a little pale."

"Yeah, I'm, uh—" *Screw it.* I whip the jacket at Alan. "I've been kidnapped! He's got a gun! Run!"

But the man doesn't run. Instead, his eyebrows rip up his forehead and he goes for his gun.

He's quick.

Alan is quicker.

The cabin explodes with noise and light. Three rapid fire shots: *BANG! BANG! BANG!*

Silence.

The cop gazes at me, then at Alan, his head finally tilting down to his stomach. His face wilts and he tries to say something, but all that bubbles off his lips is blood. With a gurgle, he collapses to the ground.

I blink, realize I'm crying.

Alan slams his fist into the dash. "Dammit, Brynn! Dammit! I told you to keep your mouth shut!"

Outside, the cop fish-gulps air. The sound is wretched. Wet. A pop of static rises, followed by tangled speech.

"Ten, nine-nine-nine... o-officer... down."

Alan groans and shoves his way out the door.

Two more gunshots follow. Two blinding flashes of light. I screw my eyes shut and shake my head. *No. No. No.*

Nooooooo.

My heart thunders in my throat, in my ears. It's all I can hear, all I can feel, until Alan starts tapping the door with the Glock. A skeletal *tap, tap, tap,* that doesn't stop; the sound of untethered madness marching through the night once more, dragging me under, pulling me with it.

CHAPTER SEVEN
HOMECOMING

I run my hand over my face. It's shaking. My entire body trembling as I stare at the shit-bag diner through the dusty windshield. Alan's out there somewhere stealing us a new car. The van is toast now. Killing a cop will do that.

I punch the seat back and my headache roars in protest. I can actually hear the blood whooshing against my eardrums with each beat.

Why'd you have to kill him, Alan? Why?

Did he? You're the one who screamed, Brynn.

No. I can't go there. I need something... anything. And I need it quick. *A pill.*

I grab the bottle and tear off the cap, clumsily shake one into my mouth. Dry swallow it. At least Alan hasn't caught onto my latest trick yet, hasn't even so much as looked at my jacket since I threw it at him. He will though, eventually, but the pills I snatched from the pocket will be long gone by then. I'll make sure of that.

A faded red Nissan Altima whips up in front of the van. A pair of fuzzy dice swing from the mirror. Beneath them, through the windshield, Alan stares at me stone-faced. I see it again—him pretzel-stuffing the trooper into the hatch of the cruiser and slamming the trunk lid down over and over. Hear the dull crunch... crunch... crunch of metal on bone until Alan thought to move his arm.

He gets out and hurls the van door open, towering over me. "Let's go." The twenty-four-hour-diner sign blinks dully behind him: Pink. Green. Pink.

I open my mouth to scream, but he flashes a syringe—probably the same one he used on me last night. "You want this shit in your neck again? Because if you say anything, if you make one single sound, it's gonna happen, got it?"

I nod and he jerks me out of the van.

"Hey! Take it easy with the lady, boss."

The voice comes from my right. I glance over at a Black man pulling himself from a gray sedan a few parking spots down. He lumbers toward us in a way that tells me he isn't afraid of a fight. Shoulders squared, chin low. My heart leaps, but I catch Alan looking at me with that slight flick of his head again, and I know I can't do anything to get this guy hurt. I can't handle any more death tonight.

"We got a problem?" Alan asks gruffly as the man nears.

"I don't know. Do we?" He glances at me. "You okay, Miss?"

He's big, but Alan has him by half a foot at least. Maybe more. Again, I see the officer and the way his face collapsed when Alan shot him. The way he looked at me with those glassy, half-lid eyes, like someone had reached into his brain and turned out the lights.

I wave him off. "I'm fine."

"You sure about that? 'Cause it don't look that way to me."

I force out a thin laugh. "We were just playing around. I'm fine, really."

"Mmm-hmm." He crosses an arm and massages his chin. For a moment, I expect Alan to pull out the Glock and pistol-whip him.

"All right then," the man finally concedes. "Suit yourself." He eyes me for a moment longer, mutters something about shit never changing, then turns and weaves his way through the parking lot toward the diner. Alan grunts when it swallows him. "Good. Let's go."

———

We stop at some broken-down motel so Alan can swap plates with an age-worn Cadillac and then hit the road. It's silence for miles. The Altima is better than the van, but not by much. It's 1990's bland: a coffee-stained dash lopper, beige seat covers, headrests peppered with grease spots. The backseat is littered with old receipts and used clumps of Kleenex. A spatter of empty pizza boxes cover the floor boards. It reminds me of Vivian's room in the trailer after a Walmart shopping spree—a bunch of blue-light-special clothes strewn all over the bed, sacks everywhere, never to move again.

I dig a nail into my forearm where an angel poses seductively in lush purple ink. The sight suddenly makes me yearn for the sweet ache of a tattoo gun. Nothing calms me like the smell of ink and smoke, or the way the blood beads on my skin and stills my feverish brain. It's beautiful how the pain makes everything disappear. In that moment, there is no fear or rage or bitterness. No future or past. No shame. Nobody like Alan fucking up my life.

Only that terrible, beautiful pain.

But right now, I don't have a gun or any ink. All I've got is my arm cuffed to the oh-shit bar and a slew of crappy options running through my head like runaway boulders. I try to slow them down, to tick them off one-by-one.

A. Make a move for the steering wheel and send us hurtling into the concrete median, or worse, into oncoming traffic. Uh, no thanks.

B. Flag down a nearby driver. Somehow get them riled up enough to call the cops. Impossible through the black nothingness outside the window. And even *if* it did work, it would mean a standoff with Alan and a bunch of pissed-off cops out for revenge. More bullets. More death. Pass.

C. Work a miracle and get loose without Alan noticing, roll out of the car, and turn myself into a slab of Grade A, highway-fresh, roadkill. Nope.

D. Shit. There is no D.

My only consolation is the buzz; a friendly, pillow-perfect reunion whispering, *Hi! Hey there! I've missed you. Come on in and stay a while. Make yourself comfortable.* I want to. God, how I do. But I *can't.* There's no time. Not this close to Denver and to Mac. I've got to find a way to stop Alan before he gets to him. Otherwise, it will be all trails west to the shelter.

I can picture it: some washed-out, lifeless concrete box. Miles of fabricated steel. Twelve-inch-thick cement walls. No one around. Just Alan and his demons and us—one big happy family socked in nice and tight, ready to enjoy his imaginary apocalypse for all of eternity.

"I'm proud of you," he says out of nowhere. It startles me, but I manage to keep my eyes locked on the road. I don't want to talk to him or look at him. Ever. Again.

"You did good back there. With the guy in the parking lot. You made the right choice this time. Listen, I know you're upset about that cop. So am I, but there was nothing else to be done about it. Not after you screamed."

I whirl on him. "Don't you dare blame that man's death on me. That's all you. I mean shit, Alan. You didn't have to *kill* him. Couldn't you have knocked him out or something? I bet the guy had kids. Or a wife." I pick at a patch in my jeans and try to hold back the tears, fail as they slide down my cheeks in warm streams. He probably took away someone's father tonight.

I can feel his eyes on me, burning through the dark like heat lamps. "You left me no choice."

My entire body clenches, the tears evaporating into anger. "*I* left *you* no choice? Really? *Really?* You have to be fucking *kidding* me, Alan. *You* killed him. You did that. Not me. And you want me to what? Just get over it? Just forget about it like nothing happened? Like you probably think nothing happened with Mom or the shitty life you left us with afterward? Forcing us into that awful trailer with Vivian for all those years? The only one who actually cared was Tasker, and even he said you were a—"

He smacks the dash. "Enough! You think I wanted to kill that cop? Don't you get it? I didn't want any of this for you, or for Mac. None of it! It makes me sick what happened. *Sick.* I *loved* your mother. I still do..." His voice cracks. "Don't you know I *hate* myself for that? Every morning since that day I've considered ending things. So don't you for a *second* think you hate me worse than I hate myself. Because you don't." He falls silent, a shadow to my left breathing deep and hard. When he finally speaks again, his voice is quiet. "You know the only thing that kept me from tying a sheet around my neck in that cell? The only thing that kept me sucking air?"

My throat glues together. Please stop. *Please.*

"You, Brynn. Sure, your brother, too. But it was *you* that kept me going all those years. It was you I pictured when I was alone in that cage. What I've done, all of this, everything, it's all for you."

The passing headlights swirl into a hazy sheen, and just like that, I'm ten again and leaping into his arms after work, the smell of him working its way out of some long-forgotten memory: sweat and grease and suntan lotion. His little girl. Tears slick over my cheeks and patter off my lap like raindrops. I won't let him do this to me again.

I *can't.*

I reach up and take hold of the grab bar, wedge my feet against the door, and strain with all I've got. Legs, arms, heart, muscles, cells. My wrist screams, but it's nothing compared to the empty ache swamping my chest, the heat filling my face.

The bar pops, cracks free.

He sees what I'm doing too late and swerves.

All around us horns blaze. Headlights knife through the cabin in crazy, erratic flashes.

I lunge for him, go for his eyes, and manage to rake his face. It's enough to throw him off balance. I swing a wild left before he can recover and connect with his neck. He howls and the car sheers into the guardrail. I fly off him and slam into the dash as he jams the brakes, go semi-conscious, everything swimming, the needle puncturing my neck before I can recover. That woozy—*Oh, God, not again*—rush swims through my veins. He relaxes his grip and shoves me back into the passenger seat, and somewhere through the encroaching fog, it hits me...

There *is* an option D. A way out.

"I warned you," he says, his voice off somehow, like he's crying too, but I can't focus on that, only on maintaining what little is left of my wits before they're gone. I dig the bottle from my pocket. Tear off the cap with numb fingers. The world flickers in and out, everything turning gray, and I just want to let it darken, let the black wash over me, but no, not yet.

Not yet...

I get the bottle to my lips and tip it back. Several pills fall in my lap, but most spill down my throat like they're supposed to. I fling the empty bottle at Alan as a song whispers its way into my head. A song we'd both howled along to in his truck on lazy weekend camping trips. I'd lived for those trips. Those special, sun-soaked days when I was his little girl and he was my idol, my hero. The melody floats over me oily and distant, but I can't retrieve the words before I'm pulled into the void.

CHAPTER EIGHT
BLACKOUT

I'm floating, drifting through big, puffy balls of cotton. You know the type: those low-hanging clouds that, as a kid, you think you can brush with your fingertips if you just stretch hard enough and high enough. The kind you want to fall into, if only for a little while. The kind that look so soft.

So very soft...

Voices drift through the mist in snatches. Suddenly, Mac is there. He runs his fingers through my hair. Hair so thick I can barely get a brush through it most days. Not like his, which is fine and blond and perfect. So perfect I sometimes wonder how we're related.

He leans over and kisses my forehead, tells me to hang in there, that everything's going to be okay. He wears his half-curve smile. So perfect that smile—the way it lights me up on the inside like a splash of sun on a cold day. I've missed it so much. I've missed *him*.

I reach for his face. "Dad's coming, Mac," I whisper. "You have to hide."

He pulls back and his face crumples.

"Mac. I tried to stop him. I promise. I'm sorry."

He doesn't say a word...and he doesn't need to.

"I didn't mean to abandon you. To leave you alone. I just had to get away from the memories. From Vivian. From all of it. My heart was breaking. *I* was breaking. You understand that, don't you? *Don't you?*"

He tells me he understands—he does, he's my Mac, my sweet, sweet Mac—and he'll see me again soon.

———

A river of fire ants chew their way up my throat. Cramps wind through my abdomen. Nausea greases my stomach. I retch. Vomit spews over my face and runs down my neck. A moment of relief and then I'm back to shaking, my whole body seizing and twitching, vibrating so hard, I'm afraid I'll come apart.

Someone shouts to hold me down. *Alan!* I lash out. Grab a fistful of his hair and pull. Hands clamp over my wrists and grab my legs. A rubber block is jammed into my mouth. My eyelids flutter—patches of color leaking through. Burnt oranges and reds that flare and fade away. And then gravity takes hold, and I'm falling, falling, falling...

———

My eyes drift open to a milk-skinned nurse hovering at the foot of my bed. A pair of tortoise-shell glasses perch on the bridge of her nose and obscure the color of her eyes. Maybe hazel? Green? I can't tell. Her acorn-colored hair is tied up in a bun, and she's writing something on a clipboard, her lower lip planted firmly between her teeth, humming some long-ago TV tune I recognize but can't place. A thought flickers through my head: I wanted to be a nurse once. To help people.

I pull myself up onto my forearms and my head spins in tilt-a-whirls. My sheets are drenched with sweat, and my legs ache like someone took a meat tenderizer to them and had a good time doing so.

"Well, you're a lucky one," the nurse says, looking up. Her name tag reads *Laurie*. "Another half-hour and you'd have been gone." She wrinkles her nose. "These painkillers have sure done a number on you kids. I see a lot of your kind in here these days. Not all of them make it. And a lot of them don't have near as much in their system as you did. You must have some kind of tolerance."

I whip my hand up. "Oh, God. G-get me a—" But it's too late. I roll on my side and heave. Laurie wrestles something from the foot of my bed and thrusts it beneath my mouth. A bedpan. I retch into it over and over again until it feels like I'm about to puke up my stomach lining. When I roll onto my back, everything is sloshing back and forth—the ceiling, the walls, Laurie's face.

Kill me.

A moist cloth whispers over my lips, my forehead.

"It will subside, I promise. Just hang in there. They've got you on methadone, which will help."

Again the thought: this was supposed to be my life. A year of nursing school wasted. My first year in Austin. And I was *good* at it. Really good.

I try to force myself up again and fail. "What time is it? Where am I?" Each word stings the back of my throat.

"Parker Adventist. Try to get some rest, okay? I'll be back in an hour or so to check on you."

Parker Adventist. I know this place. About fifteen miles from Vivian's.

Shit! Vivian... Mac!

"What time is it?"

She pushes the glasses up her nose. "It's a little after seven, why?"

"A.M. or P.M.?"

"P.M. You've been out for quite a while."

I run the math and my brain vapor locks. Let's see, I downed the pills somewhere around ten, so that makes, what…eighteen, no, *nineteen* hours since I blacked out! Oh, God. Too long. *Way* too long.

I snatch her wrist. "Listen, you need to call the police."

She frowns. "Calm down. It's not good for you to get agitated right now."

I shake her arm. "No. You don't understand. The man that brought me in last night, he abducted me, drugged me. He's dangerous. He's already killed a man…a—a police officer, a state trooper south of Trinidad, and now he's after my brother." I gulp down the panic. "Is he still in the waiting room?"

Her face pales. "Oh, I'm sorry. I have no idea who brought you in. I wasn't even on shift last night. And it wasn't last night. It was…" She slides out of my grip and grabs a clipboard hanging by the door, glances at the paperwork, looks up. "I'm afraid you've been out for two days."

———

They get a cop to my room quickly. One Mark Olberman—a vulpine-faced detective with thin hair slicked over his scalp in greasy strands. His features are delicate. A feminine nose. Thin lips. High cheekbones. The kind of cheekbones that look like they'd crack with a solid right hook.

"So, you say your father—"

"Alan."

"Okay, Alan. You say he's after your brother? That he's the one who shot that trooper near Trinidad? The same one who escaped Florence a couple weeks ago?"

"Yeah, that's him."

"Hm." He massages his chin. "Why'd he shoot the trooper?"

"He stopped us. Alan didn't want to go back to prison—look I don't know why he does anything. He's fucking crazy. He thinks the world is going to end. He used to stick me with needles as a kid."

The detective's eyes narrow. "He stuck you with... needles?"

I glance at his cell phone on the side table for the hundredth time, the one he let me use to call Mac a moment ago. No answer, so I left a message for him to call back. *Call me, Mac. Please. Dad's coming for you.*

Olberman follows my gaze. "Don't worry. We've got a unit at your aunt's place right now. They'll find your brother. And your dad. I promise. Half the cops in the state were looking for him before this. Now he'll have to hide from all of them."

I slide back on the pillow and close my eyes. Veins of light paint the insides of my eyelids in white branching streaks.

"Miss Donovan, I need to ask you a few more questions. Standard procedure. I'll be out of your hair shortly."

I open my eyes and motion for him to continue.

He clears his throat. "Have you ever abused narcotics?" He scans my arms as he says it, my tattoos. I know what he's looking for—track marks and bruises. Evidence that maybe I'm the one at fault here and not Alan. That I somehow did something to deserve this.

"What does that have to do with anything?" I reply. "All that matters is finding my brother."

He blinks.

I stare at him in silent fury until his phone rings. He snatches it up and brings it to his ear. I lean in, hoping to hear Mac's voice on the other end.

"Olberman. Yep... Go ahead. Okay, got it. Keep me posted."

His beer-colored eyes flick my way. "Your aunt's place is empty. We'll have a unit patrol the property tonight. See if anyone shows up. In the meantime, Miss Donovan, I need to inform you that you've been placed on a seventy-two-hour hold." He glances at my arms again. "It's standard course in situations like yours."

Situations like mine? A victim of abuse? Of kidnap and assault?

I swallow my rage and nod.

Think whatever you want, asshole. I'll be long gone by then.

CHAPTER NINE
E-DAY

Tolerance. My superpower.

The ability to function under conditions that would leave most people drooling in a gutter. Still, even I have my limits, and with a literal pharmacy of drugs swimming through my bloodstream, I wonder if I'll make it down the hall, much less out of the building, before passing out.

I rip the IV from my arm and stand.

Getting dressed is ridiculously hard. My entire body feels like one giant, throbbing bruise, not to mention my shirt is gone, probably cut off when they brought me in. But my jeans are there, stuffed in the mesh bag by my bed, along with Tank's spider pendant and my shoes.

I slip the pendant around my neck and pull on the jeans, then tuck my hospital gown into the waist for an awkward business in the front, party in the back, insane asylum sort of look before edging toward the door to peer down the hall.

There's a reception desk helmed by two nurses, one pecking away at a laptop while the other sorts through a stack of forms. Across from them is the elevator, which means no easy way out, but at least they're too busy to notice when I slide into the hall and totter away in the opposite direction.

It only takes a few steps before black flecks are spiting through my vision and threatening to send me to the floor. I press against the wall and remain there for a few breaths as an orderly exits the room in front of me. I toss him a floppy wave and force a smile. (*I'm fine. Nothing to see here.*)

His eyes flick up for a microsecond, find mine, and then drop back to his chart.

I press on past dimly lit rooms full of broken bodies. The blue wash of TV light filters from doorways. Machines beep and hiss from within. I'm sweating by the time I reach the door beneath the exit sign at the end of the hall and pause to vent my gown. A voice rises behind me. One that uses my name.

"Excuse me, Miss Donovan!"

My heart flip-flops. Laurie the nurse is speed-walking after me, her green scrubs swish-swishing away. She waves her hands above her head like she's an air traffic controller motioning for me to circle back and land in my room.

I bowl through the door.

The stairwell is all steel and concrete—a dark throat threatening to break all my bones if I fall. I grab the railing and stumble down the stairs as fast as I can, my knees wobbling, quads twitching. The door crashes open above me, and Laurie's panicked voice rains down. "Miss Donovan! Miss Donovan! You need to stay in your room. We haven't released you yet. It's not safe for you to be up—"

I plow into the first-floor hall and collide with a lanky kid wearing an 80's style tracksuit and red and yellow Adidas. "Whoa. You okay, lady?"

"Where's the exit?" I ask frantically, clutching his shirt.

He takes a step back and points toward a sprawling, open room with a marbled floor and vaulted ceiling. "Uh, over there, I think."

The watery onion soup I choked down for dinner sloshes dangerously through my stomach as I stride for it. I'm careful to keep my eyes low and away from the guard desk where a man in a blue uniform pages lazily through a magazine. A sudden squelch of static from his radio sends me crashing onto a couch next to a couple of kids playing with Legos at their parents' feet.

I smile at them and then risk a glance at the man in time to catch him moving in the opposite direction. I'm back on my feet and out the door before he turns my way.

Outside, it's dark and cold. A hard shiver runs down my arms and settles in my legs. Alan could have at least had the decency to kidnap me in August. September even. The end of October, with winter approaching, is just plain cruel.

I rub my arms and make for the street. The thin material of the hospital gown does little to ward off the encroaching chill. It only takes five minutes before I hit a busy intersection with traffic blowing by in both directions. A parade of headlights stings my eyes. The whoosh of rushing metal fills my ears. I squint and spot a cab, wave for it to slow down, which it doesn't. Neither do the next two.

I massage my temples and wince as my brain swells with vertigo. Consciousness threatens to leave me. How will I get to Mac if I can't even make it a few blocks before passing out? My only answer comes in the form of chattering teeth and a sudden cramp surging through my thighs. A familiar cramp—like someone slit open my legs and poured a bag of quick dry cement into my veins.

Nooo.

It hits my abdomen, and I double over with a groan. The pain is horrific, even worse than when I first came to in the hospital. My vision stains pink at the edges, my eardrums popping with the sound of a wailing horn.

I look up to a taxi van. It idles on the corner a few feet off, ugly and purple, with a bunch of faded sevens stenciled across the side. Tinted windows obscure the interior as the passenger door swings open to a billow of cigarette smoke. *Great. Just what I need.* But it won't keep me from getting in. Anything beats standing out here freezing my ass off for a second longer.

Another cramp strikes as I start for it, and I double over with a groan while managing to raise an arm. "Sorry. Just... give me a second." I half expect the van to bolt, but it doesn't. It just sits there idling as a truck pulls up behind it and revs the engine.

I force myself forward... and stop.

The vibration is quiet at first. Barely perceptible, a dull grinding sensation that rises up my legs and fills my chest. A detox consolation prize. Of *course,* it's my legs shaking, not the street.

But it's not.

A harsh crack splits the air and I crouch. Screams blister the night. I follow the sounds up the street to a massive slab of buckled asphalt. Several cars are overturned next to it, one embedded in the plate-glass window of a pizza shop, horn shrieking. Plumes of dust and smoke filter eerily through the glow of street lamps. Traffic is a mess.

A moment of silence falls over the street, thick and oppressive.

Another crack hits, this one thunderous. Deafening. I cover my ears.

What the hell is happening?

I don't have time to dwell on the thought before everything begins to tremble. Then there's an awful sound; this horrible, jagged crunch like the earth is coming alive. Like an ocean of glass is being chewed right beneath my feet.

CHAPTER TEN
GET IN!

A jagged seam rips through the cement and I slam to the ground. The impact jars my wrists. I look up in time to see a steel girder punch through the building across the street. A moment later the windows shatter. *An earthquake.* But it can't be. Earthquakes don't happen in Denver. It doesn't make—

"Get in!"

The voice is gruff, wracked with panic. I search for it as the trunk of an oak ten yards away splinters. Two street lamps to my left pop and rain down glass.

"Brynn, get in!"

I zero in on the voice. Alan.

He's leaning across the taxi passenger seat holding the door open. His eyes are wild, dilated marbles. Veins line his forehead. The sight paralyzes me. I can't move, can't feel the air rushing in and out of my lungs in quick gasps, can't reconcile what's happening around me. *To me.*

A power line snaps and whips down over the asphalt. Sparks fly. A motorcycle swerves to miss it and slams into the broadside of a Suburban. The rider whipsaws over the hood with a wicked crunch.

A woman screams across the street. It's ear-splitting. Like she's being torn apart...

Because she is.

There are these black things spinning out of the ground all around her, drilling into her, ripping through her legs, and turning them to pulp.

"BRYNN!"

I move. My feet fast-slap against the concrete and I dive into the front seat of the cab. Without warning, Alan tears away from the curb. My legs smack off the asphalt and, for a terrible second, I feel like I'm about to lose my grip. Alan grabs my forearm and rips me in as a runaway truck blows my door off its hinges. I catch a glimpse of the driver: glazed, half-slit eyes, his head pancaked against the steering wheel. A second later, the truck swerves and slams into a concrete retaining wall.

I realize Alan is shouting at me.

"What?" I yell back.

"Get your seatbelt on!"

I whip it over my shoulder and click it home with shaking fingers. "Wh-what's happening?"

He glances my way for a millisecond, his eyes harsh black pin-pricks in the low light. "What do you *think* is happening?"

Oh, dear God, no.

"Brace yourself," he says, stiff-arming the wheel. "We wreck, and we're done."

There's a series of bone snapping cracks. Ahead, several gouts of asphalt hiss into the air, and the road vanishes. A city bus jams its brakes, too late, and fishtails sideways over the lip into a geyser of steam.

Alan brakes and rips the van up and onto the sidewalk, narrowly missing a bike stand before burning back onto the street toward a snarl of traffic. Red brake lights coming way too fast.

He cranks the wheel left back onto the sidewalk and I bang to the side. My head whiplashes out into the open space where the door used to be. Icy air stings my eyes. I grasp for something, *anything* to hold onto—find the seatbelt and pull. The cold brush of metal whispers through my hair, and I'm nearly decapitated by a parking meter as I swing upright again.

We blur past shattered storefronts and mailboxes. To my right, the street is sheer gridlock. The thunder and boom of cars slamming into one another pounds my ears. A blood-curdling shriek explodes from a white Jeep Cherokee sandwiched between two cars. Those *things* are there, swarming from a sewer grate and up through the Jeep's windows. I catch sight of a skin-stretched face—a woman flapping her arms as a terrible, high-pitched tone ignites. *Skreeeee!*

The interior explodes with blood.

"Don't look at them," Alan shouts. "Look straight ahead! I need your eyes."

I snap my gaze forward as we pulverize a sidewalk display. A mental-looking clown holding an ice-cream cone smacks against the glass. Alan curses. Through the clown's polka dot legs, I see us barreling straight for a steel post. I grab his arm and yank. "Right! Go right!"

Alan cranks the wheel, and the van hurtles off the sidewalk onto the asphalt. The shocks squeal, and the clown blows off the glass and tumbles somewhere behind us. We careen through an intersection and clip the fender of a red Dodge Charger. It spins a lazy circle before plowing straight into an oncoming truck. The crunch of metal and glass trails in our wake along with a cluster of wet, distant screams. An ambulance siren wails from somewhere. The blast of a firetruck.

And through it all, that familiar high-pitched keening sound rises, a pulsing *wha-wha-wha* that I recognize from somewhere. It takes a moment, and then it hits me.

Drills. I'm hearing drills.

A snip of blue carves through the windshield. A sign: I-225. I grab a fistful of Alan's shirt and point. "There! The interstate."

He shakes his head. "No. It'll be a cluster fuck. We need to get away from the cars. From all this noise." He whips left and hammers the gas. The van shudders and picks up speed.

We weave through traffic, cars blowing past us on either side. I catch glimpses of terrified faces through windows. Mouths pulled wide. Teeth slivered and bared. Alan slams the brakes, and we squeal to a stop. Ahead, an overturned seafood truck blocks the road. A waterfall of ice pours through the open doors, mixed with silvery glint of fish scales. All around it are rows of tangled cars, some on fire, some overturned. Twisted doors and stray bumpers pepper the street. The smell of smoking rubber fills my nose.

"Shit," Alan mutters through clenched teeth.

People scatter in every direction. Running for the sidewalk. Charging toward the buildings and through the doors. They climb up trees and jump onto car hoods, all in an effort to escape the slick-black bodies ripping from the ground with terrifying speed.

It doesn't matter.

The flood is relentless.

They look like giant cockroaches mated with drill bits, legs there one moment, gone the next as they whirl back into the earth.

A woman falls and is swarmed, shrieking until she's nothing more than a writhing bulge of shells. A man leaps onto a bench, only to have it dissolve beneath him as the things rip through the metal supports... and then him.

I twist around to headlights, several of which are hurtling straight for us. My eyes click toward the sidewalk and the black gap there, nestled between two buildings. *An alley.*

"Alan," I shriek and point. "Over there!"

He jams the gas, and the tires catch. Horns blare as we slam into the alley and hurtle toward a dumpster. Alan swerves around it and obliterates a stack of boxes. Then we're through and careening onto the opposite street, whipping south away from all the chaos.

There are fewer cars here, but still too many.

"We need to get off the road," Alan says, jaw clenched.

I gesture toward a wall of shadows three blocks down—the dark shape of pine trees hemming a park. "How about that?" Something slams into the van's fender as I say it. A scooter whips over the hood, followed by its driver. Both of them tumble into the gutter where a black wave is surging through a sewer grate. The man's mouth goes wide in a frozen scream.

More of those things.

"Dammit," Alan spits. He pumps the gas again, and we thread back into traffic and then break free and angle toward the park. Alan kills the headlights as we whisper over the grass with nothing but moonlight to guide our way. The tires make strange clicking sounds like they're seconds from snapping off the axles. A dull orange glow smokes off the horizon ahead of us. I realize what it is with a shudder.

Denver is burning.

I look away. I'm cold. Freezing. Shivering not just from the temperature, but from this night and the sheer insanity of it all. My foot jackhammers the floorboard. Alan reaches over and slides a hand over my knee. "We're gonna make it, okay. We just need to get to Tasker's. It's not far from here."

I nod dumbly; I can't speak.

We idle past a playground that shines like a cathedral of bone in the pale moonlight. Faraway sounds flare to life. Collisions and screams and the intermittent snap of gunfire. Those drills, whatever they are.

I shiver.

Something flashes to my right, and I flinch, but it's only a dog. A collie with a red handkerchief tied around its neck and luminous, dark globe eyes. It looks terrified. As terrified as—

Oh, Jesus...

I whip my gaze back to Alan. "Mac? *Where's* Mac?"

"I've got him. And Vivian. They're safe."

A shudder of relief spills through me, followed by a cold realization. I look at him dumbfounded. "Wait, you were right? All this time, you were *right*?"

He waves me off. "Not now. Later. As soon as we're out of this mess."

"Fine. But how'd you find me? Back there on the corner?"

"I didn't. I followed you from the hospital. Been camped out there for over a day now." He glances at me, his face half-buried in shadow. "Been waiting for you."

I look at him numbly, the words dying on my tongue.

He was right...

We reach the far side of the park and Alan eases the van onto the street. It's quieter here. Blocks and blocks of sprawling houses. Ranches and split-levels with brick fronts and manicured lawns. All of it bathed in eerie moonlight—the electricity blown. Sudden ghost towns. A cry pierces the night from somewhere behind us and Alan picks up speed.

Soon, we're moving east on a lonely sweep of road. The houses are thinner in number here, quickly giving way to empty space and farmland. I find my wrist and turn a few anxious circles over it with my thumb. The road feels endless. My eyes scan the asphalt for movement. For the black scatter that means more of those...*things.*

Finally, I see the sight I've been yearning for looming through the dark—a dim square of industrial development: warehouses and offices and medical facilities. In the far corner, Tasker's Oilfield Supply rises with its haphazard stacks of casing and tubing piled out front. Across the road, a flare stack burns bright next to two ancient pumpjacks; giant horse heads that push and pull in a ceaseless search for more oil.

Something warm runs over my lips. I run a hand over it.

Blood. Why am I bleeding?

The flare stack erupts.

I wince as a column of flame bursts skyward. One of the pumpjacks sways and then smashes to the ground. The air burns and shimmers like a fun-house mirror. Several mounds of earth bubble up in front of it, oil leaking everywhere, thick gouts of it spilling over the sand and flowing toward the road.

I squint and my stomach clenches.

It's not oil. It's *them*.

Hundreds of them, their bodies jerking over one another, spreading across the dirt, consuming it like a living blanket of tar.

I grab Alan's leg and squeeze: "Go! Go! Go!"

The van leaps forward as they flood the road, their angular bodies covered in swirls of sharp protrusions. They drill in and out of the ground like it's made of water. And the way they move... it seems familiar. Almost like I've seen it before.

Because I have.

Dolphins. They move like dolphins dipping in and out of the waves. One jerks its head up as we pass. Its jaw splits wide, quartered into four serrated mandibles. Something long and blade-like whirs impossibly fast between them. *Skree!* The blood drains from my face.

This. Isn't. Happening.

We tear into the yard. Gravel sprays off the sheet metal we fishtail to a stop in front of Tasker's. I rip off my seatbelt and lunge for the door, grab the knob, and twist. My heart explodes. It's locked.

"Get it open," I plead to Alan. "Hurry. They're coming."

And they are. I can *feel* them.

Alan hammers his fist against the door. "Tasker! Open up, goddamn you! Open this door right fucking now!"

The smell hits me first: a sweet, putrefied stench that slides into my nostrils like the scent of rotten meat. Like day's old pus drowned in sulfur. Then the sound hits. A terrifying crackle. A million fingers snapping at once. An ocean of black chitin floods the parking lot—wave after wave of razor blade bodies rushing straight for us, moving impossibly fast.

I can't blink. Can't move.

I flash to the woman in the car again, see the way they drilled into her chest and punctured her neck. Picture her skin as it tore and split apart. The red gush of blood that coated her chest and the way she screamed...

Fingers take hold of my shoulder and rip me back. I spin around.

Tasker! Stick-thin and manic. All waving limbs and cracking joints folded beneath a black cowboy hat. He slams the door shut and shoves me toward a huge oil tank in the back of the warehouse. "There. We can hide inside!"

I bolt for it, tear between shelving units and supply racks stuffed with tools. Alan jerks next to me in a hobble-run, struggling to keep up with his prosthetic, his cheeks flushed red beneath the bright bay lights of the warehouse. A harsh whine roars against the shop's aluminum walls and vibrates through the floor.

"Keep moving," Tasker roars.

I reach the tank out of breath, stars spitting through my vision, lungs on fire. I don't have time to rest, though, because Tasker is already shoving me toward a ladder, shouting for me to, "Climb!"

I take the rungs two at a time, my hands covered in sweat and slick on the steel. I nearly fall, but he steadies me from behind, and I keep climbing until I'm over the lip and on top of the tank where I collapse.

How am I still alive?

Tasker appears and rips me to my feet, pushes me toward a rusted hatch: "No time for that, Brynn! Get inside!" He turns to help Alan, and I catch a glimpse of the things drilling through the warehouse walls behind him, their armored heads twisting in and jerking back again like they've been stung.

So *many* of them...

"Brynn," Alan yells as he hauls himself up. "Get in the tank already!"

I turn and hustle for the hatch, thinking none of this makes sense, that nothing will ever make sense again.

CHAPTER ELEVEN
THE TANK

The light is muted as I descend the rungs; a burnt-white glow from an old Coleman lantern that hisses over a mess of dirty mattress pads and blankets. A few coolers are scattered throughout along with some backpacks and duffel bags. Along the far wall, someone struggles to their feet. I'd recognize the shape anywhere. *Mac!*

I leap down and rush to him, pull him into my arms. "I've been so worried about you. Alan said you were safe, but I didn't know if he..." I pull back, my heart beating so fast I can barely speak. "He didn't hurt you, did he?"

He shakes his head. "No, I'm okay."

"Thank God." I pull him in for another hug and his ribs scrub mine. He's thin. Too thin. And taller. God, when did he get so tall? He's got me by three inches at least. Maybe more.

I step back and take him in. He's fully a teenager now with a scatter of acne and the slouch to match. The spray of freckles across his nose is darker than I remember, and his sandy-blond hair spills out in clumps from beneath a black Adidas ball cap. The dark circles under his eyes make me wonder when he last slept.

He thumbs his nose and points. "You, uh... I think you're bleeding."

I press a hand to my nose. "Oh, shit, yeah. I'm not sure what's going on with that."

"What's happening out there? We've been down here for a couple days now. Or I think it's been that long. I'm not really sure." He eyes my hospital gown and wrinkles his nose. "Man, you look terrible."

"You don't look so hot yourself," I say with a laugh that quickly transforms to a knot in my throat. "Mac, I don't even know where to start. Alan was right. About all of it. About the monsters in the ground. Everything he talked about when we were kids. He..." I notice his ankles and trail off. They're cuffed together. *Goddammit, Alan.* But at least this time I understand it.

Alan roars behind me, and I whirl around to see him rip Tasker from the ladder and slam him against the tank wall. He's got him by the neck, shaking him like a life-size doll. Tasker claws at his hands and gasps for breath, his hat on the floor, his cowboy boots banging off the shimmering steel.

"What the *hell*, Tasker?" Alan barks. "Why was that door locked? You plan on leaving us out there to die? To be eaten by those things?"

Tasker shakes his head maniacally. Alan slams him against the tank again. "You almost got us *killed*. Another thirty seconds and we would've been. You're lucky you opened that door when you did."

"Be right back," I whisper to Mac. I jog over to Alan and place a hand on his arm. "Hey, put him down, okay?" I say it with a nod, like I'm deciding for him.

He looks at me, jaw pulsing, and for a moment I think he won't, but he finally lets go. Tasker collapses to the floor and massages his throat. When he speaks, his voice is raw. Hoarse. "Those... things. Wh-whatever they are. S-saw them on the news. And then... th-the explosions. I was... just trying to protect Mac. Viv."

"Bullshit," Alan spits. "You knew we were coming back."

I brush by him and help Tasker to his feet, hand him his Stetson. He's light. A strip of the Old West in a sidewinder button-down and a black leather vest. "Cut him some slack, Alan," I say. "We're fine, aren't we?"

He glowers at me. "No, we're not *fine*. I'd say we're just about as far from fine as you can get. In fact, I'd say we're pretty much fucked."

Tasker shakes his head and blinks, spreads his hands wide. "Don't worry. Th'aint getting in here. Not through all this metal."

Alan raps his knuckles against the steel. "What? *This?* This is *nothing* to them. Nothing. They'll chew through it in a matter of minutes. Open it up like can of tuna and tear us apart."

"Will you two shut up already?" The voice carries a rasp that sends a shudder down my spine. Vivian. She pulls herself up from a nearby mattress and stumbles over scatter-haired and bleary-eyed, her perma-scowl etched on her face. "Come back to finish us off, did you, Alan?" He opens his mouth to reply, but she's already turned toward me. "I assume you're in on this little family reunion of his?"

I suck in a breath. Her left eye is swollen shut, the color of a bruised plum, the flesh beneath it stained a deep, thunderstorm black. A trail of moisture leaks from the corner down her cheek. I can picture how it happened. Her mouthing off to Alan, telling him to fuck off when he told her to pack her shit, that she and Mac were coming with him. Alan leveling her with one punch in reply and tossing her over his shoulder.

"Nice outfit by the way," she adds, glancing at my hospital gown. "Looks good on you." She looks back to Alan. "You need to uncuff me. You have no right to hold us here any longer. Not for one more minute. How dare you do this to your wife's sister? Her *sister*, Alan."

I hear something and tune her out. It's muffled but there. A sound like an angry colony of bees searching for whoever smashed their nest. And it's getting louder.

"...all these years I've had these two. Kept them fed and clothed and schooled after you killed her. The whole while you were locked up. Don't you think for an instant that you're gonna get away with coming into *my* house and stealing *my* car and taking *my*—"

I grab her arm. "Vivian. Shut up." I jab a finger toward the tank wall. "Do you hear that? That high-pitched sound out there?"

She stares at me, working her underbite back and forth. "What is that?"

"It's why you're here. Why we all are." I shake my head. I must sound as crazy as Alan. "There are things out there coming out of the ground. And they're eating people."

The words leave me feeling lightheaded, everything rushing in at once: The kidnap. The trooper and the pills and the hospital. The people getting shredded by those...creatures. Everything gone to Hell. My entire life wrecked in a couple of days. I sit down hard and bury my face in my hands.

All of this is so *fucked*.

I don't even realize I'm crying until I feel the hand on my shoulder. I look up to find Tasker hovering over me with his palm outstretched. I wipe my eyes and consider swatting it away, then, with a sigh, take it and let him pull me to my feet.

"You're looking good, Bear."

A nervous jag of laughter rises up my throat. "Riggght." I stare at Alan's best friend. At my fake dad. The man who was there for me when my real one wasn't. The man who, at times, felt more like a father than my own. He winks, eyes bright even in here, and a burst of affection runs through me. Besides some gray at the temples and his mustache, he looks exactly the same—like an extra on the set of an old Western. It's been way too long since I've last seen him.

"Either way," he continues, gripping my shoulders, "I'm glad you're safe. How you been?"

"I've been better."

"I think we all have," he says with a laugh before pulling me in for a quick hug. He even smells the same: a mix of leather and suntan lotion, grease and sweat. They're good smells. Safe smells.

"Hey, I could use a little help over here," Mac says, hopping toward us from the wall, stopping suddenly as something booms outside the tank. "Uh, what was that?" Another explosion vibrates the metal, this one closer.

Tasker looks up toward the hatch, still rubbing his neck. "I don't know. But if we're about to meet our maker, I'm not doing it on an empty stomach. Come on. We could all use something to eat, 'specially you, Brynn."

————

He serves us paper plates smothered in Chef Boyardee Ravioli and beans heated over a small propane grill along with cups of lukewarm Orange Crush and mini bags of pretzels. I should be starving but I'm not. The food tastes like chalk in my mouth, everything bland and flavorless. Tasker wolfs his like a savage, barely looks up from his plate the entire time; something else that hasn't changed about the guy. He's practically a skeleton but eats like someone three times his size, apparently even when the world is falling apart outside.

A dull thunderclap echoes in the distance, and I set my plate down. Mac eyes the far wall like it's about to split open at any minute. "Th-they're not going to get in here, are they?"

Alan scoops a final bite of beans in his mouth and pushes his plate aside, runs the back of his hand across his lips. "Don't know. They've drilled through a lot of formation to get up here. A lot of rock."

"Why not? Aren't you supposed to be the expert?" Vivian asks.

Alan's eyes flash beneath the brim of his John Deere cap. "You still think this is a joke, don't you?"

The way her eyes are bouncing all over the tank tells me she doesn't, but she'll do anything to get under Alan's skin. Even now. And I've always been happy to join in, to bad-mouth him when she did. *Screw the old man, right?* Talking shit about Alan is the only thing we've ever had in common. But right now, I wish I'd never said a word.

"No one thinks this is a joke anymore, Alan," I say.

He grunts and runs his fingers through the beginnings of a beard.

"So, what are they?" I ask. "Where do they come from?"

"You know what they are."

I do. The thing I've been running from all my life. My own personal Bogeyman. A ghastly childhood fairytale come true.

"As far as where they come from, well..." He points toward the floor. "Down deep. Source rock."

"Oil?" I ask.

He nods. "And gas. There's an ocean of it down there. Their food source. An all-you-can-eat buffet, and we stole it."

"How the hell you know that?" Tasker asks with a belch, tossing his plate somewhere behind him.

"How do you think?" Alan says, pulling up the leg of his jeans. His prosthetic glows pale in the lantern light.

"Shit, Alan. I'm sorry. Even I thought that was a bunch of

bullshit."

"Yeah, you and everyone else." His eyes find mine, something painful stirring there. "And every day since I lost it, I've tried to figure them out. I chased leads all over the country. People gone. People turned to body parts in remote areas. And they all had one thing in common."

"What?" Mac asks.

"It always happened around the basins. Always near wells. And caves. The way I figure it, these things are old. Really, really old. And we woke them up."

"We're dead," Mac whispers.

"No. I know something most don't."

"Yeah?" Vivian asks. "And what's that?"

"Hematite."

"Hema—huh?" Tasker says.

"Hematite. They can't get through it. The well that exploded on us, the one they crawled up, didn't have any hematite in the drilling mud. The company was cutting costs. Getting cheap. First well out of hundreds where they pulled that shit."

"What's mud have to do with anything?" I ask.

He shifts forward, foot tapping, fingers dancing on his knee. "Mud holds back the formation pressure when you drill. And we're talking thousands and thousands of pounds of pressure down there. Hematite is an additive. Makes the mud stronger'n shit. Nothing can get through it. When we pulled it out of the mud on that well, it went boom." He makes an explosion sound and spreads his fingers. "Just like that."

"How does hema... whatever help us, though?" Mac asks.

Alan chews on his cheek. "The shelter's full of it. I found a place I could get a truck up to. Nothing will crack through that foundation.

Or the walls. Not even an army of backhoes." He drains the rest of his drink and crushes the cup, tosses it into the dark away from the light.

The movement tickles something in my brain; a thought: *Light.* My heart quickens. It's not much, but it feels like the first sliver of hope I've had in days. Something I can latch on to. "It's the light," I mutter softly.

Tasker leans forward. "What's that?"

"The light," I repeat louder. "Up on the tank, before I came down here, I saw them drilling through the walls and pulling back again. They didn't like something about the warehouse. I think it's the light. It's gotta be." I look to Alan. "What time was it when they…" I swallow, can't believe I'm actually about to ask him this question. "When they took your leg? At the well? Was it dark?"

His brow furrows. "It was late evening. So yeah, not much sun."

I eye Tasker. "And your shop. The lights are bright. It's like the middle of the day out there."

"Yep. Full LED. It prevents theft. There's a few too many five-finger discounts out here. I always leave 'em on. Tends to keep the riffraff away."

I suck in a lip. It makes sense. "Listen. What do you hear?"

Mac's eyes tighten. "Nothing."

"Exactly. The drills are gone."

An explosion—the closest one yet—rattles the tank as I say it and sends something crashing to the floor outside. Vivian skitters back and knocks over a cooler. "Jesus. What was that?"

Alan stares at the tank wall for a long moment, scratches his ear. "Don't know. But we should all get some shut-eye while we can. No telling if or when we'll get another chance."

———

I pull a foam mattress pad next to Mac and lie down with a groan. He rolls over and stares at me, his eyes glimmering in the shine of the lantern. "Is it true? What you said is happening out there? I mean is it *really* true? You're not making this up like Dad did, are you?"

"Trust me. I wouldn't believe it unless I'd seen it myself."

"So, Dad, he's not... crazy then? Not like all the kids at school thought? Like Mom thought?"

I think of the cop, of the fine red mist coating the van door. The needles in my neck on the way here. The needles in my arm as a kid. "Oh, he's crazy, all right. Just not in the I-see-imaginary-monsters way we'd thought."

His face brightens. "I *knew* it. I knew he wasn't crazy. So, what do they look like? The feeders?"

The feeders. There's that word again. It still feels wrong—like if I say it, I'm admitting I've lost my marbles, too. I shudder, all the moisture gone from my mouth. "Kind of like a beetle I guess. But larger and super sharp."

"They're... sharp?"

"Yeah, their bodies are covered in all these crazy swirls if that makes any sense. It was pretty dark, though. I couldn't really see them all that well." I think of the mandibles with their razor-blade hooks and those horrible drills whirring between them. The awful, rotten-egg smell everywhere. The way they move through the ground like it's made of liquid. I cringe. There's no reason to tell Mac about that stuff yet. He'll find out soon enough. But there is something else I need to know.

"Hey, Mac?"

"Yeah?"

"Have you... felt anything lately? Like body aches or cramps. Your muscles going tight. That sort of thing?"

He pulls his lower lip between his teeth and hesitates. "No... not that I can think of. Why?"

"It's nothing. Forget it."

He quirks his head at me. "You okay?"

"I'm fine. Just worn out."

"So, I've been thinking about what you said about the lights. What if... well, what if they go out tonight?"

Cold fear bleeds through me. "Don't think about that, okay? Just try to get some sleep if you can. Alan's right. Who knows when we'll get the chance to rest again."

He gives me a sarcastic nod. "Yeah okay, Mom." He's trying to act brave. Like Alan. But he's nothing like Alan. He's warm and sweet and goofy, not to mention thin as a stick. He's nothing like me, either, bitter and brimming with life's poison. All things that will get him killed out there. A swoop of hair falls across his forehead, and I want to reach out and brush it aside. I want to tell him everything's going to be okay, that we'll be fine. But it would be a lie, and I don't want to lie to him. Not anymore.

A hint of a smile breaks over his chin, and he shakes his head. "I knew Dad was right. I *knew* it."

He rolls over onto his side, and I watch him until his breathing evens out. Vivian sobs somewhere behind me, making little mewling sounds that make me think of an injured cat. There's no way I'll sleep tonight. Not with my muscles cramping like crazy and my brain smoking with a million different thoughts at once. Mac's question buzzes through all of them like a chainsaw: *What happens if the lights go out?* I don't know the answer, and something tells me I don't want to find out.

CHAPTER TWELVE
DETOX

**Opiate Withdrawal Timeline:
Phase 1**

Length   1–2 days.

Symptoms Agitation, anxiety, insomnia, panic attacks, excessive sweating, muscle aches, diarrhea, loss of appetite, nausea, and vomiting.

Summary Welcome to Hell. Population: You.

My eyelids scrape open to sheer darkness. A tomb. I can't see the streetlight through my blinds, can't find the assuring glow of my alarm clock on the dresser. I peel off my blanket and attempt to sit up, then collapse, muscles aching, back to the sweat-soaked pad. I'm freezing, shivering, my perspiration turned to ice. My skin itches so bad I want to scrape it off with a sheet of sandpaper.

Where am I?

Why can't I see anything?

It's so cold...

Light fills the tank as the hatch squeals open, and it all comes roaring back: the hospital, Alan. Smoky visions of exoskeletons and heaving earth. The blood. The screams. Running for the tank with my heart in my throat.

I rub my temples and moan. My entire body is drenched in sweat. I know what it means. Withdrawal. And it will only get worse. I've been here before. The throbbing legs. The body tremors. Headaches so bad I'd rather have my brain tossed in a frying pan than deal with them. The endless, suffocating crush of hopelessness. The empty ache of despair.

Tasker's face materializes high above me through the open hatch. "Alan, get up here," he yells. "You need to see this. Brynn was right. Good news is these things don't seem to like the light. The walls are drilled all to hell, but none of 'em got in here last night. Bad news is… half the city's gone."

Vivian snaps upright, hair a tangled mess, eyes pink with sleep. "What do you *mean* gone?"

"Just that. It's burned. There's smoke everywhere."

"We don't have much time, then," Alan says, shrugging on a sleeveless black hoodie and a pair of camo cargo pants. "People will panic. It's going to be a madhouse out there. We need to get to the shelter before that happens."

"I'll start packing the Suburban," Tasker says.

"Yeah, do that. I'll be right up." He turns to Mac and me. "Get your asses moving, you two."

Mac scrambles to his feet, but I don't move an inch. I don't want to see what's out there, and I *really* don't want to face another day like yesterday. There's no way I can. Not with my body wrecked like this. Not with my brain hissing and kicking off steam.

I pull the blankets over my head, only to feel the toe of Alan's boot land between my ribs. "Get up, Brynn. Now!"

———

My joints protest as I climb down the tank ladder toward the floor of Tasker's warehouse. It's cold. *Way* colder than inside the tank. I shiver and rub my arms. There's no way I'll be warm enough in this stupid hospital gown, although it does have a nice back-alley junkie look to it with all the blood from my nose smeared over the front.

"Oh, for Chrissakes. Put this on already. We don't need you freezing to death." I turn to Vivian offering me a long-sleeved Broncos shirt—Super Bowl Champions circa 1998. *Yay.*

I snatch it from her. It smells like an ashtray, but I'm immediately ten times warmer as I rip off the hospital gown and tug it on.

"Better?" she asks. Her eye looks even worse in the morning light—a tender purple circle of bread dough rising.

"Yeah, thanks. I'm sorry about your eye."

"Me, too. Your Dad's always had a way with the ladies."

I grimace. "Really, that's so messed up. I can't believe he did that."

"Can't you, though?"

"I—" The cramp cuts me off. "I'll be right back."

I barely make it to the rear of the tank and get my pants down before diarrhea explodes out of me in a hot, razor-blade rush. My legs go weak, reality tilting in seesaws. I almost tip over but manage to steady myself and grab a nearby roll of paper towels and wipe. *Mom would be so proud.*

Mac is waiting for me when I circle back around, a strange look smeared over his face. "Uh, what were you doing back there?"

"I... nothing." Change the subject. "You doing okay this morning?"

"I'm fine. Better than you by the looks of it."

It's true—I'm still sweating despite the chill, muscles groaning, brain on fire. Even my eyeballs ache. I squint. There's something different about him, a detail I don't remember, a feature out of place. "Hey, when did you start wearing glasses?"

He frowns. "Seriously, Brynn? I've only had them for two years now. You'd know that if you ever came to visit. Or called me once in a while." A dagger of shame pierces my chest. He's right. I haven't seen him in person for *at least* two years, but it's probably been closer to three. And now that I think about it, I *have* seen the glasses on FaceTime, I'm just too screwed up right now to think straight.

I want to tell him so, and that I'm sorry, it won't happen again, but he's already walking away, toward the front of the shop. It's amazing how much it hasn't changed. The place is still stuffed with tools, every square inch of it jammed with hammers and wrenches and nuts and washers. It even smells the same: chemicals mixed with grease and the soft scent of dust.

A sliver of memory rises. Me as a kid swiping suckers from the candy bowl on the counter while Alan and Tasker loaded up the work truck and chatted about whatever it was they were getting into over the weekend, which was always something. Camping trips up near Red Feather Lakes. Football games and backyard barbecues. Hazy summer afternoons spent sipping six packs and lemonade.

But those were the early years. The good years.

Then came the deterioration. The feeder talk. Alan barging into the house during the middle of the night blinding drunk and ranting. Mom screaming at him to stop as Tasker got him to the couch. I'd wander downstairs to her shouting red-faced and Alan hollering back in a shower of spit. Tasker would spot me and carry me upstairs with whispered promises that he'd calm them down, that he'd always be there for me.

And he was. Even after Alan got put away. Tasker—my safe place in all the chaos. Tasker—a phone call away when I needed to escape Vivian and the trailer and the suffocating press of life, if only for a few minutes. Tasker—a lifeline I didn't use nearly enough.

The sun blares down over the parking lot as I step outside, everything hazy, smoke coiling toward a slice of cobalt sky. The building across the yard is so riddled with holes, I'm not sure how it still stands. Beyond it lies the highway and the pumpjacks, which aren't pumpjacks anymore, just tangled knots of charred metal. And the road itself is mangled, chunks of asphalt and dirt scattered everywhere like a bomb went off.

I search for Mac and find him standing next to Alan and Tasker, the three of them staring at a hole in the ground—one that looks like someone carved a gash in the earth with a giant chainsaw. It's massive. At least ten feet wide. Something about it makes me want to run, to get as far away from it as possible, but I edge toward it instead. A vibration curls through my legs as I near. It's electric; a hum I can feel pulsing stronger with each step, calling me closer. And Closer. My neck throbs and I suddenly think of Alan's late-night injections as a kid, wonder if maybe they had something to do with—

"Brynn! Stop. Jesus, have you lost your goddamn mind?" Alan spits. "You're gonna get yourself killed. Not to mention the rest of us." He has his palms spread wide, looking at me like I'm the village idiot. Behind him, Mac nods in agreement.

"Sorry, I—"

"Sorry, nothing. Just go inside and wait for us to figure something out."

I roll my eyes. Leave everything to the men, right? But I'm too tired to argue, so I head back into the warehouse and wander over to Tasker's office in the far corner, bang inside, and plop down in a rolling chair next to Vivian. She ignores me, her eyes glued to the TV, her face pale. I glance at the screen and suck in a breath. It's a shot of downtown Denver. Sixteenth Street Mall to be exact, but not the one I remember. The one I remember is full of street artists, flowers, and clothing shops. Hipsters on skateboards and food stands hocking overpriced burgers and hot dogs. This one's riddled with holes. Holes like the one I saw outside. Scary massive and *everywhere.* They shred the sidewalk and pock the street, run roughshod through buildings and storefronts alike.

"Holy hell," I whisper.

The camera pans out and I see the fires. *So many fires.* More than I can count. It seems like every other building is burning. Columns of smoke spill through shattered windows to stain the sky. A few firetrucks squirt streams of water that do nothing to quench the flames. The news anchors try to keep up with the camera shots, their voices tight with panic. The screen splits and I see the same thing happening in Houston, Los Angeles, and New York. Chicago...

Vivian gasps, her fingers hovering over her lips. "How is this happening?"

I don't have time to answer. I'm too busy falling to the floor.

———

"Brynn... Brynn, you okay?" Tasker.

I whimper and work my fingers to the back of my head and the egg-sized lump there, pulsing beneath my hair.

"Here, I got you." He helps me into a sitting position, and I nearly puke. His face comes into view, his eyes buried in worry lines. "Hey, kiddo. You gave us quite the scare there."

"Yeah…" I finger the knot again and look for blood on my fingertips. There's none, so that's something. "Yeah, I think so. Wh-what happened?"

"You fainted. Cracked your head pretty good, too."

Of course, I did. Withdrawal sucks. "Just give me a minute. I'll be fine."

"No, you won't," says Alan as he crouches next to Tasker. "Not without your… meds. There's a drugstore close. A couple miles out. I think we'll pay it a quick visit on the way out of town to stock up."

I blink at him in surprise. "For real?"

"Yeah—just until you aren't so… you know, sick anymore."

"What's all this talk about meds and being sick?" Vivian asks. She stands a few feet back, her underbite working away like she's chewing a mouthful of cud. Mac is perched next to her, his face coated in concern.

Tasker spits to the side and glances back. "Don't you worry about it, Viv. We got enough coming our way without you digging into other people's business like you always do."

I want to reach out and hug him. I've never wanted to hug him more.

Vivian crosses her arms. "Yeah? Well, given the circumstances, I think it's the perfect time. In fact, there's never been a better time for sharing, seeing as—"

"Good God, Vivian. Will you just listen for once?" Alan snaps. He appraises her, then looks at the rest of us. "All of you listen up. We don't have time to squabble with each other like this. We've got today and today only to get the hell out of this city. People will panic when they realize no one's coming to save them. Not the cops. Not the hospitals. And certainly not the goddamn government. Nothing's the same now. If we're lucky, people won't have figured that out just yet. But when they do, shit's gonna hit the fan real fast and real hard. It's everyone for himself now."

"And just where *exactly* is this shelter of yours, Alan?" Vivian asks.

"Close enough we don't need to worry. Far enough to count."

"She's got a point, Alan," Tasker adds. "We should at least know where we're going."

Alan scowls and shakes his head. "Not happening. We need to stick together, and the only way I can be sure none of you get any bright ideas to run off by yourself is if I'm the only one who knows the way. Look, if something happens to me, I got a map in my bag with the shelter codes. Until then"—he taps his temple—"it stays up here."

"Not sure that's such a good idea," Tasker says, straightening. "Have to say I agree with Viv on this one. Best if we all know where we're headed at this point."

Alan's eyelid twitches. "Oh, you think so, do you? Because you built it, right? You spent years studying the geology and found the perfect rock. No, wait, that's not right. If I remember correctly, you were the one who—"

Tasker raises his hands. "Hey, I was just trying to—"

"—told me I was wasting my time with the shelter, that nothing—"

"—say we should all have an idea cause—"

"—was ever going to happen to—"

Mac picks up an empty paint can and flings it against the garage door. "Shut up! Both of you! Fighting won't get us anywhere."

I wobble to my feet. "He's right. We need to go."

The ground sways a little. Tasker reaches over and steadies me. "Careful now. Take it slow."

I nod, thankful for the support, thankful for *him*.

Alan claps his hands together in agreement. "Okay, everyone. You heard the man. No more arguing. Pack your shit. We load out in thirty minutes."

CHAPTER THIRTEEN
DRUG STORE COWBOY

We drive in silence. There's no point talking. The wreckage outside speaks for itself. Cars abandoned. People who couldn't get their seat belts off in time. Drivers chewed to the bone. Feeder holes everywhere. The Rockies paint a mustard stripe on the horizon through all the smoke and remind me of the long-ago summer forest fires that would rip through the mountains when things got too dry. Except the smoke from this fire isn't because a forest burned, it's because Denver did.

We curve around a gutted truck, the driver a pillar of ash, his lips burned down to the teeth, nothing but ivory nubs peering through the char. The smell of scorched rubber and metal works its way in through the air vents, coating my tongue until I'm about to puke. I spit on the floorboard, but it doesn't help. I can't get the taste of death out of my mouth.

Tasker clucks his tongue from the driver's seat, shakes his head. "So, this is the rapture, huh? Pops always said it would come. Had this verse he'd spout off from time to time. Something like,"—his voice deepens—"'for there shall be a great tribulation, such as was not seen since the beginning of the world. The sun will go dark, the moon will not shine, the stars will fall from the sky, and the powers of the heavens will be shaken.'"

"What's that mean?" Mac asks, pale-faced.

"It means that when everything goes to hell, all you can do is hope you were good enough to punch your ticket to the afterlife." Tasker shakes his head. "To be honest, I always thought it was a bunch of bullshit. Just stuff Pops said to keep us kids in line, but the old man was right. Satan's finally been unleashed on the earth."

"Lord Almighty, Tasker. Will you can it already?" Vivian says. "There's enough ugliness as it is. No one wants to hear that right now."

Tasker whips his hands wide. "The hell you call this, then, Viv? A Sunday stroll in the park? A fall saunter to do some leaf-peeping and take in the pretty colors? Hell no. I'd say this is about as close to the end times as it gets."

I rub my face and sigh. "Can we please not do this right now? *Please.*"

Tasker kicks a boot up on the dash. "Eh, whatever. Just sayin'..."

The carnage grows as we near town: cars buckled around telephone poles, cars smashed into other cars. They lie on the road mangled and smoking, glimpses of blackened flesh flashing from inside. Corpses missing jaws and windows misted with gore. It's clear where people tried to run because all that's left of them are bones and piles of gore. Next to one, a child's teddy bear stares up at me from the asphalt with dull bead eyes. A small hand with pink fingernails is still wrapped around it, no arm.

Bile surges up my throat, and I claw at the handle. "Stop the car."

"No," Alan replies." We don't have—"

"I said, stop!"

He does, and I throw the door open and vomit. Mac leans over and places his hand on my back. "Hey, you okay?"

I flop back into my seat and shut the door, wipe a string of bile from my lips. "I'm...fine. Fine."

A hand smacks my window.

I shrink back from the greasy face staring at me through the glass, the wild, bloodshot eyes, and grim slash of a mouth. "Let me in. *Please*. I'm hurt. I-I need...a doctor." His words are muffled and clipped as he holds up his other arm. My stomach lurches. Vivian squeals. It's a stump, nothing but a wing of ragged flesh fringed in muscle fiber, dangling beneath a tightly cinched belt, the skin black and rotten.

He bangs on the window again, harder this time. "You have to help me. I've been out here all night. My arm... it's infected. I won't make it much longer."

Suddenly, I'm back on the corner by the hospital, alone on the street with the entire world falling apart around me with only Alan there to help.

We can't leave him here.

Alan punches the gas as I move to let him in. The Suburban leaps forward before I can, the man hobbling next to us while clutching the stump pathetically to his chest. "No. Don't go. *Please!*"

My heart carves through my chest as he stumbles and falls. "Alan, we can't abandon him."

"It's already done," Alan says.

Mac leans forward and grabs his seat. "Dad, Brynn's right. He needs our help. He's hurt."

Vivian clamps a hand over Mac's forearm and yanks him back. "No, Mac. He might be dangerous."

"Dangerous?" I nearly choke on the word. "Are you kidding me, Vivian? The guy's bleeding out. What's he going to do? Beat us to death with that stump of his? What if that was you out there? Or Mac? Would you just keep on driving? You probably would, wouldn't you, you—"

"Hey," Alan barks, slapping the dash. "Knock it off. Both of you. We aren't stopping for anyone. If we start playing Good Samaritan to everyone we see, we'll never get out of the city alive. The only people we can help from this point on are ourselves."

I feel my lips curl up over my teeth. "That's bullshit, Alan."

"He's right, Brynn," Tasker says softly, eyeing me from the passenger seat, then Mac. "We need to be careful. You both have good hearts, but things have... changed. It's different out there now. The only thing we should focus on is getting out of town before night hits. If we don't, it's not that man you should be worried about. It's us."

———

The only people we can help are ourselves. What a load of crap. We could have helped him, could have dropped him at a hospital or a police station at least. Instead, we did absolutely nothing. *Nothing.* Just left him there to rot with the rest of the roadkill.

"What's taking them so long?" Vivian asks, glancing toward the Walgreens for the thousandth time in the last five minutes. "They should be back by now."

I shrug. "I don't know. Why don't you go in and find out?"

She turns on me, her black eye gruesome in the morning light, her voice abrasive. "You know this is your fault. We should be on the road right now. Not stopping to get whatever it is you need in there."

Her eyes narrow. "What's your deal, anyway? What exactly did you get hooked on down in Texas? Is it drugs?"

Drugs. So she's put it together, my problem. Not like it's some big secret at this point; I'm still sweating, my hands shaking so badly I might as well have cerebral palsy. I just wish Mac didn't have to see me like this.

"Don't worry about it," I reply.

"I kind of have to, seeing as you made it my problem too." She glances back at the store. "I'm telling you; they've been in there too long."

She's got a point—they have. I count off the minutes in my head: At least ten now, maybe fifteen, since they went inside. *Come on, Alan. Get your ass out here already.* I squint at the Walgreens. It's old, the white trim pocked with rust marks beneath the gutters, the sidewalk cracked and flaking off in gray, powdered chunks. Through the windows I catch shadows weaving down aisles fighting over endcap displays. A woman shoves another woman away from a shelf and scoops an armful of whatever's on it into her cart.

The panic has begun.

"How many of those do you have?" Mac asks.

I realize he's watching me trace a fingernail absentmindedly over my swallow tattoo. I pause. "Uh, a lot." Nineteen to be exact.

"Did they hurt?"

"Some more than others."

He scoots closer. "Can I see another one?"

"Yeah, sure." I lean down and pull up the ankle of my jeans, show him the angel inked on my calf. A buxom ginger in a leather corset sporting a vicious set of daggers. Tank did it for my birthday a year ago. Twenty-three. My heart thickens. *Tank...*

Mac flashes a grin, the first real one I've seen all day. "That's so cool."

"Uh-uh," Vivian snips. "No, it's not. Those things never come off, and you have to cover them up if you ever want a real job." She raises her eyebrows on the word *real*, and I know it's meant as a jab. She funded my first year of nursing school. When I dropped out, she told me I was spoiled and shortsighted, that I was a waste of her money and her time. I told her to fuck off and hung up the phone, not that I disagreed with her.

"Well, Vivian," I shoot back. "I don't think he'll have to worry about a *real* job anytime soon."

"You don't know that, and despite what your father says, the people in Washington will get this figured out. Just you watch. When they do, you're gonna wish you'd taken better care of yourself."

"Dad's right, Aunt Viv," Mac replies. "About the government, I mean. Just like he was right about the feeders and all. You should listen to him more." He glances at me. "You both should."

"Yeah, whatever," I say, pointing at the store. "Look, they're coming."

And they are, but warily. Unnaturally. Tasker appears first with his back to the parking lot, a sack clutched in his left hand. Alan follows, and I can tell he's yelling by the way his back is jerking, his finger jabbing toward something.

No, not toward something, toward some*one* and, *shit*, it's not his finger. It's a gun.

Three men trail out of the store and press into the parking lot. One is huge and bald, almost the size of Alan. The other two are smaller but stare at Alan without fear—like they'd love to spend the next half hour slowly gutting him with a butter knife.

"I knew it," Vivian mutters anxiously. "I *knew* there was something wrong in there."

"What's going on?" Mac asks, leaning around Vivian for a better view.

I tug him back. "I don't know, but don't get too close to the window."

He brushes me off, leans forward again. "I'm fine. I want to make sure Dad and Tasker are okay."

Alan reaches the Suburban and motions Tasker around the hood, his Glock still leveled on the men. "Back! I said get BACK!"

The big man holds up his hands and stops, leans casually against a blue truck, and lights a cigarette. The other two join him, one rubbing his chin. It's lifted, one of those trucks hicks drive with the oversize grill and fog lights. The kind that sounds aggressive when revved—like it somehow soaked up all the vitriol of its owner only to spit it out through the tailpipe.

Alan gets in and Tasker throws the Suburban into gear and peels out of the parking lot. Once we reach the street, Alan sets the Glock on the console and wipes a pair of sweat marks on his jeans. "Shit, that was close."

"What was *that* all about?" I ask.

"They wanted the same thing we did," Tasker replies, his eyes ticking between the road and the rearview mirror.

"Those three had your stuff," Alan says. "*All* of it."

I rub the back of my neck. "So you took it from them?"

"Had to. It was the only choice. Apparently, you aren't the only one with a prob—" He stops, corrects himself. "You aren't the only one who needs that kind of thing."

Mac glances behind us. "Will they follow us?"

"I don't know," Alan says. "Maybe."

"Did you hurt them?" Vivian asks.

"No. Well…" Alan pauses. "Just a little when one of them mouthed off."

"Did you hit him? You did, didn't you?" Vivian asks, incredulous. "Why'd you do th—"

I catch the flash of blue a second before the collision slams me sideways. Violent motion carries us sideways across the road. My head cracks off the window. Fireworks fill my vision. Somewhere, Vivian screams.

The vague sensation of spinning down a slope overtakes me.

Spinning, spinning.

Into water, followed by the crunch of metal as we come to a sudden, lurching stop.

Time slows, and I struggle to focus. Doors tear open. Heavy steps come our way, sloshing toward us. A graveled voice barks orders. Then it's our doors being ripped open. Someone shouts at Tasker for the bag. Tasker barks back and is pistol-whipped. A hand reaches in and grabs the sack of pills. The gun comes down again.

No, I think pathetically. *Give it back…*

A moment later an engine fires, and I catch the blurry smear of a blue truck and the bald man grinning down at me from the street.

My eyes click shut.

———

Open.

My ears are screaming. We're in a ditch. I know because I can smell the decay of pluff mud and old earth. The reek of sewage.

I shake my head and clear the stars. My second concussion of the day. *Great.* Mac moans next to me and my heart flutters. "Are you all right?"

He nods. "Yeah...yeah, I think so." His glasses are cracked, the frame bent on his face. I reach over and ease them off, examine him.

"You sure nothing hurts? Nothing's broken?"

"No...no I don't think so. Just a little shaken up. Are you"—his eyes constrict—"your head's bleeding."

I finger it and hiss at the resulting sting. "It's nothing."

"Wh-what happened?" Vivian asks, grimacing and clutching her wrist.

"I screwed up is what," Alan replies. His voice is strained. Weak.

Tasker groans next to him and sits up with one hand pressed against his forehead.

Alan shifts. "*Shit.* My ankle."

I lean forward for a better view and shudder at what I see. His torso is twisted to the left, his leg buried somewhere beneath the dash and a knot of metal. He glances up at me glassy-eyed, blood weeping over his forehead. "Listen, you all need to get out of here right now. Get the shelter map and go."

I shake my head. "No."

"It's in my bag near the bottom."

"Shut up, Alan. We're not leaving you here."

He cocks his head and gives me a pained grin. "Ah, shit. I remember that look. I don't have a choice, do I?"

I shake my head. "No. You don't."

CHAPTER FOURTEEN
A CHANGE OF PLANS

Tasker places a crowbar beneath the door and strains. It creaks open a couple of inches, allowing me just enough space to work my hands around the frame to help him pull. Gaining traction in the half-foot of ditch water is next to impossible, both of us sliding, Tasker growling as we yank, my vision turning to a field of hazy squiggles that threatens to send me toppling into the muck at any moment.

"Open up, you rusty bitch!" Tasker shouts, heaving harder, until, with a tinny *BANG!*, it does.

I stutter back a step, and Mac presses by me with a horrified look splattered on his face. "Jesus," he mutters.

Jesus is right. Alan is screwed. A snarl of plastic and metal consumes his lower right leg, which is twisted at an ugly angle that means a broken bone, if not worse. Probably worse.

"Don't worry, Dad," Mac says. "We'll get you out." He glances back at me and Tasker, his eyes wet, pink at the edges. "Come on, guys. Don't just stand there. Help me."

"Oh God," Vivian croaks over my shoulder. "There's no way we'll get him out of there. *No way.*"

"Not helpful, Vivian," I reply.

Her eyes widen. "What if those psychos come back? They'll kill us this time. We need to go before they do. We need to leave right now!"

I take her by the shoulders and give her a hard shake. "Get your shit together. We aren't going anywhere without Alan. In case you haven't figured it out yet, he's still our best chance at surviving." I turn back to Tasker. "What are we waiting for? Let's do this."

Tasker shoots me a quick grin, winks. "Mac, you heard the woman. Help your sister pull when I tell you to." He jams the crowbar in between the floorboard and the dash, next to Alan's leg. "Ready?"

I loop my arm beneath Alan's armpit as Mac takes his wrist.

"Okay," Tasker says. "On three. One, two…"

Alan sucks in a sharp breath.

"Three."

The metal groans and we pull. Alan is heavy. Impossibly heavy. Anchor heavy. His face contorts, reddens. "Shit! Stop! Stop!"

I drop his arm. "You okay?"

"Hell no. Hurts like a sonuvabitch."

Tasker wipes his hands on his jeans, then adjusts his grip on the crowbar. "I felt you move on that last tug. I think with another try we'll have you out of there."

Alan leans his head back. His skin looks wet, waxen. "Wait, wait. Give me a sec." He takes a few quick breaths and grips the seat. Exhales. "Okay, do it."

Tasker cranks down on the crowbar, and I pull so hard my arms burn. Something snaps beneath the dash and Alan roars. I let go, and his head thumps back to the headrest in a spray of sweat. "No more. Please, no more."

"Well, shit," Tasker mutters. "What now?"

"We need to go," Vivian replies. "While we have a chance."

I whirl on her. "Always one to put others first, eh, Vivian?"

"Aren't you one to talk," she spits back before wheeling around and disappearing over the crest of the ditch.

"I hate to admit it, but she's right," Alan says. "My foot's jammed too deep. You guys need to..." He stops, wheezes. "You guys need to go on without me. I'm okay to... go." The resignation on his face as he says it sends a swarm of scorpions scattering through my gut. His eyes fall on me. "Get the map, Brynn. It's in my duffel bag, in the black pouch at the bottom. I'll mark the route."

"No. We're not *leaving* you, Dad," Mac says, his brow collapsing. "We just got you *back*."

Alan reaches up and loops his hand around the back of Mac's neck and pulls him close, forehead-to-forehead. "I'm sorry, bud, but you got no choice. You gotta be brave for me. Look out for your sister. Can you do that?"

Mac shakes his head. "No. No way. We're not going. I don't care what you say."

Tasker sets a hand on Mac's shoulder, his voice soft. "Mac. I don't want this either, but your dad's right. Listen, we'll call an ambulance when we can. They'll cut him out."

Mac glares at him. "Yeah *right,* Tasker. Call an ambulance? With all of this going on, no one will come! I thought you were his friend! We can't just leave him here. We *can't.*" He turns to me, face pleading. "Tell him, Brynn."

"Go. Get the map," Alan orders, this time to Tasker.

He nods and wades to the back of the Suburban, opens the hatch, and digs out Alan's bag. Mac continues to stare at me in disbelief, his hands raised. "Well?"

He's right. We can't do this.

"Got it," Tasker says, holding up the map triumphantly.

I slosh over and snatch it out of his hand.

"Hey," he says. "Give it back." It's only there for a second, but I catch it. A flash of something sour buried in the look. Something poisonous. For as long as I can remember, he's been nothing but bad jokes and smiles, someone I can count on for a quick laugh or a pick me up when I need it most. But not this version of Tasker. This version is...*different.*

"No. Not happening. Not without..." I trail off and point at the sliver of steel poking out from beneath the spare tire in the hatch: Alan's way out. "There—we use that."

———

It takes us ten minutes to lift the dash with the carjack and another ten to drag Alan up the bank and onto a patch of grass near the road. Unfortunately, Vivian is still waiting for us, pacing back and forth like a lunatic, jabbing her phone in search of a signal.

"Pick up," she mutters. "Pick up!"

I ignore her and unlace Alan's boot, then pull it off. He groans and tips his head up. "You should have left like I told you. Look how much time you've wasted."

"Just try to relax," I tell him.

Mac crouches and places a hand on his shoulder. "You're going to be fine, Dad. Brynn's got you."

Tasker hands me his Swiss-army knife, and I unfold the scissors and carefully cut a straight line through Alan's cargo pants and spread the material wide. The flesh around his ankle is purple, swollen, and hot to the touch. I run my hands over it and grimace when his tibia swims sideways beneath the skin.

Alan roars. "Christ, that hurts. Take it easy, will you?"

"Shut up. I need to think." I can't recall much about ankle injuries, except that they need a splint. Or is it a wrap? Nursing school was too long ago and buried beneath far too many hangovers. Tank would know what to do if he were here; he patched up way worse in the Middle East. But he's not, and I need to make a decision. A splint it is.

I round up the supplies: Tasker's belt, a cardboard box from the back of the Suburban, the shoelace from Alan's boot, and several T-shirts from his bag. Behind me, a car blows by as Vivian screams maniacally for it to stop. I roll my eyes at her and then take Tasker's knife and cut a flat piece of cardboard from the box and fold it into thirds. Next, I line it with two of the T-shirts before glancing at Tasker and Mac. "Lift his leg and set it down when I tell you. Gently, though, okay?"

They nod.

"Alright, let's get this over with."

Alan grinds his teeth as they ease his leg up. I slide the cardboard under his calf and motion for them to set it down. "Here," I say, cutting several strips from the last T-shirt and tossing them at Tasker. "When I set the bone, you wrap the splint like this." I make a cinching motion. "Tight, okay? It can't move. Mac, you finish it off with the shoelaces and the belt. Wind them around the entire thing."

He looks glassy eyed and distant—like he's about to faint. "You got this," I tell him, then to Alan: "This is going to hurt, but just for a second. Ready?"

He winces. "Not really."

"Too bad. I'm doing it anyway."

I take hold of his foot and pull. It takes longer than it should, but finally the bone grinds into place. Alan howls the entire time, pounding the asphalt with both fists, begging for me to stop. I keep the pressure on his ankle as Tasker goes to work on the knots. He's quick, his hands steadier than mine, and he's done before I know it. Mac follows after him, winding figure eights around the splint with the shoelace, and then with the belt. When he's done, I set Alan's foot gently on the ground. "How's it feel?"

"Like heaven." He wheezes. "W-we need... need to find a car. Got to get back on the road. We can still make the shelter by afternoon if we... hurry." He looks like hell, his beard drenched in blood, his eyes dilated and unfocused.

And he's pale. *Way* too pale. He looks like someone just rolled him off the set of a bad zombie movie, blood streaming from his forehead into his eyes. He's so fucked. We all are. Each and every one of us. But on the bright side, at least we're still together... for now.

CHAPTER FIFTEEN
A DETOUR

There are no cars to steal. None concealed or old enough to hotwire, anyway. Just a bunch of endless cul-de-sac neighborhoods sprinkled in between crumbling strip malls and neighborhood parks. We hobble down the street in a rag-tag parade past other sorry-looking clumps of survivors, tattered families lugging wide-eyed children, bums that beg us for money like it can somehow help. Like nothing has changed, and if they can have a few bucks—*Hey!*—everything will be just fine.

The sun hangs overhead in a bright yellow disc turned orange by all the smoke. It's so thick, I feel like my lungs are close to catching fire. We move at a tortoise pace, taking turns playing crutch to Alan, all except Vivian, who shuffles ahead of us with her shoulders tucked into her red cardigan sweater.

The houses deteriorate as we push further west, well-maintained exteriors giving way to walls of peeling paint and yards that are more dirt than grass. Alan groans with each step, his hair plastered to his forehead with sweat, his beard crusted with blood.

And there are holes *everywhere*.

Pocking the streets. Riddling the yards. Every time I see one, I can't look away fast enough. I tell myself they don't exist, that they're not real.

If only I were a better liar.

Hours pass. The strip malls become pawn shops become gas stations become bars. We limp past one with blacked-out windows framed in velvet red curtains, the kind made to soak up grease fumes and smoke. I try to ignore the man leaning against the wall outside, a paper-sack bottle cradled in one in one hand, a cigarette in the other.

I look away as his lips crease into a smile, but not fast enough that I can't see him shamble after us. His gaze burns into my neck for blocks, pours over every inch of my skin until I finally turn around and realize he's gone.

Near mid-afternoon, I stop to puke again, this time into a clump of shrubs. I catch a flicker of a face staring at me through a nearby window, a flash of teeth.

"You aren't going to make it much further, are you?"

I glance up. Vivian is looking at me with something close to concern in her eyes; an emotion I'm not used to coming from her, and one that fills me with an unexpected flood of shame.

"I...need to stop," I say. "We can't go on like this."

"Finally, something we can agree on." She holds out her hand. "Come on, I'll find a place we can rest."

———

A half-hour later, I crash down on a picnic table, sweat-soaked and shaking, at some needy-looking park with a concrete basketball court and rusted-out swing set long abandoned to time. The sun screams over the mountains that we have two, maybe two-and-a-half hours left until sunset.

Until death.

I work my tongue over my gums. They feel like dried strips of jerky.

"So, how long have you been on this stuff."

I glance at Vivian, feeling lightheaded. "What stuff?"

"Your pills. The drugs."

"Leave her be, Viv," Tasker says, passing me a water from his backpack. "Only thing that matters right now is figuring out our next move."

"Which should be getting to one of those community shelters they were talking about on the TV." She says it like it's a fact, like the decision is already made.

"Don't be stupid," Alan snarls. "Crowds are dangerous."

Vivian snorts. "Why? Because they'll have food and water? Protection? The news said the National Guard will be there. Why would we go hiking off to this shelter of yours when there's a better option down here."

"Because it's not better, Aunt Viv," Mac says. "Crowds will draw the feeders in." He looks at Alan for confirmation. "Right, Dad?"

"Exactly," Alan says, clapping him on the back, his eyes still narrowed at Vivian. "Exactly..."

"So, what do you suggest?" I ask. "Wander around until your foot falls off or someone collapses beneath your weight and you jack up your ankle even worse? Because that's what's going to happen if we keep this up."

"Here, dig in," Tasker says, dumping several granola bars, two apples, and a bag of beef jerky onto the table. Some chips. "It ain't much, but it's what I had time to pack. Thought we'd be locked up safe and sound by now with all those supplies Alan was going on about." He uncaps a bottle of water and takes a long drink, waves at the table. "Don't be shy. We all need the calories. No point in starving just yet."

I grab one of the bars and gag it down. Mac and Vivian do the same. Alan nibbles on an apple. The sun warms my neck. A breeze chimes above us, through what's left of the fall leaves. A finch chirps from the branches. I pull in a lungful of air and close my eyes. I could almost lose myself in the moment. *Almost.* It feels like every other Colorado fall. Even the tang of fresh chimney smoke fits.

Except it doesn't.

It's rotten, tinged with the smell leaking from the two feeder holes on the corner; the ones I can't stop looking at. The ones I can *feel.* No one says anything, but I know they smell them, too. The stench is unbearable—like cattle decaying in a vat of curdled milk, or blood left to congeal on the floor of a Texas slaughterhouse in mid-summer. And I *know* they see the half-gnawed femur propped against the trunk of the ash tree a few feet away. Mac has glanced at it twice now, like he half-expects it to be gone every time he looks, like maybe he can change the channel if he simply blinks hard enough or long enough.

We need a plan.

I straighten. "Vivian's right. We need to find a place to bunk down for the night."

Alan shakes his head. "No. We can still make it to the shelter. I can get us a ride. All I need to do is—"

"Rest," I finish. "You're messed up Alan. You need to elevate your ankle before it turns into a balloon."

Mac points across the street: "How about in one of those?"

I follow his finger toward a public storage complex. Rows of semi-sized crates stacked behind a massive orange lattice-work gate.

Tasker taps a finger on the picnic table. "Hmm. That might just work if we can break into one." He gives Mac a slug on the shoulder. "Good eyes, kid. See, you never needed those glasses, did you?"

He grins, shrugs. "I guess not."

"Let's get going, then," Alan says. "Breaking off one of those locks won't be easy."

I move to stand, and then stop, my gaze drifting left toward an office a block up the street with a sign in the yard that stops my heart when I read it.

"It's going to have to wait," I say. "We need to make a stop first."

———

Mountain View Vet Clinic.

The name's a load of crap. No mountains, no view, unless you count the orange stacks of storage pods next door. The place looks rundown—more house than office—but it's not entirely devoid of charm. Someone took the trouble to hang a few baskets of flowers over the door, which are frost-burned, but still, it's the thought that counts.

I clomp up the wooden steps and onto the porch where a mat shouts: "Welcome to the Little Clinic!" There's no doorbell, so I knock; a polite rap that even I have trouble hearing. "Hello. Anyone home?"

No answer.

I knock again harder, banging until the stained-glass sidelights rattle in their frames.

"No one's there, Brynn" Tasker says. "And if they are, you've scared 'em off by now for sure."

Screw that. Someone had better be here because I cannot *stand* another second stranded outside with these goddamn holes and their goddamn smell, wandering around these barren neighborhoods with my skin itching so bad, I want nothing more than to collapse to the ground and tear it from my bones.

That, and I have this feeling that there's something wrong with the streets. A persistent voice in my head telling me we need to get off them. Right now.

I step back and give the door a solid kick. The wood splinters.

"Brynn, wait," Mac says, rushing up the steps. "Maybe we can find another way in." He shrugs toward the backyard. "Maybe one that isn't quite so *obvious,* if you know what I mean."

I do, and I don't care to sneak around back right now. If there was ever a time for discretion, this is not it. I swing my foot back, ready to send it straight through the wood, when the door opens.

"Stop. Please. You will break it." The man who says it is the oldest Native American I've ever seen, clothed in a crisp white dress shirt and a tan leather vest. White hair drifts in braids past a face cracked by time, and hangs over his chest, along with a beaded turquoise necklace. He flashes me a set of teeth pressed into the shape of a smile or a grimace, I don't know which. "What do you want?"

I step back with an awkward wave. "Sorry about that. We, uh— sort of have a problem you might be able to help us with."

He stares past me, at Alan, and the lines around his eyes deepen. "Yes. I can see that. But I'm in no position to help." He frowns. "Especially when the person asking is trying to destroy my door."

He moves to shut it, but I step forward and jam my palm against the knob before he can. "Wait, wait. You're a vet. A doctor, right?"

"Yes, but—"

"Please. We need your help. If there's nothing you can do, we'll leave. I promise."

He stares at me, his eyes slitting before he sighs and opens the door.

"I suppose you can come in for a moment. But don't make me regret this."

CHAPTER SIXTEEN
THE VET

The place is warm inside, everything painted in beige and lavish grays. Naturescape photos pepper the walls. Mountains draped in fog. Forest lakes surrounded by trees. A collie with a bandana wrapped around its neck, seated near a meadow pond.

"What happened?" the man asks as we enter.

Mac is the first to answer. "These guys followed us, and they—"

"We were in a wreck," I say, flashing him my best *shut-the-hell-up* look. No need to let the good doctor here know about our little adventure to the drugstore hoping to score some pills for the screw-up daughter. "A hit and run. We were trying to get out of town when a truck broadsided us." I nod his way. "They fractured Alan's ankle. I tried to set the break, but it's swelling." I pause, consider if there's anything else. Vivian coughs into her elbow. "Oh, and this is Tasker, Mac, and Vivian."

Tasker tips his hat, Vivian and Mac wave.

The man stares at them blank-faced and then returns his attention to me. "Sounds like surgery. I'm not trained for something like this. Not on a human. The bone will have to be stabilized. Plates and screws. Antibiotics. The works."

"*Please,*" I say, hating the desperation creeping into my voice, "we have nowhere else to go. Not with night on the way and those things—"

"The nayee."

"The nay—what?"

"The creatures from the ground. From the holes."

"Yes. Them."

He scowls. "Man's greed has woken them. We have poisoned the earth."

"Yeah...well, we don't stand a chance out there against those monsters. Not with Alan banged up like this."

Tasker removes his Stetson and runs a hand through his curls. There's a sizable knot on his forehead where he was pistol-whipped. A soft, fleshy pebble rising beneath the skin. A wave of guilt washes over me; none of this would have happened if weren't for my addiction.

"Look, truth is, we're in a bad spot here, Doc," Tasker says. "We don't exactly have another option."

I step forward. "Will you help us, Mr...?"

"Tsosie." He rubs a few circles over his eyelids, opens them. "I sense something off with your group. Something wrong. But I will not send you back outside. That is not my way. My wife would have wanted me to try. Please, follow me."

He leads us down a cream-colored hall, past a battered oak staircase, and into an operating room covered in anatomical posters of cats and dogs and horses. Two stuffed rabbits sit on the counter. Unlike the reception area, everything here is sterile: white cupboards, white paint, white tile, white light buzzing from the ceiling. *Light.*

"How do you still have power?" I ask.

"It's solar. I had it installed a couple of years ago in case of emergencies. Never planned for something like this, however." He shakes his head and runs a leathered hand over the back of his neck. "Please, bring him here."

Tasker and I help Alan up and onto the metal exam table. It creaks beneath his weight. Dr. Tsosie nods at the splint. "Remove it. The boot, too. I need to assess the injury."

Tasker beats me to it, one of his fingers catching on a shoestring and jerking the boot to the side. Alan grunts and slams his fist on the table. "Shit! Break it again, why don't you?" A tray of implements crashes to the floor in a glassy volley of *ting-ting-tings* that leaves my ears ringing.

Tasker steps back, his hands flashing up. "Sorry."

I slide over and guide him toward the door. "Tasker, why don't you take Mac and Viv and wait outside?"

"You sure you don't need my help in here?"

"No. No reason to watch this."

Dr. Tsosie snaps on a pair of rubber gloves, doesn't bother looking up. "She's right. I cannot have you in here. There is a waiting room down the hall."

"If you say so." He frowns. "Take care of him, Doc."

"I will do my best."

Mac brushes by me with a wary look, and I grab his arm: "Don't worry. He'll be fine. I've got him."

"I hope so," he says, glancing behind me once more before disappearing down the hall. I shut the door and turn back to Alan.

"This is going to hurt."

He nods. "Just make it quick."

I start with the belt, unwind it, and then cut through the shoelace and strips of shirt with a pair of scissors. Sweat glistens on Alan's forehead, his eyes dancing away from his ankle as I gently, slowly, rock the boot and roll it off. The bone clicks beneath the skin in a way that makes my head spin. Alan exhales in a long, slow hiss and thumps back onto the table. "Holy hell."

"You have good hands," Dr. Tsosie says. "And the splint is well constructed." I can't help but smile. "Here, let me have a look," he says, easing by me. I hand him the scissors and he snips his way through Alan's cargos and pulls the fabric wide. My stomach boils. Alan's ankle is huge—plum-colored and shining. It's like someone cut it open with a scalpel, stuffed a grapefruit beneath the skin, and sewed it shut.

Dr. Tsosie runs a hand over his chin. "Mm. There's a hospital not far from here. I can give you a ride."

Alan seizes his wrist. "No. Hospitals aren't safe. You take us there and you kill us, simple as that. They're overflowing with injuries right now. People way worse off than me. The feeders will be drawn to all that blood."

"The feeders?"

"Yes...the nayee or whatever you called them. They'll be back soon. There's not enough time to get to a hospital as it is. So, you got no choice but to try, Doc."

The vet pulls free. "I—I don't know."

I cut in. "Look, you *have* to have seen this before, right? On an animal or whatever?"

"Well...yes, with canines. Never a human."

"But you've done it? Fixed something like this?" My voice rises with the question. Cold, fluttery panic slides through my veins.

"I have."

"Then do it again. *Please.*"

He rubs his chin and appraises the injury. "Why did I let you people in? Why?" He eyes Alan. "You understand the risk, yes?"

Alan nods and manages a painful grin. "Fully."

"I will try, then." He glances at me. "You must leave now. I work best alone. Do not enter again until I call for you."

———

I avoid the waiting room—the thought of more idle chatter too much to bear—and settle instead for a leather recliner in a small room further down the hall. Dr. Tsosie's office. Or at least that's what it looks like. Stacks of paper and shelves full of medical books surround me. A grimy green lamp with no light bulb sits on a rickety desk in the corner under a window bleeding late afternoon sunlight.

I grab a blanket from the ottoman and pull it up to my chest. My skin is doing the hot-cold-hot-cold thing that means I'm about to pass out, my chest leaching sweat. A sour scent works its way into my nostrils, and I glance accusingly at the trash-can beneath the desk before I realize it's me. I'd kill for a shower right now, but I'll have to settle for a nap.

I lean back, and close my eyes—

"Hey."

—and open them to Vivian settling into an armchair across from me. She tucks a strand of hair behind her ear. "How are you feeling?"

Terrible. Awful. Hideous. "Fine."

"Right."

Most days I would gladly rise to the occasion, but I can't handle a battle with her right now. "What do you want, Vivian?" I ask wearily. *Go away and let me sleep.*

She smooths her cardigan and stares into her lap for an uncomfortably long moment, then looks up. "We need to talk."

Please, God, no. "Right now?"

"Yes. I...don't know if we'll get another chance." She leans forward and plants her elbows on her knees. "You know, I'm not quite the monster you make me out to be."

"Oh, no?" I ask. *This should be interesting.*

"Okay, it's true I wasn't happy about taking you and Mac in when your mother passed. I was forty-two and way past thinking I'd have kids. To be honest, I was never really cut out for them. It was Laura who was supposed to be a mother, not me." She swallows and glances out the window. "She was the better one in most things, really. School, sports, boys." She smiles. "Oh, how the boys loved her. God, it made me so jealous. Everything came so easy for her. It all seemed to just fall into her lap. But then she had you and Mac, and I couldn't be jealous anymore." Her hazel eyes find mine. "You know why?"

I shake my head.

"Because anyone who saw her with you two knew it was God's purpose for her life. To be a mother. And how can you be jealous of *that?* It was a divine thing. Brynn...you made her so proud. You should have seen how she'd light up when she talked about you."

The words worm their way into my chest where I don't want them. My eyes burn. *Not now. Please, not now.* I can't handle thinking about this—about Mom.

"She talked about you all the time. How funny you were. How bright you were and what big things you were going to accomplish. Then Alan did what he did, and everything fell apart."

Her face crumples, and my heart unwinds at the life she's lived. It's etched in the wrinkles that line her forehead, baked into the way her shoulders curl toward her chest—like if she can just keep them there long enough, it will prevent her from experiencing any more pain. And the truth is, to her, I *am* that pain. I get it. Loving someone is hard to do when all they remind you of is everything you've lost.

A clang bleeds through the wall followed by Alan's muffled howl. I glance toward it, a chill working down my spine. Vivian looks too, pursing her lips. "He'll be fine you know. Your father's a tough one. I'll give him that."

"He's also a bastard," I say with a nod toward the sickly bluish-yellow corona swamping her eye.

Her fingers float to it. "Absolutely. First class."

A laugh bubbles up my throat, and she joins in. It feels good to laugh. Normal. She shakes her head. "Who knew he was right, though? Never in a million years would I have guessed that."

"Me neither."

"So, what do you think they are?" she asks.

"I'm...not sure. You?"

She doesn't hesitate. "Something aliens planted in the earth to wipe us out when the population got out of control."

I start to laugh and stop. She's serious. I can tell by the way she's staring out at the sky like a UFO is about to appear at any moment. A week ago, I would have rolled my eyes and told her she was out of her mind. A day ago, even. But today...today it's as good a guess as any. I shiver and hug myself. "Yeah, maybe."

"Let's have it," she asks with a smirk.

"What?"

"Your guess. What they are."

I pause and consider whether I should share the next part. "All I know is I can...feel them."

"How do you mean?"

"Like when they're close I get these weird sensations. These body aches. Electrical jolts down my legs and stuff. Bloody noses."

"You sure it's not your, uh"—she thumbs her nose—"your condition. Getting over something like that, well, it ain't easy even in the best of circumstances."

I think about arguing with her, telling her it's not really *that* bad. That it just got a little out of control is all. But she's right, and I'm tired of lying to myself. It is that bad. *I'm* that bad. "Maybe part of it. But these sensations are...different."

She tugs a loose string from the sleeve of her cardigan and flicks it to the floor. "I believe you. These days I'd believe anything."

"Same."

"Listen, I'm going to go check on Mac and Tasker. Get some rest while you can. I'll let you know if I hear anything."

"Vivian," I say as she stands to leave.

"Yeah?"

"Thanks."

She gives me a small smile. "Anytime."

I lean back and close my eyes. When I open them again, Tasker's outlined in the doorway, his mouth set in a grim line.

"Hey," I say. "What's up?"

"He's done. Doc wants us."

———

Alan looks like death warmed over, his skin the color of overcooked fish, his eyes muddy with pain. He's naked from the waist down, save for a pair of boxers, and his ankle is bound in a gluey-looking cast.

On the table next to him is a mound of crimson gauze stained dark with blood.

Dr. Tsosie strips off a latex glove and tosses it in the trash. "His malleoli were fractured. All three of them. Two seriously. I applied reduction and pinned them. Two plates and a screw." He strips off the other glove. "He fractured his tibia as well. His recovery will not be easy."

Alan moans as if in response, one hand flopping off the table.

"Is he going to be okay?" Mac asks. His eyes dart to Dr. Tsosie. "He's not going to die or anything, is he?"

"No. I gave him a few tranquilizers for the pain. He's just now coming to. I've done my best. He will need to keep the ankle elevated and iced. You can stay here tonight. Upstairs. There's some ice in the freezer." He shakes a bottle and tosses it to me. "He'll need to take these as well. Two twice a day."

"What is it?" Tasker asks.

"Clavamox. It's Amoxicillin for dogs. I doubled the dosage based on his weight. It should do the trick. Works as well on humans as it does on animals."

I pocket the bottle and lay a hand on his arm. His skin is warm and rough, papery. "Thank you for this. It means...a lot."

He nods, offers a hint of a smile. "You are welcome. Now we must get upstairs. The day is fading. Everyone grab a lamp. Anything we can use. We'll need as much light as we can get."

CHAPTER SEVENTEEN
HORSES

We round up every light on the first level—a torchiere floor lamp, two bronze table lamps, a green piano lamp, two packs of LED bulbs, and three flashlights—and head upstairs. I'm the first to reach the second story, and as soon as I crest the landing, I realize I was right; this isn't just an office, it's Dr. Tsosie's home.

It's nothing like the first floor and surprisingly modern in comparison. The floors are beetle-kill pine with soft blue streaks swirling through the wood, the walls deep rust-red brick. A leather sectional with a chaise lounge looks ready to leave me sticky-skinned with sweat the instant I sit on it. Through a set of white French doors, I glimpse a granite-layered kitchen and a dark hall beyond.

I set down my lamp and wander over to several portraits on the wall: Dr. Tsosie in what I guess to be his late thirties, his arms draped around the shoulders of a pudgy-faced boy and a girl clad in a deer-skin Navajo dress, an eagle feather entwined in her hair. Next to it is an ancient wedding photo of Dr. Tsosie and his wife. A brunette with a warm smile and ample hips. A bouquet of tulips sprouts from her delicate hands as she gazes up at her new husband. Another photo of the kids, teenagers now, the boy still pudgy-faced and looking like he'd rather be out smoking a joint, but the girl beaming and now as striking as her mother. Skin the color of desert sand. Almond eyes so brown I can't help but lose myself in them.

"My daughter."

I jolt. For his age, Dr. Tsosie moves like a cat.

"Forgive me, I did not mean to scare you." He points at the picture. "That is my daughter Natasha."

"She's beautiful."

He cocks his head, his face softening. "She has two boys of her own now. Lives in New Mexico with her husband." His eyes dim, and he shakes his head. "I haven't been able to reach them since all this started."

"Keep trying. She looks like a fighter."

"She is, just like her mother. I lost her to cancer two years ago, but it should have been seven. She fought like a banshee. Never gave up."

I go silent, unsure of what to say. Luckily, there's a clatter at the stairs, and Tasker and Mac appear carrying Alan—Tasker by the arms, Mac supporting his legs. Behind them, Vivian lugs an old floor lamp that looks as brittle as her, like it might split in half at any moment.

"Where should we set him, Doc?" Tasker asks.

Dr. Tsosie waves across the room. "There, the recliner."

I let them pass, then head back downstairs to the operating room where I pause and then quietly slip inside and turn on the lights. It looks the same, except Dr. Tsosie took the time to wipe off the metal table and stuff the gauze into the trashcan along with Alan's pants, which are so drenched in blood I can't look at them. I'm in here for a different reason, anyway: *Where, oh where do you keep the good stuff, Doctor? Because I know you have it.*

I start with the medical cabinets on the far wall. My hand trembles in anticipation as I reach for the closest. My muscles are screaming, my head swimming in fog. I'm half comatose and would do just about anything for a pill right now. Claw someone's eyes out. Punch a baby or two. Whatever, as long as it means my skin will stop its junkie itching, and my head will feel a little less like a pressure cooker ready to explode.

The first cabinet is all hand sanitizer and disinfectant. Packs of surgical gloves and masks. Strike one. The next is more of the same— along with some cleaning pads and bottles of disinfectant. Strike two. I rifle through the rest of them, tossing everything on the counter, not caring if anyone hears—no pills. Strike three. Four. Five.

Where are they?

I turn my attention to the drawers. I need something. *Anything.* Some Feenies or Special K. I don't even care that they both suck. Anything will do at this point. My fingers jitter their way around boxes of bandages and climb over suture packs. There are shiny sharp things for which I have no name. Useless things. Things that don't mean shit to me right now because I only want one *thing*, and that one thing *has* to be here.

"What are you doing?"

I whirl around and clutch the counter, nearly fall. Mac is looking at me suspiciously—like he just walked in on me masturbating. His gaze flicks to the open drawer.

My cheeks burn. "I, um—nothing. Just looking for more lights."

"In there?" He raises his eyebrows. "Well, when you get done with *that*, dinner's ready."

———

Everyone but Alan is gathered around the kitchen table when I walk in. I take the seat furthest from Mac and keep my eyes off him. I can't handle his judgment right now. *When you get done with that.* Like he's so perfect...except that he pretty much is. A thought that doesn't help ease the heat in my cheeks as I stare at the bowl of canned chili steaming in front of me. After today, I should be starved, should be absolutely ravenous, but I'm not. The scent of reheated meat and beans only serves to further turn my stomach.

"Doc," Tasker says, shoveling sloppy bites into his mouth so fast I can barely understand him. "It's mighty nice what you've done for us here. I can't thank you enough for your hospitality."

"Mm-hm, this is so good," Vivian says, swiping a dribble of sauce from her chin with a napkin. "A warm meal is just what we needed."

"Please, call me Gene," he says, rolling up the sleeves of his dress shirt.

"Okay, Gene. You got it. You're good people in my book," Tasker replies. "You need anything before we head out in the morning, you just ask."

"That is kind of you. Where will you go?"

Tasker wipes the back of his hand over his lips. "We've got a... place."

"Hey," Mac says, grabbing his arm. "Maybe Dr. Tsosie can come."

Dr. Tsosie raises a hand. "No, no. I will not leave my home. This is where I raised my children, where I built my life. That room down there—" he points toward the hall "—is where my wife passed away. This place is all that's left of her. That, and her horses. If I abandoned them, she would return to haunt me, and I would deserve it. I'm still not sure why she married an old grouch like me."

Vivian grins. "Don't worry, Gene. You're not alone there. Every woman asks herself that question after getting married."

They all laugh except for me.

"What? Not hungry?" Mac asks with a smirk on his lips.

I glare at him and then jam a spoonful of chili into my mouth with a grimace, follow it up with a bite of cornbread. Smile. "Starved actually."

———

We sit huddled in groups. Vivian with Dr. Tsosie in the kitchen, Mac paging through a magazine by Alan, who's catatonic in the recliner, and me near the large bay window overlooking the backyard. It's not fully dark yet, but Dr. Tsosie's back porch floodlights are already illuminating the grass, and further back a small cream-colored stable. I've been hoping to see the horses, or even hear them, but so far there hasn't been a sound.

Tasker strolls over with a sleeping bag in hand and hangs it over the curtain rod, blacking out the view.

"Hey," I protest, swatting at his leg. "I can't see anything."

"That's the point. Light's dangerous now." He settles into a nearby chair. "At least up here where other people can see it, it is. It could bring attention we don't want."

There's a sudden roar overhead, and I grab Tank's spider pendant so hard, it stings. Helicopters whooshing past in a series of cold *thwap, thwap, thwaps.* Pressure on my knee. Tasker reaching over with a reassuring squeeze. His eyes are the color of antifreeze in the stark lamplight. "Don't worry," he says. "We're safe in here. Plenty of light. Thank God the Doc's got solar."

"No kidding." Mostly the eco-friendly crowd annoys the shit out of me—too self-righteous, too many banner-swinging nut jobs who just want to see themselves on TV—but he's got a point. I've never been more thankful for green energy in my life.

"And we'll make it to the shelter. Tomorrow. All of us. Even the Doc. I've thought on it some. We can't leave him here. We'll drag him up there if we have to."

"Good." I fall silent for a moment, something I've been meaning to ask him picking at my brain. "Tasker?"

"Yeah?"

I nod at Alan, who's snoring softly, his eyelids fluttering. "Why didn't you call the cops when he kidnapped Mac and Viv. Why didn't you turn him in?"

He rubs his mustache. "I thought about it. Almost did, but I couldn't. Not when I had you to consider."

"What do you mean?"

"Alan didn't tell me where you were. Just that he had you stashed away somewhere. After I lost your mother." He clears his throat. "After what Alan did to her and all, well, I was worried about what might happen to you. That, and when he showed up at the shop out of the blue, I froze. Couldn't think. I mean *shit*, the man was supposed to be in jail for another decade or two. I didn't want to set him off. At least not until I had a chance to think things through. Besides, Mac and Viv were where I could keep an eye on 'em, you know?"

I fall silent for a moment, then say, "Thanks, Tasker."

"For what?"

"For watching out for them. For doing what you did to keep them safe. All of us. Even before this happened. You've always...been there for us. For me and Mac."

His ears redden, and he shakes his head. "No need to thank me. You guys...'specially you and Mac, you're about the only family I got left."

———

I find a soft fleece blanket and curl up on the floor next to the couch where Mac is already dozing. I don't want to go to sleep. It means another day facing God knows what. Maybe one of us dying. Maybe Mac? Maybe Vivian or Tasker? Or Alan?

And if it *is* Alan, how will we survive? How will *I* survive if I don't get the chance to tell him that I'm...what, sorry? Or that I'm still angry with him? Still pissed? Because I am. He destroyed my life. He destroyed Mac's. And worse, he was right...

About all of it.

And I'm pissed at him for *being* right. It would have been so much easier if he'd been wrong. So much cleaner. I could still hate him, could write him off and not have to think about him in this new, fucked-up light. But there's more to it than that. This thick tar bubbling up in my chest every time he looks at me that feels like guilt, but so much worse than guilt.

It feels like...*shame*.

Shame because *I* abandoned *him*. Not the other way around. *I* left him in a cage to decay. *I* never opened his letters, never called him, never brought him up. To *anyone*. I just wanted to hate him—*needed* to hate him—because it was so much easier than hating myself, even though all he was trying to do was protect me and Mac. Trying to protect Mom, who'd still be here today if I'd only listened to him, if I'd never gone for that gun...

I try to picture her and can't—all that comes to mind is a faded smudge of blonde hair and a set of blurry, ocean eyes...

Something brushes against my cheek.

Something plastic. Hard.

A foil packet in a shape I recognize. My pupils dilate. *A pill!* Tramadol. A solitary, beautifully engineered combination of chemical salvation. I snatch it from Mac's hand and dig at the corners. "Where did you get this?"

"In the operating room. You missed a drawer."

I'm not even listening as my fingers tremble and tear away the paper. I punch the pill through the foil, jerk it toward my lips...and stop. Look at Mac.

"I, uh—"

"I'm not a moron, Brynn. I'm in high school, remember? I'm not the same dumb kid I was when you left me with Vivian. I've seen it before. My friends do it, too."

"Do you do it, Mac?" Suddenly, I can't handle the thought of him touching this poison. "Please, tell me you don't."

"*No.* I'm not stupid like...look, I just can't stand to see you all messed up like this, so just take it already."

Every molecule of my being screams to do as he says. To taste the sweet dust of the pill on my lips. On my tongue. One quick swallow is all it would take.

My brain screams for me to do it. *Do it, Brynn. He wants you to do it.*

It's a lie I want to believe. Intensely. But I can't. Not with the way he's watching me, his eyes full of disgust, his mouth curling down in disappointment.

A moment of clarity: I can't take it. I can't ever touch another pill again. Because if this isn't enough motivation, hurting Mac, disappointing him again and again and again, nothing is. If I do this, I'll never stop.

I hand it back to him. "Get rid of it."

His eyebrows disappear beneath his bangs. "Really? You sure?"

I nod and struggle not to cry.

"Positive?"

"Yes."

"Okay." He stuffs it into his pocket and settles onto the couch, looking at me like I might ask for it back at any minute, which I want to, have to, *need* to...

So badly.

I stare at the ceiling until he's asleep, still fighting the urge to grab his wrists, shake him awake, and fill his ears with more false promises.

This is the last one. I promise...just one more.

———

A sound.

I lurch awake with a gasp. Something's wrong.

Tracers dance at the edge of my vision as I sit up and take in the room. Mac's out, dead to the world on the couch. The same with Alan, who's covered by a mound of blankets on the recliner. Tasker is in a sleeping bag by the window, and Vivian is crumpled and snoring in the papasan along the far wall.

The sound comes again, distant and shrill. Drills.

And something else. Something unearthly. It's the horses. They're screaming.

Footsteps smack against the floor—a snip of white hair

disappearing down the stairs. Dr. Tsosie. I pull myself out from underneath the blankets and follow him, pins and needles dancing through my legs with every step. By the time I reach the bottom, he's already at the back door.

"Dr. Tsosie," I say. "Wait. Don't go out there."

His eyes find mine—two tender pools of desperation. "I must. They're all I have left of her. Of my wife. I will not abandon them. I slept with them last night. I expected to die with them. But they saved me. The nayee never entered the stable. The filthy cockroaches." He makes a spitting sound and presses his hand to his chest. To his heart where he makes a fist. "If I die, so be it. I'll be with my wife and the Creator. Take my truck. Take whatever you need. Trust yourself, little one. You are far stronger than you think."

Before I can respond, he opens the door and slides into the night...and I'm left wondering if I'll ever see him again.

CHAPTER EIGHTEEN
TRAPS

<pre>
Opiate Withdrawal Timeline:
        Phase 2
</pre>

<pre>
Length: 1-3 days.
Symptoms: Abdominal cramping, fatigue. Excessive
          nausea and vomiting.
Summary: I'd rather swallow a bucket of nails.
</pre>

I'm in Natasha's room, taking cover from all the noise in the living room, the sour taste of bile on my tongue threatening to send me back to the toilet for the third time this morning. My stomach clenches at the thought. Any more vomiting and I'm pretty sure chunks of it will start ripping off, too. I envision them in the water, delicate pink scabs of tissue floating in all the stomach acid, everything blending into a muddy green as it whirls down the bowl...

As bad as the thought is, it's better than the alternative—going outside to discover what became of Dr. Tsosie. Maybe he's okay. Maybe he's in the stable with the horses, feeding them a bucket of oats. Or maybe he's in the kitchen, dressed up as Santa Claus, waiting to tell me this is all one bad dream, that my stocking's not actually full of coal.

The truth is, I already know what happened to him. There's been no knock at the back door. No *Hey guys, open up already!* In fact, there's been no sound at all. Not even from the birds, so I'd rather just lay on Natasha's bed and stare at her old boy band posters and forget about the outside world for as long as possible. Where did Dr. Tsosie say she was? Arizona? New Mexico? It's hard to retrieve the memory through all the wet cement clogging my brain.

"Brynn, we gotta go," Tasker shouts down the hall.

I don't respond, hope if I'm quiet enough, he'll leave me alone. He doesn't.

"Brynn, seriously. Get a move on."

"Ugh, *fine.*" I roll off the bed with everything going woozy around me and catch a glimpse of myself in the full-length mirror on the wall: matted hair, face sunken in, crazy, meth-red eyes screaming *If you know what's good for you, you'll FEED ME A FUCKING PILL!*

But I can't. Those days are over.

Or are they? The thought feels like a lie, like one of those promises you make as a kid with your fingers crossed behind your back so you can break it later when no one's looking.

I button the Levi's I scavenged from Natasha's closet and then pull on the sweater I snagged from her dresser. The jeans barely fit, way too tight, and the sweater is something I would have avoided even in my needy trailer-park days—a rainbow of clashing color, all puke greens, and dirty browns and reds—but after trudging around in my vomit jeans and Vivian's ashtray of a Broncos shirt, I'd go naked and be happy.

The sound of a diesel engine coughing to life outside pulls me over to the window. I slide it open and taste smoke. It's even worse than yesterday. The sky is streaked with it, a sick yellow wash that sets me to squinting. I can't make out the city from here, the northern horizon a smudged haze of ash and soot. To the west, beyond the sprawling suburban crawl, a bank of clouds rolls off the mountains like an angry strip of seafoam. It could be rain on the way. Or snow. Probably snow. October in Colorado—anyone's guess.

"—got it! ...need to drive... almost sixteen, Aunt Viv."

The voice pulls my gaze to the street, to Mac. He's in the driver's seat of Dr. Tsosie's red Dodge Ram with an elbow flung out the window, his head twisted back at Vivian as she hops in the truck bed with a box and pushes it toward the cab.

I cup a hand to my mouth and yell, "You guys need some help?" *Say no... please say, no.*

Vivian squints up at me and offers a weak flutter of her fingers. "Uh—yeah, sure. Come on down. We got lots of supplies still to load." She turns back to Mac. "Okay, back it up onto the driveway closer to the garage. Nice and slow."

Mac nods and the truck shudders into reverse, the rear tires thumping from the street onto the sidewalk. It's a sight that fills me with an unexpected bolt of optimism. Maybe we'll make it to the shelter after all, if we can just—

A thunderclap splits the air.

My gaze snaps toward the sound. Another crack hits and the asphalt buckles beneath the front of the truck. I don't wait to see what happens next. I explode from the room and slam past Tasker. Shove him spinning to the side.

"Where do you think you're going?" he shouts after me.

I ignore him and pound down the stairs. The screen door clatters against the clapboard as I leap off the deck and race toward the truck. The rear wheels are floating an inch off the curb, with the front of the truck tilting down through the rapidly dissolving asphalt. My nervous system short circuits. I can't believe what I'm seeing. There's a hole forming in the street, a hungry mouth ripping wide in the blacktop.

I reach the tailgate and peer over. Vivian is curled in the truck bed, looking up at me like a lamb before the slaughter—eyes stretched, nose flared. "Listen," I say, trying to keep my voice steady. "Whatever you do. Don't. Move. I'll figure out a way to get you—"

My words are swallowed by a sudden rock-on-rock grinding, a grating rumble that shivers through the road. The truck tips forward, the back tires rising further off the cement. Vivian screams and clutches the railing. Another crackle rips through the earth and it hits me: weight. The truck needs more *weight*.

I leap onto the bumper, and it dips slightly. Someone thumps down on the bumper next to me and the back half of the truck drops a few more inches. Tasker. He stretches an arm toward Vivian. "Crawl to me!"

She nods but doesn't move, her face paralyzed with fear.

A dull pounding pulls my gaze toward the truck cab—the sight ripping a hole in my chest. Mac has his face pressed to the glass, his lips spitting words I can read: *Help, help, help!*

A savage *CRACKAM!* sends the front of the truck smashing through the blacktop. Metal squeals, and I nearly lose my grip. Tasker's chest slams off the tailgate. He groans and pulls himself straight. Mac pounds the glass, jerking back and forth with the motion, rocking the truck forward. My heart beats faster.

"Mac," I scream. "Stop moving!"

He's pure panic as he turns and shoves the door open, nearly falling out in the process.

"Jesus, Mac," Tasker shouts. "Hold still!"

Fat chunks of asphalt crumble beneath his swaying feet. He looks at me, face white, his entire body rigid and stiff as the truck tilts.

He has to jump.

My voice explodes up my throat: "Jump, Mac! Jump!"

"It's too far. I-I won't make it."

He's right. *Jesus Christ. He's right. He won't.*

Another chunk of street dissolves and the fatal pull of gravity takes hold once more.

Tasker leans forward and extends his arm again. "C'mon, Vivian, move your ass!"

She starts for his hand and then stops, a strange look rolling over her face. "I—I can't. I'm sorry." Then, before I know what's happening, she flips over and spider-crawls back to the cab. The truck groans beneath her weight, the bumper rising and rising, everything happening in slow motion.

We're three feet up. Four.

She plants her feet against the truck bed and reaches for Mac with both hands. "Grab on!"

He shakes his head, his eyes saucers.

"Mac, do it," I beg. "Please!"

He snakes a hand up and Vivian grabs his wrist.

He jumps.

Vivian swings him toward the sidewalk with a strangled cry. My heartbeat slams in my ears, everything happening in slow motion.

Not far enough!

I leap off the bumper and dive for him. My fingers scrape his, miss, and latch onto his forearm instead. His weight snaps me forward toward the hole. The ground dissolves. Vivian and the truck whip past in a shower of rock and dirt, her screams ripping into my eardrums.

My grip weakens. I can't hold on!

Tasker thuds down next to me and snatches the back of Mac's shirt, then his hand. "Got you!" Together we pull—pulling as my arms shake and my back cramps, pulling until my very muscle fibers feel like they'll fray and come apart. And then he's scrambling for the grass with his hat gone and his hair powdered in concrete dust.

"Oh, God, oh, God, I thought I was dead," he blubbers. "I thought that was it."

I wrap my arms around him and tell him he's okay—*You're okay, Mac. You're okay*—and keep them there until we both stop shaking, until it no longer feels like the entire world is coming apart around us.

———

This hole is different.

No saw-tooth swirls of mud here. No corkscrews of earth churning down, down, down into black nothingness. Just shattered asphalt—like a semi fell from the sky and busted through a sheet of ice—but instead of cold water beneath, it's all dead space and dust motes mixed with that now familiar rotten-egg stench; a long, dark throat running straight to Hell.

I lean forward trembling, ready to bolt back at the first sound of another piss-your-pants crack and cup my hands to my mouth. "Vivian!"

No echo. Nothing.

I try again and the hole devours my words like it devoured her screams. She's gone, and I'm suddenly certain that if I stand here long enough, it will swallow me up, too. I retreat and collapse on the lawn.

"What did you see?" Tasker asks.

"Nothing."

"You sure?"

"Look for yourself."

"No, I'll take your word for it. But damn. Vivian..."

I glance once more at the hole, then at him. "We're done with cars."

"Why?" he asks.

Because that cold prickle of fear from yesterday, the same one sweeping over my skin right now, was no coincidence. "Those bastards have been digging beneath the streets. They're setting traps."

———

"Wait, *what*?" Alan asks when I tell him, a chill spreading over his face. "Vivian's... *dead*?"

"Yes. She—"

"—saved me," Mac answers, the words frothing out of his mouth. "It was awful. The street it, it just came undone. The truck started sinking, cracking beneath the tires when I backed it up. I thought for sure—" There's a sudden hitch in his voice. "I thought I was dead. And if it wasn't for Viv I—I..." He shakes his head and turns away. I place a hand on his back, realize he's trembling. Realize I'm trembling harder.

"Shit," Alan mumbles, blinking hard. "Shit..."

"Yeah. And there's something else," Tasker replies. "Cars aren't safe anymore. Those things. Whatever they are. They're smart. They set a trap. It's how they got Vivian." The statement hurts worse than

I thought it would. I picture her face as she turned to help Mac—the determination there, mixed with fear. A few days ago, I would have happily ditched her funeral. Now all I want is to bring her back.

Alan frowns. "We can't make any rash decisions. The shelter's too far to make on foot."

Mac wipes his eyes. "I don't care. There's no way I'm getting in another car. *No way.* They were waiting for us, Dad."

Alan opens his mouth to respond but is cut off by a sound I recognize bleeding through the window: a snort followed by a few deep chuffs. Hooves on grass.

The horses.

They're alive.

CHAPTER NINETEEN
HIGHWAY TO HELL

My eyes are hungry for any sign of Dr. Tsosie as I step outside. The stable is wrecked. Half a door hangs from one hinge, the other gone. The roof is buckled in, looking like it might come apart in a gentle breeze.

"Oh, hell," Tasker mutters. I follow his gaze to a nearby aspen. Beneath it are the remains of Dr. Tsosie's leather vest. It's shredded, crusted with blood. Next to it lies an empty boot and the remnants of an ankle.

No, No, No.

I should have stopped him, should have pulled him back inside and held him there, should have done...something. *Anything.*

But instead, all I did was *nothing.*

Warmth runs over the back of my hand as blood seeps from my truck stop scab through my clenched fingers and into the grass. I watch it drip and squeeze harder.

Tasker grips my shoulder. "Brynn, you can't save everyone. Let it go."

"I can't."

"You have to. Now let's go see to those horses."

They're hemmed in by a pair of massive feeder holes, trotting anxious circles in the corner by the fence. One is a chestnut mare, the other a stallion, pissed-off and charcoal black, blowing sharp bursts of air from his nostrils as we near. They're both haltered, the stallion already saddled with the billet strap hanging loose like Dr. Tsosie gave up securing it halfway through.

Probably because he was eaten…

Tasker blows in his hands, and I notice the chill hanging in the air. It feels wet. Heavy. Definitely snow on the way. Shit. "All right," he says, "I'm not sure how the hell these two are still alive, but I'm going to try for the mare. You stay here." `

I pull deeper into my sweater as he eases forward and clucks out a few *easy girls* and *there, theres.* The horse watches him through dark-glass eyes, backing up a step and clacking her teeth. Still, he approaches, forcing her to the fence where she snorts. A pink strip of tongue works out over her lips. The stallion brays and edges away.

"Whoa, whoa. Easy there, girl. *Easy.* I'm not gonna hurt you, I promise." He sets his palm on her cheek and holds it there until the horse's nostrils go round and soft, her lips curling down at his touch. "See. I'm not so bad." With his other hand, he grabs the halter and gently guides her past the holes toward me. He grins and strokes her back. "She's beautiful, ain't she?"

She is. Her coat is glossy and speckled with creme-colored patches that glisten in the morning light, her muscles gliding beneath my fingertips as I run my hand over it.

"The other one's not going to be so easy," I say.

As if in response, the stallion hammers a hoof into the ground and snorts.

"Good thing I'm always up for a challenge," Tasker says, handing me the mare's reins.

I hand them back. "I'll do it. You try, and I'm pretty sure you'll have a pair of shoe prints stamped into your chest."

He chuckles. "You? You don't know a thing about horses, Brynn. He'll trample you to death."

He's wrong. I took riding lessons when I was ten. A blissful six-month period before oil prices crashed and Alan said we couldn't afford them anymore. That we needed to buckle down and save. Translation: another childhood dream trashed.

"I'll be fine," I tell him. "He needs a soft touch. Trust me."

"No way. I'm not letting you anywhere near that stallion. One wrong move and—"

"Tasker," Alan barks from the window. "If she says she's got it, she's got it."

His eyebrows patch together like he's about to argue, but then he unfolds an arm toward the horse. "Fine, your highness. Be my guest. But don't say I didn't warn you."

"Brynn, wait," Mac says, running through the back door in a blue and white Nuggets jersey. "I found these in the fridge. Maybe they'll help." His eyes shift to the stallion as he hands me the carrots. "Be careful, okay?"

"I'll be fine. Wait here."

He nods, and I start forward, my legs greasing over with sweat as I pass the holes. I can't look at them. One glance and I'll lose my nerve—I can barely handle the smell of their sweet rot as it is. I keep my eyes on the horse instead, who has his ears pinned back and a *get-the-fuck-away-from-me* look splattered across his face.

I draw close and hold out a carrot. "Hey there. You look hungry."

The stallion swishes his mane and steps back with a snort. His legs are shaking, his hindquarters trembling like he's about to collapse.

Jesus, he's more terrified than me.

It's all I need to know. I slide forward and quickly guide a carrot under his nose while bringing my other hand to his cheek. "You don't like those holes much, do you?"

He lips the carrot and lets it fall to the ground.

"Oh, c'mon, don't be that way. They're good. I promise." I grab another and take a bite, "Mmm, see?" then press it to his jaw. This time he takes it, his lips working it into his mouth an inch at a time.

"Told you," I say as I take hold of the reins. "Let's get you away from these nasty holes." I give a gentle tug and ease him back toward Tasker with a grin.

"Well, I'll be damned," he says.

Mac cracks a smile. "She used to ride."

"I can see that."

"But Dad said she got bucked off a lot."

"Oh, shut up," I say, elbowing him when I draw level. "Like you know anything about horses."

Tasker laughs. "Well, either way, I'm impressed, Brynn. Didn't think you had it in you."

My gaze drifts to Dr. Tsosie's vest as he says it, and I look away, suddenly feeling hollow. "Whatever. Let's just go. I can't stay here any longer."

———

We head west. The mountains mock me in the distance, so far away I wonder how we'll ever reach them. The plan is to make it to some oil company field office near Morrison before nightfall. Tasker helped outfit it years ago. Says he installed the generator himself. *No way it could fail.* Even Alan knows the place, so it sounds legit enough... if we can actually make it there. The problem is, we're not the only ones trying to escape the city.

C-470 is packed. People surge all around us, weaving in between abandoned cars and gutted trucks. Those missing arms and legs shuffle along at a snail's pace, looking like they're already dead. Most probably are based on the patches of blackened skin left behind by the feeders and the dark ink rivers that web from their wounds and flow through their flesh in the form of poisoned veins. Their faces are masks of pain, their bodies pale and shriveled things sprouting limbs that look like tubes of boiled meat ready to slip from their packaging.

Men shoulder overstuffed backpacks and shove their way through the crowd, clad in thick coats and fleece-lined pants. Mothers drag bawling kids behind them, their eyes wide and terrified, their brains absorbing sights they were never meant to process. Dogs dart through the crowd and snap at people, at each other. I pass one gnawing on a severed arm, its snout a dirty red, its hair matted and greased in blood. It snatches the limb when it catches me looking at it and bolts away into the brush like I might reach out and take it for myself.

A sudden thought at the motion: *Where are all the gutted dogs? Or the livestock gnawed to the bone? Where are the deer sawed in half, or any dead animal for that matter? Because I haven't seen a single one...*

A rash of feeder holes materialize. We do our best to avoid them, but that doesn't stop my skin from crawling. Each step feels like a spin of the chamber, a pull of the trigger, hoping my brains stay glued to the inside of my skull. Each step a gamble and a prayer that a hole won't open beneath my feet and swallow me whole.

And the smell, *God*, it's beyond awful—all smoke and gasoline and sulfurous, rotten-egg air. It has me gagging, wondering if I'll ever be able to smell anything aga—

An elbow jabs my ribs. "Watch it, bitch."

The voice belongs to a woman with a rodent-like face shining beneath a thick set of glasses. A man lumbers next to her, keeping his gaze on his feet like he's been expecting this for some time now, and I'm the lucky winner.

"Screw off," I mumble through clenched teeth.

The woman's eyes turn to slits. "What did you say to me?"

"She told you to fuck off, or weren't you listening?"

The woman snaps her gaze up to Alan and her mouth falls open. She stumbles back and raises her hands. "Sorry, my bad. We don't want no trouble."

"Best be on your way, then."

She grabs the man, and they disappear into the crowd. I don't even need to look at Alan to know he has the Glock in his hand. On a horse, he's intimidating enough. Toss in the gun and he might as well be the Terminator.

"You okay?" he asks, stuffing the pistol back into the waistband of his jeans. It's the question I should be asking him. Skin drawn and sallow. Desiccated cheeks. The gash on his forehead scabbed over and angry looking, his long-sleeve cotton shirt riddled with ribbons of sweat and yellowed at the pits.

"I could've handled that, you know," I reply.

"Uh-huh. How about a thank you?"

I press my wrist to my forehead and fake swoon. "Thank you, my liege. Thou hast defended my honor. How, oh how, did I ever fare without you?"

He twists his mouth to the side and stifles a laugh. "Give me a break. Listen, why don't you double up with Mac and ride the mare for a bit? You don't look so hot."

I give him a weak smile. "I can walk a little longer. We probably shouldn't wear out the horses just yet."

He stares at me for a moment and his chin tightens. "Fine. Another mile, then you ride."

I nod, and he teases the stallion past a feeder hole and trots ahead. I watch the animal's gait, the way the muscles flex with each stride, the saddlebags swaying.

Swaying, swaying.

Swaying like me...

My stomach gives a sudden lurch, and I collapse next to an overturned truck and vomit. Bile splashes over the road and spatters across my shoes. Half-digested chunks of apple and toast pepper the asphalt. No one stops to gawk. Apparently, the end of the world has changed what constitutes making a scene.

Alan circles back, followed by Mac and Tasker. I raise a hand as they near. "Don't worry about me. Just go. I'll catch up."

"Like hell you will," Alan says. "Get on the horse."

I straighten and take a slurp of ashen air. Overhead, the clouds twist in dark gray coils, moving fast, and the thought comes again: *Snow. Definitely snow. And soon.*

I shiver and rub my arms. "No, I'm okay."

Tasker draws uncomfortably close. I can taste his breath as he speaks—stale coffee and warm chew. "Do what he says, Brynn. Ride with Mac. We need to pick up the pace." He glances at Alan and gestures toward the frontage road curving away from C-470 toward the foothills. "We should get off the highway. It's too slow with all these people."

Alan raps his knuckles on the saddle and stares at him through flesh-bag eyes. "No. We've been over this. No one will try anything out here. No ambushes. And the highway's a straight shot to the field office. You said so yourself."

Tasker spits. "Well, I've changed my mind. You look like hell warmed over, Alan. We need to speed things up before you die of blood poisoning and leave us stranded out here with no clue how to get to that shelter of yours."

"That won't happen."

"But what if it does? You ever think about that?" He waves at two stragglers shuffling past—a man and a woman, the woman missing an arm. "You want us to rot out here with the rest of the meat? Have you seen their skin? You want us to wander around aimless and catch whatever it is they got?"

"We'll talk about it later," Alan replies.

Tasker spreads his hands wide. "Later? There is no later. This is it. I'm done with all your secrecy shit, Alan. Either give me the map to the shelter and the codes or—"

"I said *later*," Alan hisses through gritted teeth. His eyes flick to the side, toward two men standing a few feet off, one a dirty white kid somewhere in his twenties with tight cheeks and gravel-colored eyes, the other older and heavyset, his neck shining with sweat.

Alan turns to them. "Something we can help you with, gentlemen?"

The thicker one steps forward and raises a hand. "Morning. The name's Randall. Couldn't help overhearing you're all heading to a shelter? That right?"

Alan serves Tasker a burning look. "Yeah, we got a place. The community shelter near Golden they've been advertising on the radio. You hear about it, too?"

The man blinks, and I imagine the little gears in his head smoking with effort, trying to determine if it's a lie. "Hm, Golden, huh? Sure sounded like it was a place of your own. That really where you're headed?"

Alan's mouth tightens. "Where we're headed's no concern of yours."

The man's hands shoot up, the skin lines black with grease. "Whoa, we don't want any trouble. Look, all I was trying to say was me and Benny here"—he claps the younger man on the back—"need somewhere to ride all this out." He winks. "And we've got a lot to offer folks who might be able to help, ain't that right Benny?"

Benny sucks his teeth and smiles. His hair is thin, straining at the temples even though he can't be a day past twenty-five, his eyes flat and lifeless. When he speaks, it's a little too fast, the words blurring together like he can't wait to get them out. "Yeah, my uncle's place is a few miles off the highway. There's food stored out back. Canned goods and rice, and a bunch of those packaged meals the army uses. Oh, and"—he raises a finger—"we've got guns. Lots and lots of guns. The real heavy stuff. We can provide you all with some protection."

Tasker pulls his vest to the side and points at the pearl stock of his pistol. "Nah. We're good."

Randall scratches his face, his eyes narrowing on the handgun. "That don't look like much to me. At least not against those things." He gestures at a nearby feeder hole. "Saw a bunch of 'em tear a man clean in half last night. I believe he was shooting at them with something like what you got there."

"Like he said, we don't need your help," Alan echoes.

The man stiffens and what little light is left in his eyes winks out. "Suit yourself. You all be careful now. You wouldn't want the wrong people hearing about that shelter of yours. Lots of bad folks out here. You never know what might happen."

Tasker crosses his arms. "That a threat?"

"No, not at all. Just some friendly advice from one traveler to another." He nods toward Benny. "You heard them. They don't need our help. Let's go."

Benny flashes me a smile as they pass, his left incisor gone gray at the root. "We'll see you around, sweetheart. You can be sure of that."

I want to tell him to go to hell, that he doesn't want to see me again because it will mean him lying on the road bleeding from his throat, but it's all I can do to stand my ground and watch him until he turns around and melts into the crowd.

CHAPTER TWENTY
DEAD END

The going is slow, even on the mare, and I can't help but wonder if Tasker was right in wanting to get off the highway. He guides the horse on foot, reins in hand, past skeins of fallen transmission wire and cars turned to charred metal skeletons. Alan trails behind us on the stallion, his face ashen, his cheeks sagging like puddles of melted candle wax.

I lean against Mac and try to avoid looking at the carnage. It's impossible—death is everywhere, all around us. We pass a sedan with a half-devoured corpse still buckled into the driver's seat, jaw severed, eyes vacant. Intestines spill through the door in lavender coils, only to be trampled into the asphalt by the passing crowd.

A legless torso lies on the shoulder of the road with chalk-colored ribs peering out through gills of shredded flesh.

My gorge rises—I want the images to stop, to melt from view and never return.

They continue for miles.

A head turned to a skull tucked into a patch of grass with a few tufts of hair still sprouting from the crown and a glistening length of spine from the base.

The ruined body of a woman lying naked in a culvert, cradled in the arms of a man who pleads for someone—*anyone*—to help him drag her up the incline and carry her home.

No one does.

People shove through choke points and argue why they should go first: *My daughter's sick! My wife is pregnant! I can't find my son!* No one cares. No one backs down. Two men exchange words and then blows. One of them tumbles down the bank with a face turned to hamburger, while the one who did it screams down at him with bloodied fists.

It's noon. We have six hours.

I blow into my hands and press them to my ears. It provides a moment of relief before I have to blow and do it again. The cold always hits my ears first. You'd think my hair would help with how thick it is, but it doesn't; the chill knifes right through it every time. It's one of the reasons I chose Texas. No cold fronts. No sub-zero temperatures. Just miles of beautiful, sweltering heat tucked beneath blankets of endless humidity.

I draw closer to Mac and try to soak up some of his warmth only to realize he's shivering too.

"You okay?" I ask.

He glances back, his ears tinged red beneath his ball cap. "What do you think?"

"Hey, don't stress. We'll make it to Tasker's place before dark."

"No, it's not that. It's..." He grimaces. "I didn't even try to help her."

"Who, Vivian?"

He nods. "She saved me, and I did...nothing."

"There's nothing you could have done, Mac. I was there, remember?"

"Maybe. Still, all I thought about was saving myself."

"Mac..."

"I hated her. Or at least thought I did. She didn't deserve to die like that." He bites his lip, shakes his head. "She's the only one who never abandoned me."

The comment guts me—*I left. He's talking about me.*

"I'll never forgive myself," he continues, looking back at the road.

I want to comfort him. I want to scoop all of the pain from his chest and swallow it whole, but I can't—not when I'm already brimming with cancer myself.

———

I hear it before I see it: megaphones. Voices bubbling somewhere ahead like a bad stew. The sound of shoes scraping asphalt. And then it appears—a thick mass of bodies strung across both lanes of C-470, people stacked up against a metal barricade intersecting the highway. Behind it, the green and black camouflage of National Guard trucks mixes with the red and blue flare of police lights.

The mare stiffens and looses a shrill whinny. Alan pulls up next to us and blows into his hands. "*Shit.* Now, this we do *not* need."

Tasker whistles low through his teeth. "Huh. A dead end. On the highway of all places. Imagine that."

"Can it," Alan says, spurring the stallion forward. "Let's go see what this is all about."

We follow, Tasker guiding the horse through the fringes of the crowd toward the side of the road where I dismount and step onto the guardrail for a better view. A bloom of panic fills my lungs. Beyond the barricade, a jagged chasm splits the highway in two. A massive gorge, carving west to east from the foothills and running down the valley slope toward the shitty little lake at the bottom that I'd sometimes see people water skiing on as a kid. Except it's no longer a lake. It's a glistening sheen of mud puddles and trash, split wide by the festering black scar.

"What *is* that?" Mac asks, staring at the chasm.

"I don't know, but I don't like the look of it," Tasker replies.

"Whatever it is," Alan adds. "We need to get around it quick."

Tasker kicks a rock off the road and whirls on Alan. "No shit. I knew this damn highway was trouble. I *knew* it." His eyes ice over, form pale blue daggers. "So, boss man? What's your grand plan now that this one's tanked?"

Alan glares back, his features hardening, turning to stone. "Like I just said, we find a way past this mess."

"And how we gonna do that? This right here"—Tasker spreads his hands and pulls them wide—"is the definition of a cluster fuck if I ever saw one."

He's right. I can practically feel the air throbbing with panic, angry faces everywhere I look. Tight, strained voices and furtive glances. Balled fists. People shouting. The scene reminds me of the slaughterhouse, all the semis packed with cattle. Their hopeless mooing and futile stamping. It's what this feels like—a bunch of warm meat waiting to be butchered.

"TURN BACK! THE HIGHWAY AHEAD HAS COL-LAPSED!"

I search for the voice and find it perched on the hood of one of the military trucks. A buzz-cut pile of muscle in army fatigues busy assaulting a megaphone, the veins in his neck popping with each command as he raises a square sheet of paper and jabs at it with his finger.

"DESIGNATED COMMUNITY SHELTERS CAN BE FOUND ON THIS MAP. TAKE ONE AND EVACUATE TO THE CLOSEST LOCATION IMMEDIATELY."

I spot several soldiers passing boxes of maps over the barricade, gesturing for them to be distributed through the crowd. Anxious hands grab for them, most spilling to the ground before they travel five feet.

A rumble tears through the earth, and the mare clacks her teeth.

"What the hell was that?" Tasker asks.

"I don't know," Alan replies, stroking the stallion's neck. "But it's time to go. We'll backtrack and find a different route."

Tasker scowls. "No, backtracking will take time we don't have." He glances my way. "You see anything up there, Brynn? There's got to be a way around this shit."

There isn't. Three massive cargo trucks are parked lengthwise behind the barricade with police cruisers filling the gaps. Pop-up tents speckle the tarmac and house packs of nervous-looking soldiers who look ready to give their trigger fingers some exercise—probably on people like us looking to break the rules.

My eyes jerk left toward the foothills and the jags of scrub brush there, interspersed with baby pine and prairie grass yellowed by the weather. A few boulders rest in their midst, none large enough to hide behind, no real cover to speak of. Sneaking past the soldiers without being spotted is impossible, especially on the horses. They'd never make it, even if we tried. They're spooked enough as it is. We have to go back.

I hop off the guardrail and yank Tasker's arm. "Come on. We can't get around this."

"THE HIGHWAY IS IMPASSABLE. IT IS IMPERATIVE

YOU SEEK SHELTER BEFORE NIGHTFALL!"

An angry voice spikes to my left. "There isn't time!" It belongs to a Black man, holding a girl in his arms. Chunky twists of hair sprout from her scalp, her eyes wide as she clutches the man's neck.

Another voice rises: "Yeah, either help us or let us through!"

And another: "Let us through!"

"Save us!"

"Government bastards!"

I catch the lazy arc of a glass bottle as it spins through the air and explodes on the hood of the truck. The soldier flinches back a step, then barks into the megaphone: "STAND DOWN, CITIZENS!"

Another bottle shatters on the hood. An apple core whips sideways over the barricade, followed by a half-eaten orange.

"Fuck you!" someone cries.

A flurry of rocks and trash darken the air and rain down over the troops. A thousand voices shrieking like we're about to bear witness to a medieval hanging.

And then.

And then...

Cramps rip up my legs and tear through my arms, causing me to double over. A river of pinpricks spills down my spine.

No...

The sound that comes next is unlike anything I've ever heard. It's primal. Raw. Ancient rock grinding and splitting apart, tearing through the earth like a cannon shot. Half the crowd slams to the road. Both horses jump, the stallion bucking skyward with a snort. Alan cusses at him to settle.

Another rumble hits and the mare rears back, sending Mac tumbling to the road where he groans and clutches his side.

Silence.

A siren ignites.

The crowd explodes. People grab wailing children and crash past each other, dashing for the hills, leaping the guardrail, and running down the slope, desperate to be anywhere other than here. Reality slows and spins past in a series of violent snapshots: A woman in a purple dress trampled to my left. A toddler screaming and flapping his hands one second, swallowed by the throng the next. Mac, lying next to me on the road, trying to regain his feet.

My mind clears.

Move!

I surge for him too late. The next crack sends me to the blacktop, my knee smacking down with a white-hot flare of pain.

"Get up," Alan booms behind me.

A terrible roar fills the air as I surge to my feet and watch in horror as the road dissolves, great sections of it vanishing at once, devouring everything in its path, the trees and asphalt and rock evaporating with terrifying speed. All of it gone in an instant and rushing straight for me.

CHAPTER TWENTY-ONE
SPLIT

The asphalt buckles. Fractures race past my feet. There's dust every-where—caking my tongue, clogging my sinuses. My eyes water as screams fog the air; horrible wild things that rise up all around me in discordant harmonies. Somewhere through the haze, the National Guard trucks topple to the road, their metal frames rending and screeching like living things being devoured alive.

Because they *are*.

The mare squeals and rears up riderless, her hooves crashing down a foot from Mac's head. I scramble to reach him, to cover him with my body and take the blows, but the ground won't let me. It's liquid. Alive. Tossing me back against the stallion, who, like the mare, is bucking and snorting like a demon—Alan still somehow in the saddle, fighting against the reins as he shouts for the horse to settle.

I lurch for Mac, but Alan seizes my arm and heaves me back.

"Get on!"

"No! Not without Mac!" I rip at his fingers. His grip is iron, impossible to escape. My heart supernovas in my chest. "Let me go!"

"Brynn!" His grip tightens, and he spins me toward him. "Tasker's got him!"

I glance back. He *does*, somehow prying Mac from the ground with one hand and yanking down on the mare's halter with the other. The horse gnashes at the bit, her gums flashing pink as Tasker mounts her and pulls Mac up after him.

"Now get on!" Alan roars.

I leap for him.

He catches my arm and rips me higher, onto the horse, and we launch over the guardrail and barrel downhill, the saddle horn smashing into my sternum as bodies windmill past us and vanish into clouds of dust. To our left, the ground splinters, fissures tearing through the earth like it's made of ice, the gorge swallowing great chunks of soil and dirt, all of it vanishing into empty black nothingness.

The stallion sways right with a savage jolt, and the motion nearly whips me from the saddle. Alan grabs my sweater and thrusts me back into place.

"Stay low and hold on!"

The command burns hot in my ear. Patches of earth blur past. Stacks of deadfall and weeds and grass blending into a violent sludge of color. I grow dizzy with the speed of it before another jarring lurch sends my teeth crashing through my lip in a bright burst of pain.

Blood fills my mouth. My vision wavers. A stray boulder obliterates a tree to our right with a thunderclap of sound, sending sharp splinters of wood into my neck. It's happening everywhere I look— the earth fracturing, the world fraying and coming apart. Through it all, the stallion surges, pure rocket fuel powered by a raging furnace of muscle.

Hooves pounding soil.

Head bobbing with fluid motion.

Ears pinned back.

The slope levels off and we blast into a strand of cottonwoods, the stallion devouring the trail as, behind us, another roar rises. The savage *SNAP! SNAP! SNAP!* of trunks splitting apart. I can *feel* the sound, can *sense* its hunger, its rage at our potential escape. I screw my eyes shut and clamp my fingers tighter around the edge of the saddle.

Branches flash past above us.

Cold air frosts my lips and fills my lungs.

And then it's just my runaway heart throbbing in time with the thunder of the stallion's hooves.

Ba-da-dum, ba-da-dum, ba-da-dum.

We explode from the timber and fly over the valley floor, carving a path through waist-high grass, the stallion's coat slick with lather, his ears still pinned back as though Alan tacked them there with nails. The sound of grinding rock fades to a dull buzz and then, a moment later, snuffs out completely. Alan yanks the reins and the horse wheels around, neighing and whipping his mane.

I stare at the tree line and pray for Mac and Tasker to emerge, to charge from the thicket on the mare and join us in the field.

Please be behind us. Please.

They aren't.

My eyes dart up the hill, frantic for any glimpse of them, for any sign at all of Tasker's stupid cowboy hat or Mac's white and blue Nuggets jersey. But there's nothing—just plumes of dust and smoke drifting sideways over the freshly ruined earth. My throat constricts. The gorge is so *big*. An evil, gaping maw darker than any feeder hole I've seen yet—so black it seems to swallow the light and the flecks of motion filtering through the haze on either side.

Flecks of motion that mean...

"Survivors!" I twist around and grab Alan's shirt. "We *have* to go back! We have to find them! Mac and Tasker. They could be—"

"Hang on. Take a breath. We—"

"—hurt!" I make fists of my fingers and hammer them into his chest. "C'mon, we have to go!" My vision turns to grease. Tears spill through my lashes as panic swells in my chest. "We *have* to find them. They need us…"

Alan pulls me into a hug. I try to shove him away, but he only squeezes tighter in response. I grind handfuls of his shirt between my fingers as the sight of Mac flopping off the ground plays over and over on repeat in my mind.

I did it *again. I abandoned him.* Left him when he needed me most.

Alan takes my shoulders and eases me back. He's nodding, his eyes strained, his mouth grim. "Okay. Let's go find them."

———

What we find is a graveyard. Bodies everywhere.

Groups of survivors caked in concrete dust and grime poke hopelessly through the rubble. Ashen-cheeked zombies that look like coal miners after a month trapped without sun—their faces skin-white, lips bloodless, as they squint up at the sky. Pitiful wails for help pepper the air. Dull, muffled cries I can't place that seem to come from everywhere and nowhere all at once.

We keep our distance from the chasm. The ground near it is vicious looking; a hungry mouth packed full of sharp, broken teeth. Every few minutes the earth groans, and my heart gives a painful twist, the sound eerie and alien—like a giant gargling rocks.

A woman with sunken cheeks cries out to me for help. We drag her husband from beneath a huge block of granite. His right leg is bent at an impossible angle, his chin dribbling a fountain of pink froth. He's in shock, his pulse slow and weak, his skin sweaty-cold. I set the break and tell her to wait for help, that he'll be okay, but he won't.

He has thirty minutes. An hour at most.

More voices rise. I help where I can and clean wounds with the rubbing alcohol from the saddlebag. Dress them with the spare strips of clothing and towels their loved ones shove into my hands. Panicked men who beg for me to resuscitate their loved ones. Wives who plead, *don't let him die, please, don't let him die.* I soothe those I can and lie to those I can't—tell them they'll be fine, to be strong and to wait for help to come. But help *won't* come, and right now, lies are the only comfort I can spare.

A woman in a tattered dress collapses at my feet. Her eyes shine with fear as she raises her arm and grasps my sweater. I gape in horror at the two angry puncture wounds in her shoulder and the sleeve of decaying flesh moldering beneath.

"Don't leave me here," she moans, clutching my sweater.

I open my mouth to respond and stop. Behind her, lying partially obscured in a rubble pile, I glimpse a tuft of straw-colored hair and a slice of freckled cheek.

Mac!

"I'm sorry," I say as I shove past her.

For a moment, it's him—the round face, the soft curve of the jaw—Mac resolving in bites as I pull the rocks free, my brother lying before me, lifeless and ruined. *I'm ruined.* Without him there's no point in taking another breath, another step. But then I realize the eyes are too wide-set, the lips too thin, the hair a shade lighter than Mac's weak blond. I lean back on my knees and moan in relief. Above me, the sky swirls ashen and hopeless.

God, Mac, where are you?

I move on, Alan following behind on the stallion as I dig through pile after pile of rock and dirt, digging, digging, digging until I can no longer feel my hands, digging until my fingers bleed.

"We have to go, Brynn. They're not here," Alan says, finally pulling me back.

Terror surges through me. "They are. They *have* to be!" My voice cracks—raw from screaming Mac's name over and over and over. "We can't leave them."

"We have to. They're not here. And they'll find us." He nods as if trying to convince himself, his beard caked in grime, his forehead pulsing sweat. "They will, I promise. They'll find us…"

CHAPTER TWENTY-TWO
LOST

My lip has a heartbeat of its own where I bit it. The pulse makes it painful to talk, to think. I spit a glob of blood to the side and watch it congeal on the sidewalk, the stallion swaying beneath me as we trail along the edge of the crevasse through neighborhood after ruined neighborhood. The houses on both sides cling to the earth like barnacles made of kindling and vinyl siding, several split in half, retching the guts of bedroom closets and ruined living rooms over yellowed lawns. Couches, chairs, and tables strewn about like a class five tornado just rolled through.

The scene reminds me of the dollhouse Alan gave me as a kid; the one I spent hours playing with, my fingers carefully maneuvering the cheap plastic furniture into place one moment, trying to arrange them just so, spilling everything to the floor in anger the next when I couldn't.

I pick at a loose string on my sweater and feed it to the wind, think of Vivian as she swung Mac from the truck. How her hair flew out behind her like a comet, her face a mask of terror as she heaved, forever burned into my brain with the force of a sudden camera flash. The slow, terminal tilt of the truck, and that horrible, awful scream as the earth swallowed her whole...

Vivian—scourge of my youth, dead. Another one of my victims. Just like Mac and Tasker. Shit, all of us. Even Alan. If it wasn't for me swallowing a fistful of pills outside of Denver, we'd be safe in the mountains by now, locked behind several inches of steel and concrete. Just the five of us—one happy family with a front-row seat to the end of the world.

I kill the thought and inch my sleeves lower over my hands, hunch against the chill. I've been gone years, but I'd know the feel of snow anywhere. The wet hang of it in the air—like someone left a massive refrigerator open for the cold to spill out. It's sure to make our trek extra miserable. Or what's left of it, anyway, before the sun dives behind the mountains and the feeders come out to play.

Alan clucks at the horse to slow, and I take the opportunity to slide off and stretch, the insides of my legs screaming for lotion, my thighs chafed raw from the saddle. I stare at a ruined McMansion with a buckled roof hanging low over a pair of shattered windows, sitting on a patch of burned grass, looking hopeless and broken. Alan pushes a long, slow whistle through his teeth. "Bet this wasn't a part of anyone's retirement plan."

"Probably not." The hair on my neck rises as I say it, the creeping sensation of someone watching us—maybe the two freaks we met on the highway. I think of the younger one and how he seemed to devour me with his eyes as he passed. How I couldn't shake the chill his gaze left for miles. The same chill I feel now as I turn and scour the devastation behind us for movement, for a hidden face or a stray figure ducking for the shadows.

"...fine, you know."

I realize Alan is still talking, appraising me with his gluey pink eyes. "What?"

"Mac. He's fine. He's with Tasker."

"Why doesn't that make me feel any better?"

"Well... you got a point there, but in all seriousness, there's no one I'd rather have watching my back when the shit hits the fan."

My bullshit detector blinks red, my mouth moving before I can stop it. "Why didn't you tell him where the shelter was, then? At least they'd have a chance that way. Now they're just as screwed as we are. If they're even alive."

Alan grimaces. "Something was off with Tasker when I first got to his shop. He was acting out of sorts. Strange, like maybe he wasn't too happy to see me. Shifty. Wouldn't hold my gaze. Stuff like that."

"Didn't you just say there's no one else you'd rather have watching your back?"

He looks at me, jaw bunched, nods. "Yeah... still. But you're probably right. He's always been the closest thing to a brother I got." His lips work into a half-smile. "You know he kicked Vivian some cash every month, right? All those years I was locked up, he never missed a month. Every payday, a couple hundred bucks at least."

I frown. Vivian always acted like we were a twenty-dollar bill away from the homeless shelter. A foggy memory rises—her flipping a pack of food stamps across the counter at a bored grocery store cashier, her eyes locked on Mac and me. *Only trash have to use these. Lazy people. See what you two've done to me.*

Alan's eyes narrow. "You don't believe me, do you?"

"No, I do. It's just that, you know, Vivian never seemed flush with cash."

"Knowing her, I wouldn't be surprised if she spent it all on cigarettes and wine coolers. But that didn't stop her from telling me Tasker paid every time I called to check in on you guys."

A sharp cringe at the memory. I never took his calls. I hid under the bed. In the closet. Ran outside to hunch behind the bushes. Anything to avoid talking to him. I suddenly need to change the subject.

"How much longer until we get there? To this field office of yours?"

"We're not far off now. Still plenty of time before dark."

I'm not so sure of that. The flat angle of the sun hanging on the horizon tells me otherwise, but I keep the thought to myself and drift after him as he takes the reins and nudges the stallion forward once more.

———

I flinch when the first snowflakes hit my skin. They're gray, worthless things. Dirty flecks of white swollen with smog. Cold bits of matter that make it hard to see as I stumble after Alan, my legs stiff planks clacking numbly off the sidewalk, my feet swollen anchors dragging behind. He slows the horse and pulls next to me, extends a hand. "Time you get back up here."

He's right. And I want to, terribly, but something tells me we might need the horse's strength before the day's out. After what he's been through, riding double will only further drain him. I straighten and push on. "No. Not yet. I'm good for a few more miles."

"Uh-huh, we've been down this road, remember?"

I shrug and keep walking.

"Brynn, goddammit." He spurs the horse forward and circles back, forcing me to stop. "Will you just—God, you're impossible, you know that? You get that from your mother."

"What?"

"That damn stubborn streak of yours." He exhales through his nose and shakes his head, his eyes going distant, soft. "Man, I loved that about her. Her independence. Her fire. And I hated it, too. She was the first woman to stand up to me. She wouldn't back down from anyone. It's why I fell for her. Didn't go too well in the end, though, did it? I couldn't convince her all this"—he spreads his arms—"was coming, no matter what I said." A dimple flashes through his beard. "Couldn't convince you either, could I?"

My throat constricts at the comment, and I choke down a slug of guilt. I try to return the smile, but my face won't play along, the corners of my mouth twitching in and out.

I did this.

Me.

My feet drift to a stop. I will them forward, but they won't obey. And it's not just the snow blurring my vision as I press the flat of my thumb and forefinger to my eyelids and will myself not to cry. *Don't you do it, Brynn.* The tears come anyway, flooding around my finger pads like a burst dam.

I turn and drift over to a curb and sit down. My shoulders heave. The sobs follow. Blaming Alan all this time has been so much easier. So much more...*convenient.* A bandage I could slap over any wound.

It's his fault. He did this. He made me this way.

But it's not his fault, and I think I've somehow always known that, ever since I swung down on that gun all those years ago.

The day I killed her.

There's an awkward clatter behind me, a painful grunt, and then Alan is crouching next to me, his arm wrapping around my shoulders. He pulls me close, and I give him a weak—*I don't need you*—shove, but it's no use; he's too big and I'm lying to myself. When he leans in, his voice is soft, his breath brushing warm against my ear.

"*Hey, hey,* I was just giving you a hard time. I didn't mean anything by that."

I pull away and bury my head between my legs. Heat stings my cheeks. Salt floods my tongue. I'm vaguely aware of his hand patting my back. I can almost imagine him clucking, *there, there...*

I've killed us, I've killed us, I've killed us.

Alan. Tasker. Mac. Vivian.

Mom.

Me...

My skin itches like it's home to a hive of termites. *God,* withdrawal sucks ass. If I had a knife, I'd gladly cut it off and toss it in the gutter.

I need a pill. A shot. A line.

Anything to numb the pain sheeting through my chest.

I did this. *All of it.*

I lean back, let the snow pelt my face—

A razor blade. A gun.

—and *scream.*

CHAPTER TWENTY-THREE
ALL APOLOGIES

Fingertips brush my shoulder. *Alan's.*

"Don't touch me," I say, shrugging him off.

He pulls away, and I spot the angry strip of skin glaring at me from beneath the hem of his jeans, the gauze yellow and crusted over. The shame is instant as I lean forward and gently slide off his boot and set it aside. His foot looks frozen, his toenails blue where they protrude from the cast. My mouth goes sticky.

"How's your pain level?"

"Mmm, not great, but nothing I can't handle."

Strain lines cut away from the corners of his eyes as my fingers trace over the swollen flesh. I snap my gaze up. "Is your foot numb?"

He winces. "A bit."

I stand and stride over to the stallion, who's busy nibbling at a patch of dead grass, and rummage through the saddlebag, find the Advil, and shake six pills into my hand. I grab two bottles of water and hand one to Alan along with the pills. "Here, take these."

"No. We need to conserve our—"

"Take them. We have to get that swelling down. It could lead to something worse."

"Like what?"

"Nothing you want. Trust me."

Compartment syndrome. Uncontrollable swelling. Muscle death. I remember it from nursing school, the instructor hustling into class one morning in a huff, waking me from my hangover with news that a pro football player had just lost his leg to it. A high-ankle sprain. Leg there one moment, gone the next. Cut off. Career over.

I sit down shaky and hard, gulp some water.

Alan massages his calf and looks at me. "What's bothering you, Brynn?"

I drop my gaze, unable to hold his any longer. It's how he used to look at me when I was young and sticky fingered, begging for him to chase me around the house after a weekend breakfast.

Jesus, when did it all go so wrong? When did *I* go so wrong?

"Brynn, I—"

"I'm sorry."

"Sorry? For what?"

"For not believing you. For...abandoning you like I did. For killing Mom." My lips tremble. I turn away. I can't stand it, all these thoughts rattling around in my head like stray marbles. There's too much...*feeling* with no way to drown it out. No pills. No booze. No escape. Only the wind and the snow and Alan.

I have to get away from here. Be anywhere *but* here.

My thumb finds my wrist. Spins.

"Brynn, look at me," Alan says gently.

I can't. If I do, I'll fall apart. Cold swirls of snow spit down around us. My nose is frozen, my cheeks numb. I can't even feel the flakes hitting my skin anymore, can't feel anything except drunk, and it's a shitty sort of drunk. The kind you get from too little sleep and no food. The kind of drunk that would normally leave me passed out on the couch for days, my adrenaline shot, my heart unable to keep up with the stress any longer. Just like here, now.

I'm going to conk out soon… and hard, whether I want to or not.

Alan cups my chin and turns my face toward his. "Is that what you think? That you killed her?"

I give him a queasy nod.

"No. Don't for a *second* think that. You didn't kill her. That's on me, not you."

"But—"

"But nothing. You were protecting her. You were doing what you thought needed to be done. Just like you always have." He squeezes my hand, his eyes intense brown pools. "You know what I love most about you?"

Nothing. There's nothing to love.

His hand slips lower, hovers over my heart. "This. What's in here. Truth is, you're the bravest person I know." He pulls me close, his breath warming my ear. "Don't you ever forget that. *What* you are. *Who* you are. You're the best part of me, Brynn. The best thing I've ever done."

The smell of him—all sweat and dirt and tobacco—somehow calms the grief soaking my lungs. For a nanosecond, I'm eight years old again with my head lying in the crook of his arm as he reads me to sleep, the recliner rocking out those smooth, assuring motions, and there's no danger anywhere, no monsters slinking beneath my feet, nothing to fear; only me and him and the sweet ignorance of childhood.

After what feels like an eternity, he pulls back and takes a deep breath. "We need to get going, but first I need to tell you something. Something important. Something I need you to pay close attention to, understand?"

I pull back and nod. He begins to speak.

CHAPTER TWENTY-FOUR
TICK TOCK

"You *knew* him? You actually *knew* him, and you never said a word?" I nearly laugh, the sound turning to a choked strangle before it hits my lips.

Alan pats the stallion's neck. I'm riding behind him, resting my cheek on his back, trying to duck the snow.

"Saved his life in the clink."

I can't speak, my brain struggling to keep up. He *knew* Tank...

"How? I'm the one that—"

"—found him? Yeah, me and him made it seem that way. I knew you were into tats. Vivian told me. That, and you've always been one hell of an artist. Why do you think you scored that apartment right by his shop? With that rent? In Austin? Why do you think it was so easy to get that job?"

My mouth turns to chalk. I'd always thought I'd just gotten lucky... finally stumbled upon a break after years of slogging through crap. I should have known better; luck and the Donovans don't mix.

I run a hand over the sleeve of my sweater and bring it to rest on my forearm where the swallow lies inked beneath. The *key* to the shelter. An optical scanner. The only way in. And all along, I thought the tattoo was *my* idea. A tribute to Mom. Jesus did Tank ever play me.

Alan clears his throat, says, "I needed someone to look after you. Someone I could trust. And Tank was blood to me."

Was. A cold ache prickles my chest as my fingers drift to the spider pendant.

"I hope he's okay," I mutter. He has to be. Most of me doubts it, but a smaller part can so clearly see him stomping those armored little assholes, splitting their jaws wide and ripping out those awful bone drills by the handful, all while telling them to fuck off.

"Me, too," Alan says. "Me, too."

We ride in silence. The clouds hang above us dark and angry—a thick blanket of cold sucking what little light is left from the day, snow spitting down in droves. I guess at the time. Four o'clock, maybe? Five? Who knows, and I'm not about to ask. When you're on death row, what's the point in knowing how much time you have left? You're dead either way. Still, I can't seem to stop the countdown in my head, the blaring *tick-tock* of each second slipping past, summoning the dark.

My breath frosts out in front of me in thick crystal plumes, obscuring the mountains; a thin slice of purple swimming through the gray film. It's impossible to tell how close we are to them, or how far we've come, only that it feels like we're on a conveyor belt going nowhere.

Alan coughs, and I pull closer and try to drink in his heat. I'm shivering so hard it feels like I'll split apart. I hunch lower in my sweater and force my mind to focus on something else. Skin and ink. The sun. Distant beach daydreams. Texas summers. Sweaty sex. Anything but the cold.

A clump of fabric whomps against the side of my head, and I look up to Alan passing back a grease-splotched hoodie. A Carhartt.

"I snatched it from Tasker's before we left. Put it on," he orders. "All your shaking is making me cold."

I take it and slide it over my head. I'm five feet, eight inches—five-nine on a good day—not small by any measure, but this shirt makes me feel like I'm a little girl playing dress-up, which, in a way, I am. But despite the fit and the thing's smell (all stale dirt and oil) I've never been so grateful for anything in my life. I already feel ten degrees warmer as I cinch up the hood and blow a hot jet of air into my hands.

Alan tugs on a beanie and hands me a bottle of water and a granola bar, which I reluctantly take. I'm not hungry, but I know I need the calories. And the water. I haven't peed all day, and my head is starting to spin. I dig into the bar as Alan unwraps his with his teeth.

"Hang in there," he reassures between bites. "Shop's just up the road."

I'm pretty sure the shop isn't "just up the road" based on the fact that we spent most of the afternoon backtracking east, finally working our way around the rift near a demolished neighborhood car wash a few hours ago. The place was wrecked—vacuum machines poking up through piles of rubble like a group of prairie dogs.

I tuck my chin to my chest and pray he's right.

We pass people slipping into buildings, people on foot who clutch their chests and blow into their hands, trying to escape the chill. A drifter stares at us with coal-colored eyes that flick out from beneath a thick wool beanie. He gives me a barely-there nod and a flash of his wrist, and he's gone—a shadow melting into the spinning flakes. A moment later and I wonder if I imagined him.

Office buildings turn to apartments. The modern kind—all glass and glossy metal meant to attract the attention of hipster kids along with their parents' money. Angular status symbols that no longer matter, now lifeless husks fading in the gloom.

More stragglers. A mother and two children huddled in blankets. A bespectacled couple bundled in a single coat, pressed together as though they're one shuffling creature, their legs working over the asphalt in perfect synchronicity. Groups of men who stare too hard and too long at the stallion before spotting Alan in the saddle, his sizable bulk enough to deter them from seizing the reins. People who scurry past like wraiths as they flee the worsening storm and the one building beneath our feet. The black things churning there, waiting for the sun to set.

And all along, the feeling of eyes scraping my neck.

The eerie sensation that we're being followed.

Little things that keep me on edge. A bottle breaking a few blocks over. The gruff whisper of voices carried on the wind. Dark silhouettes in windows that flicker and vanish as we pass.

A sudden clatter startles me, and I turn in time to catch a coyote nosing through a trashcan on the sidewalk, pale pink tongue lapping hungrily at the tin lid. Behind him, a strand of trees hulk, some still speckled in leaves, others bare and thin. The street works away ahead of us, lifeless, clumped in ash and snow.

"You okay back there?" Alan asks.

"Yeah, barely. How much farther?"

"A few more miles."

"You said that an hour ago."

"Listen," he says, glancing back. "There's something I've been thinking about. The light thing you brought up. Why the feeders don't like it. I met a man in Arizona on one of my trips. An Indian. Tracked him down in some shit town way out in the desert. A reservation legend. A shaman or something."

I roll my eyes. "Seriously, Alan? A shaman?" I flash back to the van as I say it, to the picture of the sun-cracked native standing next to Alan, both of them staring down at that *thing*.

"Anyway, one afternoon this guy loses his grandson on a camping trip. Finds him two days later near a cave system huddled next to that feeder you saw in the picture." He winks. "Thought I missed that, didn't you?"

"You're a real Sherlock Holmes, Alan."

He laughs, says, "So, apparently this kid scrambled up on a boulder to escape it, and the rock rolled on the feeder. Trapped it. Kid said it went nuts trying to get to him. Wanted him so bad, it practically tore its body in half. Then the sun came up and it stopped moving. Sort of just shivered and locked up."

I cough. "What's your point?"

"These things have been underground for, what, millions of years?"

"I guess."

"At least that long. They aren't made for the sun. I think it fries their DNA. That's their weakness. It's where we hit 'em. Once we're up to the shelter, we'll get word to the government somehow. Maybe they'll have it figured out by then, but if not, we'll tell them how to—"

I whip a hand up. "Shh. Quiet. I heard something."

And I did. A crack. Barely perceptible but there. A sound out of place in all the falling snow.

I scan the sidewalk, the trees. Broken shadows spill across the street. Alan reins in the horse and tilts his head to listen. I strain for the sound again but only hear the soft blow of wind in its place and the steady patter of snow hitting my shoulders. The stallion shakes it from his mane with a chuff.

"I don't hear anything," Alan says.

The back of my neck tingles, a now-familiar ache running down my spine, flooding my thighs

Feeders.

I grab Alan's shoulders and squeeze. "They're coming."

"We're okay. We got another hour before sunset. At least."

"I'm telling you, there's no time. We need to ride."

"Okay. Done."

Alan spurs the horse with a *HAW!* and the stallion kicks into a trot. The noise tickles my ear again. It's quiet at first, an irregular crackle I've heard before...in movie theaters and at home, bleeding from the microwave.

Popcorn.

Alan stiffens and whips his gaze up the street, then to the side. His beanie and beard are frosted white with snow, his eyes casting solar flares of panic as he slows the stallion. Movement pulls my attention to the greenbelt across the street toward a mound of earth shifting higher in unnatural, arthritic movements.

I blink, certain I'm seeing things.

I'm not. The mound jerks again, and I clutch Alan's shirt and point. "Over there."

He follows my gaze, his forehead crumpling. "Oh, no."

They're hard to see at first, their movements timid as they drill through the frozen earth in droves, hesitating for a moment as though testing the strength of the sun, retracting, and then climbing higher.

Pop! Pop! Pop!

The horse dances in place, gives a high-pitched whinny. Paralysis fills my veins.

"Go, Alan," I whisper, my eyes still locked on the mound of earth and the others now rising up around it. Dozens of them. Hundreds.

POP! POP! POP!

Alan nudges the horse back into a trot. Drills blare to life all around us. The stallion's ears snap back as he gnaws on the bit. Alan leans forward and strokes his cheek. "Easy, boy..."

More drills slice through the air—*RRUUEEEEE!*

The horse explodes.

I'm nearly unseated but manage to twist my fingers over Alan's belt before I fall off. He howls in pain as we pick up speed, his cast smacking off the stallion's ribs. Streetlights blur past. Trees become brown smudges buried in all the falling white. The stallion pounds over the blacktop like a runaway freight train, like a bullet barreling down an empty chamber—moving with so much speed it steals my breath.

It doesn't matter.

One glance ahead, and I know it's too late. Feeders leak from the ground and bubble up through storm drains in torrents, their bodies all segmented armor and fast-working legs. The piercing shriek of their drills saws into my ears as they swarm the street in tangles of chaotic motion—their glistening, black-glass bodies everywhere I look.

Coming together like a tide of death.

One that's rising and about to engulf us.

CHAPTER TWENTY-FIVE
HUMANS AND ANIMALS

They're everywhere.

Plated armor bodies. Legs there one moment and then gone the next, retracting into their abdomens as they whirl back into the earth. Quartered mandibles that bloom like terrible pink flowers, those drills extending from within to soak the air with their awful whine. My head burns in response, my ears threatening to burst and run over with blood. Being this close to them is like standing in the middle of a beehive after kicking the nest.

And the stench... pure rot. Cloying and sweet; a mass grave left open to bake in the sun. I clamp my sinuses shut and force the air in through my mouth as we barrel straight for them, Alan heaving on the reins, shouting for the horse to stop.

"Whoa!"

But. He. Won't. Stop.

I screw my eyes shut and brace for the fall—

I'm sorry, Mac. I'm so sorry.

—which never comes.

My eyes click open.

We should be dead.

The feeders flow around the stallion's legs like a thousand terrible mouths—*open, shut, open, shut*—like the horse is punching holes in a foot of black water with each step.

How is this happening?

"Whoa!" Alan yells, still fighting the reins as we surge toward a UPS truck lying on its side—massive and strung across the road—wedged against the brick retaining wall of an overpass. Cars surround it, piled high in a glimmering crush of metal. No way through.

"Stop, goddammit!" Alan yanks the reins again, and this time the horse wrenches sideways, his rear slamming into a truck, sending me over his flank and onto the hood.

Metal buckles beneath my shoulders. Glass spiderwebs. Stars scatter through my vision and form crazy, spiraling patterns.

The world dips and sways. There's no light. Anywhere.

Why can't I find the light?

A voice: "Brynn!"

Prickles of sound: the savage scrabble of legs. On asphalt. On metal. Frantic for something. Frantic for... *me.*

My eyes rip open, and I roll onto my side and push up. My hand brushes against something cold, something hard and moving.

Something...*alive. Oh, shit.*

I scramble to my feet as the horse materializes in front of me, Alan stretching out his hand with a desperate scream: "Jump!"

I leap and my leg clangs awkwardly off the saddle, my momentum carrying me across the horse and over his back—toward the river of drills frothing below.

Twisting and falling...

Time slowing, bathing me in second after horrible second...

As I hurtle for the street.

A hand grabs my wrist, another wrapping around my waist.

"Grab on!" Alan barks, steadying me.

I seize the pommel and catch a flash of what I just escaped. A hood writhing in feeders, more bleeding through the gaps between the fender and the tires, the truck looking like the dead rabbit I stumbled across when I was five—nothing but slivers of bone and gristle peering back at me through a carpet of fire ants.

A drill shrieks behind us, and the stallion brays and begins to spin. High-stepping and turning circles, whipping his mane as we turn faster and faster—spinning, spinning, spinning—until we're a drunken merry-go-round rotating through a meat grinder.

Drills everywhere, burning all around us.

Shrieking and hot.

Hungry to pierce our bones, our flesh.

Hungry to tear us to pieces.

The horse bucks, and I nearly lose my grip.

Alan sends the heel of his boot crashing hard into the stallion's side and cracks the reins—"*HAW!*"—and we're moving again, working away from the truck and toward a grass incline on the other side of the road, the stallion fighting Alan every step of the way, snorting and whipping his head, eyes bulging as we climb.

Higher and higher.

Leaving the madness and chaos.

Struggling to breathe or think.

Until we're perched high above all the crackling armor—the river of dark chitin flowing below.

Alan's fingers hammer the saddle as he shakes his head, his voice coming in low and breathless over my shoulder.

"What. The. *Fuck?*"

The question hangs there, another resting beneath it, unspoken. *How are we still alive?*

It's what I'm wondering, too. Why didn't they tear into the horse? Why didn't they strip it to the bone, along with us? It's a question that's been eating at me since we found Dr. Tsosie's horses dancing through his scraps in the backyard. It's why I've yet to see the bones of a single bird on the road. Or those of a dog or a squirrel. It's why we haven't stumbled across a herd of cattle turned to ground beef, or a deer with its body gutted and cleaned.

A chill knifes down my spine. These *things,* the feeders, they aren't here for them—for the animals.

They're here for *us.*

CHAPTER TWENTY-SIX
FAMILY REUNION

"Could that be it? That they're after us?"

Alan sucks the air in through his teeth and grunts as his cast bounces against the horse. He's looking worse—unsteady—like he might tumble from the saddle at any minute. "Maybe. Tsosie said we woke them. So did that shaman. Said it was all the drilling. Our greed that did us in. Never heard of any animal attacks either now that I think about it. Only people." He eases the horse to a stop and quirks his head, points at something up the street. "Looks like we've got company."

It's hard to see at first. A trick of the light, a last ray of sun slipping through the clouds and reflecting off a bit of dirty glass. But no, another look confirms it.

A building with the windows glowing.

"We're here?" I ask.

"We're here."

The place is surrounded by a razor-tipped fence—a chain-linked outpost with a broken gate and a sign that informs us we're trespassing as we amble past and into a yard overflowing with stacks of pipe and rows of dormant machines. Faded mustard yellow bulldozers and forklifts. A red pallet jack languishing half buried beneath a pile of tires.

Frozen swaths of grass jet through the snow in spots as we wind our way around car-sized generators and toward a beige, adobe stucco building that looks pointless and out of place—like it should be housing an art gallery in Santa Fe rather than crews of Colorado roughnecks. Light seeps past windows covered in plywood; what looks to be a hasty job, and one I pray was done by Mac and Tasker.

It *has* to be them.

Has to be.

Tasker said no one else knew about the generator he'd installed. Only a few out-of-state regional managers who'd insisted the shop have backup power in case of an emergency—and if this doesn't qualify as one, nothing does. But there are no horse tracks in the snow to confirm my hopes. No shoe prints anywhere. At least not ones I can spot.

My scalp prickles with anxiety. *BehereBehereBehere...*

"Alright," Alan says, dusting the snow off his beanie, his shoulders. "Now we just got to find a way in."

I stiffen. "You mean knock?"

"No. We don't know if that's them in there." He rubs his neck. "Just give me a minute to think this through."

"Okay," I reply, planting my pinkies to the corners of my mouth before unleashing an ear-splitting whistle.

He grabs my hand and rips it back: "Brynn, what the hell?"

"They're either here or they're not, Alan. And if they're not, we're screwed as it is. Where else are we gonna go? The Holiday Inn? The Radisson? We need food and water. And you need to rest, not to mention how hard we've worked this poor horse." I pat his rump.

"He's half dead as it is. We keep riding like this, and we'll kill him. We have no other choice."

"Not now we don't." He cups his hands and blows, stares past me toward the window where there's movement—a sliver of motion between the planks, eyes peering back at us, furtive and shifting. Ones I recognize: *Tasker!*

He shouts something and points at three-bay garage doors further down the building. I'm almost off the horse and about to sprint toward them when Alan catches my arm.

"Uh-uh. Don't," he says with a nod. "Look."

I catch the black flash of armor as it torpedoes through the snow, cutting under the horse and disappearing beneath the fence.

I go woozy at the sight. Feeders, even *here...*

A motor springs to life, and the closest garage door rotates open. A flurry of movement gravitates toward the sound. More feeders. One. Two. Five trails. More. I lose count as they whisper through the snow, deadly silent in all the powder. A sudden blast of light sends them tunneling away, and I cup my eyes to the dark outline of Tasker motioning us closer as the door rattles to a stop.

"Quick, get in here! And stay away from the lamps!"

Alan teases the stallion forward. He squeals and snorts, shifting sideways as the feeders wind around his hooves, diving in and cutting back again like little darting sharks, until we're safely standing on the cement bay.

Tasker smacks the garage door button, and I catch flickers of motion beyond the cone of light; intersecting tracts that lace through the snow like vapor trails as the door clicks shut. A wave of relief spills over me—we shouldn't be here right now, not after what we've been through.

We should be dead…

I let the thought fizzle and take in the garage. It's large, industrial, with a car lift and rolling tool cabinets scattered all over the concrete. Hydraulic equipment and yellow barrels are stacked in one corner next to several workbenches covered in tools—wrenches and hammers and saws—so much metal, I can practically taste it. Fluorescent lights buzz from the ceiling, set in between red steel beams, that flicker in time with the muffled sounds of a generator coughing somewhere beyond the back wall. It's doctors' office light. The blinding, sterile kind of light that sucks the color from everything it touches, the kind that leaves rooms looking stripped and bare.

A hand brushes my knee, and I jerk my gaze down to Tasker who's got a nasty gash on his forehead, leaking a muddy trail of crusted blood past his eyes. They glow an electric blue in contrast as they shift between us and the garage door.

"What happened?" I ask. "To your forehead."

"We had a spill back there after we lost you two. It's nothing to worry 'bout, though. I'm okay."

We. I leap from the horse in a swell of panic, grab him by the vest, and jerk him forward. "Where's Mac, Tasker? *Where?* Tell me he's here. Tell me he's safe."

"Brynn!"

I twist around to my brother emerging from behind a bucket truck, his face creased in concern, his arms spreading wide as I rush over and pull him into a bone-crushing hug.

"I thought I lost you back there." Tears prick the corners of my eyes. I can't help it. I'm crying again. Blubbering. "Jesus, I thought you were gone. I tried to reach you. Tried to get to you, but I couldn't. The road…it just came apart. Mac, I'm so sorry. I tried…I really tried…"

His grip tightens, and he pulls me closer. "I thought I lost you, too. It's my fault. I couldn't control the horse. I wasn't strong enough. I almost got you killed."

"No, you didn't," I whisper, barely able to push the words out. "And you're not going to lose me. *Ever* again. We stay together from here on out, okay? No matter what."

"Promise?" he says.

"On my life."

He nods into my shoulder, and I squeeze harder. He winces and pulls back, wipes his eyes. "Careful. I think I cracked a rib or something."

"Where? Let me see." I move to tug up his jersey and he stops me.

"No. It's okay. Just a little sore."

"How about the horse? Is she—"

"She's safe." He points toward the far corner where the mare is tethered to the wall with several empty Quaker Oats cartons strewn around her hooves. "I think we've about used her up, though. I gave her a ton of water when we got here. You should've seen it. She wouldn't stop drinking. Oh, and I made her a bed with some blankets I found in one of the trucks."

I pause. "Did you see any feeders on the way here?"

"No, we made it here before the sun set. Why? Did you?"

He doesn't know. "Mac. They don't attack them."

He squints. "Attack who?"

"The feeders, they ignore the horses for some reason. And not just them. *All* the animals. They aren't here for them. I think they're here for us."

He doesn't answer, his gaze shifting past me as I spin around to Alan hobbling toward us with Tasker supporting him from behind.

In the light, Alan looks like hell. His shirt is plastered to his ribs, the whites of his eyes the same dull yellow as egg yolks, his hair poking out from beneath the beanie in sweat-greased clumps. And his face... it's off—his features twisted in a way that makes me think it's from more than pain.

From something else...

"It's best we get inside," Tasker says with a nod toward the door. "Your dad's not going to hold up much longer on this ankle."

Alan's eyes darken at that, and he stares at me in a way that makes me nervous. His head tilts and rotates in a slow shake. It's a warning. One I can't interpret.

Tasker steps to the side and my throat flushes with acid. He's got the saddlebags hung over his shoulder, his right hand gripping Alan's collar, his left palming the pearl-grip pistol he flashed at the rednecks earlier. The same one that's now pointing at me and Mac.

He nods at the door again, his face melting into a pile of leathered lines as he frowns. "Like I said, I think it's best we get inside."

CHAPTER TWENTY-SEVEN
JUDAS

Afer all I've been through, my muscles sizzling for drugs and my brain crackling like it's been thrown into a greased frying pan, my skin stil ten degrees colder than it should be, the feeders and Vivian and losing Mac. Finding him again. *Actually* finding him. And now Tasker has the nerve to march us into this place like some asshole with his stupide gun shoved in my face when all I want—*all I need*—is some food and sleep and a few hours without wondering when my next breath will be my last.

He flips lights on and orders us left into a break room, motions us toward a cracked leather couch in the corner. We pass some folding tables and a scatter of metal chairs, a pair of vending machines, and a row of cabinets hanging above a sink. The ceiling is all tile, several squares blooming weak coffee-colored water stains, everything looking as tired and beaten-up as us.

Tasker dumps the saddlebags on one of the tables along with his Stetson and then jabs his pistol at the couch. "Sit."

It's an order. One I don't feel like taking. I whirl on him. "What the hell, Tasker? We're exhausted and we're hungry and we're freezing. Haven't we all been through enough today without this shit, too? I—"

The barrel wags my way, and he slides a finger up to his lips with a slow, pissed-off *shhh*. "I'll explain everything." He waves at the couch. "Once y'all sit. You too, Mac."

Mac crosses his arms "Tasker, what are you doing? You said they would make it here. You *promised*. And I believed you. And now they're here and you pull your gun on them? Why would you—"

"Oh, for Chrissakes." Tasker flicks his wrist and the pistol flashes. Plaster rains over the couch, over Mac. He stumbles back as if sucker punched and thumps down without another word. I join him, my ears ringing, my abdomen pulsing in sympathy with the long-ago ache of Alan's bullet—Mom yelping out those wet, injured puppy sounds from some dark corner of my mind.

Alan doesn't budge. His upper lip is twisted into a snarl, his eyes on the gun. He's got a good half-foot on Tasker, but right now it feels like a scam, like he's not sheet-white and balancing on half a leg about to collapse.

"This is some real first-class bullshit, Tasker," he spits.

The gun swings lower and comes level with his chest. "You don't want me to shoot again. Now sit."

I reach out and tug Alan back onto the couch. Pain lines stretch from the corner of his eyes and his forehead is bleeding sweat, but he locks his jaw and waves at Tasker like nothing is wrong. It's a dismissive gesture, one that comes midway through an argument over who gets to control the TV remote. Something to be worked out over a couple of beers and a football game.

"Okay, get on with it, then," Alan growls. "Tell us what you gotta tell us."

Tasker smirks and steps forward, digs something from his back pocket, and lobs it at Alan. Handcuffs. *My handcuffs.* They smack off the cushion and clatter to the floor, lay there ugly and glinting.

"Put 'em on."

Alan stiffens, and for a horrible moment, I think he's going to force Tasker to shoot him, but with a slow, exaggerated lean he scoops the cuffs off the floor and slaps one over his wrist.

"Mm-mm, nope," Tasker says. "Behind your back."

"Like hell."

"Like hell is right. Do it."

Alan's eyes go cold, but he threads his hands around his waist and clicks the cuffs shut. I stare at Tasker, dumbfounded. Sure, he's a jerk sometimes, a bit full of himself, but this? Never *this*. Which means there has to be a reason—something I'm not seeing.

He slides a hand into his vest and retrieves a pair of zip ties. Tosses them at me. "Put one on your brother first. Then you."

My temples pound. I grab the ties and throw them back. "Are you serious with this shit, Tasker? Are you fucking kidding me? This is insane!"

His lips narrow, and he nods at the ties. "Do it, or I put a bullet in your leg."

"Don't you threaten my daughter!" Alan roars, attempting to stand.

Tasker spins on him and the gun recoils. Alan topples to the couch, and I stare in horror at the dark wing of blood spreading across his left thigh. He whips his gaze at Tasker, his teeth bared, a vein pulsing near his ear, ugly and purple. "*Jesus*, Tasker, you shot me. You *actually* fucking shot me, you fuck!"

Tasker runs a hand over his face and groans. "You had to do this the hard way, didn't you, Alan? *Had* to play the hero. It's always the same shit with you. You never listen. To *anything*. To *anyone*. Never see what's right in front of your face. All this time and you're still clueless."

"What the hell are you talking about?"

"I *loved* her. She meant everything to me. *Everything.* And you took her away."

Alan glares at him, speechless.

"Laura, you idiot." Tasker spits the name out like a mouthful of acid. "I'm talking about *Laura*."

Alan's eyes turn to slits. "Don't you bring her into this…"

"She's all this is about! She was going to leave you. We had it all planned out. Meet at my place with the kids. Move somewhere you'd never find us. You and that sick brain of yours." He dips his head and the cut above his eyebrow throbs with a fresh ribbon of blood. "I told her you were dangerous. Told her, 'he's gonna break someday. There's nothing you can do for him, Laura. He's not stable. We gotta go before he snaps.' On and on, I tried. But did she listen? Oh, no. Not 'til it was too goddamn late."

Alan pales further. "You lie."

"Really? You think I'd lie? About *this?*" He stomps over to Mac and clamps a hand to his chin, pulls his face close. "What do you see, Alan? Tell me what you see." Mac claws at him and tries to pull back, but Tasker just smashes his face closer in response. "Look at him, Alan. Look at his eyes, his lips. Notice any similarities?"

My blood fills with slush. I spin my thumb over my wrist and think, *they look alike…they look exactly alike.*

"Let me spell it out for you: he's my goddamn son. Not yours."

Tasker's words are flames, Alan wilting beneath their heat—his eyes, nose, cheeks, shoulders—everything going lax at once. *"No…"*

Tasker shoves Mac back and stands. "Yes."

A cold rage fills my soul—a rolling thunder that starts in my toes and rushes up my legs like a warm wind, rising through my waist to my chest, where it expands until all I can see is a boiling, faceless red.

Tasker lied to us. He lied to *me*. For years...

And he won't get away with it.

I spear forward and take him mid-rib. There's a satisfying crunch and a warm *whoosh* of air as we sprawl to the floor. His elbow smacks a chair, and the pistol skitters beneath the table. I lunge for it, pull myself forward like a snake, threading past the table legs before fingers dig into my hair and yank me back. My scalp shrieks as Tasker's wrist passes close to my mouth...too close—a mistake.

I bite down and grind my teeth, feel them pop through his skin.

"Shit! You little—"

Mac screams and leaps onto his back, wraps his fingers around Tasker's forehead and rakes his eyes. And then I'm free and scrambling for the gun, limbs pistoning off the cheap vinyl, knees knocking together like hammers. So close.

My palm on the grip.

My finger curling around the trigger.

As I roll over and—

"Drop it."

Blood weeps from Tasker's wrist over the front of Mac's jersey. Mac, who's struggling to breathe as Tasker strangles him with one arm, the other pressing Alan's Glock to his head, and suddenly Dr. Tsosie is whispering in my ear: *I sense something off with your group...*

It was Tasker. All along it was Tasker.

My fingers unwind and the gun slips free.

"Slide it over. Nice and slow."

I obey, my eyes still on Mac. He's choking, his lips turning to pale blue rubber bands, his legs thrashing.

"Let him go, Tasker," I beg. "Please. This isn't you."

He blinks and stares at me—shoves Mac, gasping, to the couch. "Tasker..."

"Get up."

I do. Shaky and unsteady, my muscles sloshing like water in my legs, my arms limp as he stomps over and loops a zip-tie over my wrists and cinches it, binding it so tight it feels like the plastic will saw right through the skin and sever the bone.

He spins me around, grabs my collar, and brings the gun to my temple, his voice spitting hot in my ear. "Shit, Brynn. Why'd you make me do that? *Why?* After what he did to your mom...to *you? Jesus,* I thought you hated him. Thought you were on my side. I was gonna bring you with me."

"L-let her go," Alan says, shaking. His face is clammy, his chest working in and out in irregular spasms—like a trout flung onto the bank of some great river left to die.

I stiffen. "Tasker, he's going into shock. You have to let me—"

He jabs the barrel against my skull. "Quiet." Then to Alan, "Where's the shelter? Tell me, or I hurt her."

Alan nods toward the table. "In the saddlebag. The map on the bottom..."

Tasker caveman drags me backward by the hair and dumps the bag all over the table: antibiotics, bottles of water, the first aid kit I snatched from Dr. Tsosie's operating room, a roll of duct tape, food. Finally, the map. He grabs it and forces me onto the couch, then unfolds it and jams it in Alan's face. "Where is it?"

"Why are you doing this, Tasker? There's room for all of us up there."

"Not for you there ain't. You took the only good thing I ever had when you killed Laura, the only thing I ever loved. I'll be damned if I'm not gonna return the favor." He shakes the map. "Now *where* is it?"

Alan grimaces. "About fifty miles off. Where I used to take the kids camping. Thirty-six south, ninety-five west. Near Rampart Meadows. I bought three acres. Y-you came with us once, I think."

Lie. He told me where the shelter was, and that's not it.

Tasker swipes a Sharpie from a table and snaps the cap off, jams it in Alan's mouth. "I remember. Mark it with your teeth." I glance at Mac. His eyes are bloodshot, his hands curled into fists as he stares up at Tasker like he's thinking of having a go at him. He's coiled. Ready to strike. I shake my head at him, mouth a *no*.

Alan spits out the marker with a phlegmy cough. "There."

"And the codes?"

"It's his—Mac's birthday. Eleven, nine, oh-eight." Another lie. Sort of. That's only the first part. My tattoo is the rest.

Alan clears his throat, continues: "Look for the big stack of boulders next to the river. There's a utility shed behind them with a control panel inside. Doesn't look like much, but that's it."

Tasker stares at him for a long moment, his nostrils flaring. "You're lying."

"*No.*"

Tasker swings the gun my way, his knuckles dirty and trembling. I shrink back, mouth dry. The barrel is black and endless. I can already feel the bullet ripping through my chest.

"I'll do it, Alan. Don't want to. But I will."

Alan leans forward, his eyes wide and desperate. "I'm not lying. Goddammit, Tasker! Ask her," he says, staring at me. "I told her where it was. Just today. Same thing I told you."

I nod wildly and pray he doesn't see the lie in my thrashing pulse. "He did. He's telling the truth."

Tasker appraises me, eyes unblinking. Says nothing.

"Tasker. It's *true,*" I repeat. "Thirty-six south, ninety-five west. Look for the boulders."

His lips twitch and he finally drops the gun. I exhale as he stomps over to the table and grabs the roll of duct tape, flings it at me. "Tape him up before he bleeds out."

I scramble for it, tear off a long piece using my teeth, and awkwardly wrap it around Alan's leg with my zip-tied hands. The blood is dark and seeping. Not the bright arterial red that would mean he's bleeding out, but still too much of it, and the color means he's low on oxygen.

"Lay down," I order. "We need to elevate this."

Mac pulls close and cups Alan's shoulder, his face the picture of panic—all stretched skin and wild, darting eyes. "Listen to her, Dad, please. She knows what she's doing." He looks at me. "Right?"

I don't. Not really, but I nod and lift his injured leg over the armrest, tear off another piece of tape, and wrap it around his inner thigh, keeping at it until I've constructed a makeshift tourniquet. It's his prosthetic leg at least; less muscle to keep alive, less blood flow, so there's a chance if I can just—

Mac jerks sideways. I look up to Tasker, who's wrapped an arm around Mac's chest and is now dragging him kicking toward the door. Alan bucks beneath me, twisting his face toward Tasker. "You let him go! Goddamn you. I swear I will hunt you to the ends of the Earth you sonuvabitch!"

The Glock roars. A bullet pierces the wall a few inches from my head. Mac goes limp. "Tape his mouth," Tasker tells me, nodding at Alan.

"Wait," Alan says. "I—"

Tasker levels the gun at him. "Say another word, Alan, and I kill you. You're lucky I haven't already." He glares at me. "Do it."

I slap the tape over his lips with a limp *I'm sorry*, everything in me going tense, electric rage throbbing through my skull in waves—*I will kill you for this, Tasker.*

"Good," Tasker says. "Listen, I'm sorry about all this, Brynn. I wasn't lying. I'd take you with me if I could, but it's clear where your allegiance lies. I can't have that kind of insubordination up there. But I promise you this. I'll take care of your brother, keep him safe." His eyes snap to Alan. "He is my son, after all."

Alan writhes and thrashes, gives a muffled cry.

Mac twists hard and nearly breaks loose. "No, I'm not! Dad! Brynn! Help me!" Tasker clamps a hand over Mac's mouth, and a cold sheet of panic slides over me. I feel like I'm drowning.

"Tasker, *please...*" I beg, stepping forward. "Don't do this. It's not safe out there. Not at night."

There's a muffled bang, and the ceiling lights sputter, click back on. Tasker glances at them with a twist of his mouth. "No, but safer than staying here. The generator won't last much longer. I couldn't find enough diesel."

I lob a final Hail Mary—the only play I have left. "But they'll kill you. At least in here, there's a chance."

"I don't think so. I saw you two ride up on that horse. Saw how those things avoided him like he wasn't even there. You weren't going to tell me about that, were you?"

"You didn't give me a chance." I take another step, my hands slick with sweat. If I can just get close enough...

He points the gun at my feet. "No closer. I know what you're doing, Brynn. And don't follow me. I don't want to have to shoot you, too."

Alan smacks his head against the couch: *"Mmm! Mm-mm-mmm!"*

Tasker stares at him, looks back. "Listen, there's a ladder in the garage. Climb up to one of those storage racks near the ceiling once we leave. They're high enough you'll be safe for the night. After that, well...you're smart. You'll figure things out, I'm sure. You always have."

"Tasker," I plead, my hands up and trembling. "Please..."

"Like I said, I'll keep him safe. You have my word."

With that, he's gone, Mac's foot lashing out and spilling a water dispenser as they round the corner, the bottle coming free with a wet glug. A few minutes later, the lights sputter out.

CHAPTER TWENTY-EIGHT
SKIN AND BONES

"Mmm! Mmm-mmm!"

I follow Alan's voice back to the couch where he's going batshit, thumping up and down and straining against the cuffs like a man possessed. The darkness is total as I feel my way up to the tape on his mouth and rip it free.

"Stop them! You…have to"—he struggles for a breath—"stop them."

"Slow down," I say, cupping my hand to his cheek. "I'm not leaving you here like this."

"You have to," he protests. "Listen to me. You remember camping up at Rampart, right?"

"Vaguely."

"Do you remember what else is up there? What w-we hiked to? What we went in?"

Caves. He's talking about the caves. Miles and miles of them, near the river. He took me in one once, convinced me it would be fun after downing a few beers. *It goes right through to the other side, Bear. There's nothing to worry about.* The dank smell smothered me the second we entered, the silence of the stone and the sheer blackness immediately forcing me back toward the light. I hated it—swore I'd never go in another one again.

"I—I—" He seizes, his muscles going stiff, teeth chattering.

"Shhh. You're okay. I'm here, Alan," I say, leaning close. "I'm here. *Breathe*. You have to breathe."

He inhales a lungful of air and releases it with a hot *whoosh*. "Wanted to screw Tasker. I didn't think about... M-Mac. You have to—"

A metallic *CLANG!* echoes down the hall, and he falls silent. The slow *glug-glugging* of the water bottle fills the room once more. Another clatter...

Drills.

"*Go,*" he rasps. "Find a light. Check the cupboards."

I push up and stumble backward, spin around and shuffle across the floor as fast as I can—smacking into a chair, bumping against a trashcan and a table, before finally brushing against the counter. My fingers tear open a drawer and dive into a forest of metal: forks and spoons, sharp things.

A knife.

I slide it free, reverse the grip, and work the blade under the zip-tie, sawing back-and-forth, back-and-forth—thinking, *C'mon you stupid thing! C'mon!*—cutting frantic-fast, my hands cramping with the effort, until at last, the plastic band snaps.

"Hurry, Brynn," Alan shouts.

Fingers tingling, I search another drawer, bang through it like a blind man looking for his cane, digging out serving utensils, a cork-screw, several coffee bags, and a few packets of creamer. Everything I don't need. Those stupid wooden stir sticks. A box of pencils and some tape. No flashlight.

Where are you—where, where, where?

And then, near the back—*Yes!*—the right shape. Glorious, cylindrical metal. A Mag Light. I nearly drop it as I fumble it free and hit the switch. A brilliant beam of light spears through the room. One I swing over the floor toward the door…which is still hanging wide, wide open.

Shit.

I rush for it, sprinting around the table, and slam it shut. It's solid metal—the only thing about this place that's not cheap—*but will it hold?* Alan watches me retreat back to the couch with watery eyes, his skin ashen, his hair sweat-clumped and matted to his forehead in chunks.

He coughs as I climb onto the couch with him, his body tensing with the effort, the crunching sounds in the hall getting louder. Closer. My stomach twists, my mouth bone dry as I whisper, "We're not getting out of this one, are we?"

"You are," he replies. "You remember how to get up to those caves, right? The spot where I sent them?"

"Sort of." It's a stupid question. I have no idea. It's been years.

"Take 285 west—"

"Stop it, Alan. Don't you do that. Don't you dare."

"What?"

"Talk like you're already dead. You're coming with me. We'll go together."

"I'm not going anywhere, and we both know it. Now pay attention. There isn't much t-time. Head up to Conifer. There's a fly shop on the way. JD's. A big white cabin next to an old…rotted-out oak. It's huge. You can't miss it. Once you're there, you'll see a dirt road h-headed north. T-t-take it. Rampart's another ten miles from there. The open field next to all the p-ponds." He cranes his head to the side and coughs. Something thick spatters over the floor. "Then, once you got Mac, three miles east to Carter Lake."

Carter Lake. Where the shelter really is.

"Remember... the tattoo. It's the key, Brynn. The only way in. Now get up to those storage racks while there's still time."

"No! I told you I'm not leaving you." I struggle to mask the sudden swell of emotion flushing my throat. "Not when you've never left me."

He gurgles out a laugh. "'Cept for all those years in prison."

I dig a fingernail into my wrist. "I'm sorry I never believed you."

"Doesn't matter as long as you make it." He smiles at that, and my heart shatters. I'm going to lose him.

I nod, try to keep it together. "Don't go. Please. I... need you. I've *always* needed you." My voice is small, trapped somewhere behind my ribs.

His eyes compress. "*Hey, hey.* I'll always be with you, Bear. Nothing can change that. Even when things seem the darkest, there's always a little light if you just look hard enough, understand?"

He's wrong. There's no light in this moment. No brighter tomorrow. Nothing but the encroaching dark. I look at him, numb to the growing whine in the hall, tears fogging my vision. It's all too much, all of this...*shit.* Finding Mac—*actually finding him*—when I thought for sure he was dead, then losing him after I promised it would never happen again. Tasker messing everything up. Shooting Alan. The feeders and the cold and my body throbbing away like one giant bruise.

"Tell me you won't give up," Alan says, his eyes suddenly intense. "Promise me."

Giving up is all I've ever done—the only thing I'm good at.

"Say it, Brynn. Say you won't give up. *Ever*."

I lean back and stifle a scream.

"Say it!"

"I won't! Okay? I promise."

"My girl."

I stare at him, brush my thumb over his forehead and pull it down to his chin, then lean in and wrap him in a hug. His beard tickles my cheek, his smell sliding into my nose, so familiar—dirt and pine and days-old grease. Words rise and swell against my ribs. Important words. Words I haven't said to him since the day I lost Mom. Ones that jam in my chest and stack together until they finally break loose and drag my heart with them.

"I love you, Dad," I whisper. "I love you so much."

A sound works its way up his throat, and when I pull back, his face is broken. Ruined. He nods, his lips tight, tears spilling over his smile lines. He blinks them away and says, "That's... all I needed to hear. Now go!"

I move to—am halfway off the couch—when the drills hit metal. *Too late.*

I swing the flashlight toward the door as the first slick black body bursts through the drywall. Another follows... and another... so many, it looks like a glass waterfall bubbling down the sheetrock and crashing onto the floor.

"Keep the light on 'em," Alan chokes beneath me.

I try, but I can't—they're too quick; little blurs of motion that won't stay still long enough to pin down, drilling into the floor and popping up again as I whip the shine at every awful snap, at every movement and sound.

They surge closer and crash into the base of the couch. I play the light over them, and they skitter back as if stung, then dart forward again. There are so many, the floor now a rolling boil of motion, black glass bodies everywhere I look.

Too many. It's useless. I can't hold them back.

Alan's leg sweeps over my chest as I think it and pins me against the cushion. He gives me a hard look, his gaze scanning my face like he's trying to take a picture, like he's trying to memorize every last feature and line. It's a look I recognize, one he used to give me before he'd head out on a work trip or to the field for a few weeks with Tasker—a final goodbye.

"Dad... no!"

A smile creases his lips. "Give 'em hell, Bear."

He rolls off the couch and thuds to the floor, and I move to pull him back, to tell him he's the one who's giving up, and that I still need him, that I've never needed him more, but his legs are already buried in a writhing mass of shells, several feeders working up and onto his chest... *into* it, rearing back and spearing down with those terrible hooked jaws. Firing those drills...

Bone snaps, and his jaw clamps shut. He's in pain—unspeakable, awful pain—but his gaze stays locked on mine, his face somehow soft as it twitches again and again and again. He glances behind me, and his eyes go wide, blood frothing over his chin as he speaks.

"It w-w-wor... ked."

My fingers unclench and the flashlight pings to the floor.

Spatters of light play off the ceiling in a sick puppet show of motion before they black out altogether. It hits me then—what Alan was looking at. *Them.* The feeders. They're all over me, too. I can feel the hard scatter of their legs against mine, hear the angry *WHAA! WHAA!* of their drills as they work closer to my ears. I can smell their rotten-egg scent as it coats my nasal lining...can taste it pooling at the root of my tongue, sour and thick.

I close my eyes and lean back.

Fuck it. There's no point in fighting any longer—I'm already dead.

Something slick laps at my palm, runs over my hand, and razes the skin. It's rough and smooth all at once—like water so hot it feels cold to the touch. It retracts and a drill ignites above my head: *Whee! Wu-Wu-Wuheee!* Legs clatter up and over my abdomen and...

Nothing. Happens.

I snap upright. This is all wrong; I should be dead.

But I'm not.

Terror blankets me, and I lurch off the couch and stumble-run for the door. Drills blaze and waver in pitch, sounding like they're running on burps of nitroglycerin instead of gas—a thousand engines revving at once—filling my blood with adrenaline and my stomach with acid. A bright flare of pain surges through my elbow as I trip and fall, pick myself up again...and push on.

Banging through chairs.

Crashing into tables.

Bodies whirling over my feet and crunching beneath my shoes.

Crazy, whirring shrieks piercing my eardrums—that cloying stench invading my nose.

I need to get out of here, right aw—

My head smacks against hard metal, and I slam to the floor.

Webs of light paint the backs of my eyelids like a lightning storm. Vague sensations prick at my legs, my chest, bodies swarming over me, my blood boiling in my veins at their touch...so hot. Sound *everywhere.* So much sound. Too much. And then none at all...

I wake to a fog of sour air, my head swimming, my lips glued together with spit. Everything hurts—my quads and stomach, my shoulders and biceps and neck. Every coil and strand of my brain. All of it singing in agony as I open my eyes to a shower of grainy light lancing through the swiss-cheesed wall.

I'm alive. *But how?* How the hell am I alive?

It worked. Alan's final words bang through my head like a freight train, and I suddenly know the answer. His dark form at my door as a kid. The late-night shots. His "vaccinations." Me bleary-eyed and shoving him off with a limp scream. The heat of the injection as it pierced my arm. His hand clamping over my mouth as he whispered, *"Don't tell Mom, Bear. This is our little secret, okay? Just me and you."* Me nodding, wanting something that was just ours, because even back then, I knew I was losing him. That he was slipping away...

He saved me. Even then he was saving me.

And now he's gone.

A sob bubbles off my lips. My eyes burn. I need light... air. *Escape.*

I stand, and something twitches at my feet; a feeder with a quarter of its body torn away, its mandibles working open and closed in sick jerks. My stomach lurches, and I scramble past it through what's left of the door and bang down the mud-splattered hall. The carpet is shredded to the cement, the walls to the studs, wisps of insulation fluttering like strands of hair as I pass. Glass is everywhere, strewn over the floor in a glittering, haphazard spray, looking like a grenade went off.

And then I'm outside, the frigid air stealing my breath as I squint up at the sun. The sky crackles a fresh blue. A few slate-colored clouds linger on the horizon. It hurts to inhale, to breathe, but I drink in the air like a newborn—like an infant taking its first breath. Oxygen fills my lungs as a thought spins manic through my head: my promise to Mac. My *lie.*

We stay together from here on out.

I don't blink, don't move. Just stare at the mountains and mentally map my route—the last thing Alan gave me. A way to get my brother back.

I'm coming for you, Tasker. I'm coming. And I'm going find you, you bastard. I'm going to make you pay.

CHAPTER TWENTY-NINE
BURN, BABY, BURN

I scavenge what I can, tearing through offices and lockers with shaking hands, throwing anything that looks remotely useful into a big pile in the middle of the garage. I can barely think straight, can barely focus. I'm on autopilot, my body moving, hands grabbing, my mind numb—somewhere else.

I can walk among them...

The thought feels like a lie, like a bad dream, but it's not, and I'm not sure what it means or how to use it. And now isn't the time to figure it out. Not when I'm hyperventilating with fury, my head so swollen with it, I can barely see straight. All I want to do is wrap my hands around Tasker's neck and squeeze until his face turns black and his eyes burst from his skull.

Stop it, I chide myself. *Think. Get your shit together.*

I walk back to the pile and sort through the supplies one at a time, organize them into categories. Hydration: a jug of water and three Gatorades. Food: a couple cans of soup and a sleeve of canned tuna fish. A can opener. All the nuts and candy bars I could grab. Warmth: a gray-wool blanket and a box of matches. Safety: a pair of flashlights. The first aid kit Tasker left behind and another I found in the back office jammed full of bandages and painkillers. Advil and Tylenol; nothing stronger.

Good enough. I stuff everything into the tool bag I found under the workbench and waterproof it with the dusty blue tarp that, until a moment earlier, covered the ATV parked next to the trucks: a black Yamaha with wide tread tires. It's a dangerous choice, sure to be loud as hell, ready to let everyone within two miles know right where I am the second I fire it up. I have no idea if it weighs enough to trigger the feeder traps, but there's no alternative. The trucks are way too heavy and not nearly as versatile as the four-wheeler, which is something I'll need where I'm going.

I use bungee cords to lash the tool-bag to the back rack of the ATV along with a five-gallon container of gas, crossing and crisscrossing them, until I'm certain everything is secure, and then glance at the battery-powered clock on the wall: almost ten A.M. How much of a head start do they have? *Ten hours? Twelve?* There's no way to be sure. All I know is the horses will struggle in this cold with no rest and little to no food or water. If I really press it, keep the thing red-lined, I might be able to catch them before they reach Rampart.

Before they reach the caves.

A torrent of wind greets me as I pry the garage door open. Like last night, the air is frigid, the sun doing little to melt the snow, but this time I'm ready for the chill. I zip myself into the thick fabric coat I found in the closet and pull an oversized beanie over my head. The key to the ATV glints at me from the ignition and my breath catches—*If this thing doesn't work, I'm fucked, and so is Mac.*

I say a quick prayer, turn it, then press the starter button. The engine rolls over once, twice, my ears straining for that magical catch, willing it to happen, my entire body trembling in anticipation—*C'mon, you stupid thing! Start!*—and then, on the third cycle, it gives a throaty cough and rumbles to life.

Yesssss!

It's the first stroke of good luck I've had since arriving at this miserable hellhole, this makeshift graveyard I can't wait to put behind me as fast as possible. I rev the throttle and nudge the Yamaha into gear, ease it out of the garage and onto the snow, which crunches beneath the tires like a layer of Styrofoam.

I've driven these things before—a couple of times with Tasker the summer after Alan was put away. I picked up how to work the clutch and gas fast enough, spent the rest of the day tearing down trails with careless speed. Even Vivian came, and she was *happy* for once. I remember her whooping as she nearly rammed a tree, Tasker barking at her to slow down. Mac was there, too, going on and on about missing Alan, and how much he would have loved being there with us.

Alan.

I *can't* leave him here—not *like* this.

A flat button of despair settles behind my sternum and spreads through my chest as I kill the engine and grab the gas can. The break room is destroyed. Holes everywhere. The walls. The floor—entire sections of it missing or turned to pulp, giving view to wide swaths of severed wires and broken pipe. The scent of sulfur fills the air, the stale reek of old dust and wood.

I uncap the container and splash gas over the tables, slosh it over the chairs and walls and the hole-riddled floor, keeping my gaze low and away from the couch—away from Alan. I don't want to remember him this way. Not like *this*, torn to scraps. Stripped to the bone—a gut pile in place of my father. A glistening coil of entrails and clothes. Tears snake down both sides of my nose. Why didn't he use the serum on himself? Why did he use it on me? *Why?* What good am I without him here to guide me? To show me the path?

A memory soaks my mind: just the two of us at Lake Granby casting for trout, me somewhere around eight watching him loop the line out over the water just so. The bobber floating there as he handed me the pole, the summer air hugging us as warm and sweet as honey. Then that first tug, him yelling behind me as I reeled, *Tight! Keep it tight! Don't give him any slack!* Me whirring my heart out, hand moving as fast as it would go, the tip of the rod bending, bending, until the trout was up on the beach and flopping over the rocks in a spray of silver and pink light.

He popped off a quick spout of laughter as I stood there, unsure what to do next. A—*Ha! You did it, Bear!*—kind of laugh, and I remember crying at that, watching the fish struggle to breathe, fighting its way back toward the water. And then he was there, kneeling next to me with one hand on my shoulder, *We don't have to keep it.* Me turning back to him and snuggling against his chest: *It's mean, Daddy! Put it back. Please, put it back before it dies!* The sound of the fish as he lowered it into the water, and the flashing *plip-plop* of its tail as it swam away, everything right with the world once more. That moment of pure love. It's how I'll remember him—for who he truly was, the only man who's *really* ever loved me...even when I couldn't love myself.

I cap the gas and light a match, drop it. The resulting *Whoomp!* is instantaneous as the flames catch and leap over the floor like some terrible serpent. My heart melts when they reach the couch. Everyone I've ever loved has either died or abandoned me.

Everyone except Mac—and it's been my job to abandon him.

With a final look, I turn and go.

———

I start the engine and glide forward. The air is cold against my face, glacial. So cold it feels like if I inhale hard enough, my lungs will crack. The yard is drenched in a lake of white. Bits of metal sparkle out at me through the glittering frost, winter beautiful as I coast toward the gate.

Highway 285 isn't far from here. A few miles at most. I can see it winding up through the foothills—a thin gray strip swallowed by all the snow. It's where they went, the only way to reach the meadows and the shelter without a plane. It's where I'll go. It's where I'll find them.

I near the fence and slow, bring the ATV to a stop. The gate is bound shut—the chain tangled around the metal posts. A final *fuck you* from Tasker. A message repeated: *Don't follow me. I don't want to have to shoot you.*

Asshole.

I slip off the four-wheeler and go to work. It takes me nearly five minutes to free the chain, my fingers turning clumsy with cold beneath my new rubber-palmed gloves as I unwind the metal. When I'm done, I shove the gate open in a big angel-wing of snow and turn back toward the ATV, registering the crunch of boots behind me too late. The rapid movement of footsteps. A pair of hands clamp down over my shoulders and squeeze. The grip is strong, too strong to escape, a man's voice leaching into my ears with coils of cigarette smoke dripping off every word.

"I've been looking *everywhere* for you."

CHAPTER THIRTY
A STRANGER

A single thought blares through my head.

No one is taking me. *Ever* again.

I shriek and whirl down, snake a hand into the pocket of my man-jacket, and wrap my fingers around the knife I snatched from the shop—a wicked thing meant to gut fish—and twist up with the blade jutting out.

The hands fall from my shoulders and the man leaps back, the knife whispering an inch past his abdomen, slicing his jacket. I lunge for him as he stumbles back, his arms whipping up, his mouth splitting wide in surprise.

"Brynn, stop! It's me!"

My arm goes limp. *It can't be.* But the platinum hair and the so-brown-they're-almost-black eyes...the stubbled, sandpaper jaw, tell me it is. The knife slips through my fingers and plunges into the snow as I gawk at him. "*Tank?*"

He's still got his hands out, his eyebrows notched halfway up his forehead: "Holy hell, Donovan. Calm down. Jesus!"

My lips go slack. I must be hallucinating. I've finally cracked. Gone mental. I blink. Hard. Count to three and open my eyes again fully expecting him to be gone. But he's not. He's right there, clothed in his black and yellow motorcycle jacket, wearing a pair of Gore-Tex pants, and shaking his head at me like I'm nuts. Which I most definitely am. Because it's him. It's *really* him.

My tongue unwinds itself—remembers how to speak. "But how did you—"

"—find you?" He taps his chest and my hand floats to my collarbone, to the spider pendant. The corners of his mouth tilt into a smile and his meaning dawns on me.

"You mean you've been *tracking* me? All this time you've been tracking me?"

He pulls out his phone and waves it. "And that surprises you? You didn't think I actually trusted you, did you? I mean, c'mon, I like you and all, Donovan, but I wasn't about to let you run off with my entire pill stash someday."

"You asshole!"

"What?" he says, one eyebrow popping. "I thought you'd be happy to see me. I mean, I did just risk my life to track you halfway across—"

I bowl him over with a squeal. We crash to the snow. The smell of him washes over me, all cigarettes and leather and cheap lotion. And the feel of him, the fresh scruff of his chin rubbing against my neck, his six-foot frame pressed to mine—it's almost more than I can take.

Laughing, he tries to roll out from under me, but I clamp my legs over his torso and hold him in place, then grind a handful of snow down the back of his shirt. "Why'd you sneak up on me like that, you jerk!"

"Ha, ha, ha! Happy to see you, too, B." He props himself up on his elbows. "I didn't want you shooting me or anything. Admit it, you know you would have. I mean, some creepy dude screaming at you in the distance, telling you not to worry… c'mon." He's right, I probably would have…if I actually had a gun. "Figured I'd stand a better chance if I got a little closer first."

"Well, congrats," I say, jabbing his chest with my finger. "You almost got yourself stabbed."

"I had it under control."

"Riggght."

"Can you let me up already? I'm freezing my ass off here."

"No." I shove him back to the snow. "You *knew* Alan? You knew my *fucking* dad and never said a word? Not one word, Tank? You *know* how much I hate…" I pause, a fresh wave of grief spilling through my chest at the word. "Hated him."

"Of course. Why the hell you think I never said shit?"

"So, you figured you'd just babysit me all those years? *Lie* to me the entire time? About *everything*?"

He shrugs. "Well… yeah. Pretty much."

"I should kick your ass right now."

He cracks a bright smile, eyes glittering up at me, hair still spiked like he's fresh from his morning shower. "Please. I'd like that."

I try to stay mad at him, but a bubble of laughter works its way up my throat, and I can't, not even now. I've never been able to. He could tell me he just blew up an office building full of people and still find a way to make me laugh about it a few minutes later.

I roll off him with a groan and help him to his feet. "How'd you even get here?"

"My bike," he says with a nod toward the white Harley Softail propped against the fence. "Got a flat yesterday, though. I patched it a couple times. Barely made it."

"Leave it," I tell him. "Get your shit. We'll ride together."

"Where we going—wait, where's Alan?" He glances through the gate, hopeful, like a boy hoping to spot his lost dog, and notices the smoke drifting off the building's roof. His eyes flash back to mine. "What happened?"

I look away, gutted. "He's dead."

"What? Alan's... *dead?*" His hand climbs to the back of his neck and hovers there. He blinks. "How, when?"

"Them... the things. The feeders. They got him last night. In... there." I bite my lip. "We gotta go."

"Where?"

"After my brother." A bright flare of panic rips through me at the thought. "Tasker—Alan's friend, betrayed him...look, never mind. Just get your shit. I'll explain everything on the way."

The ATV wails as I fill Tank in on the last five days. The abduction. The cop. My overdose, the horses, Tasker, and the rest of it. I leave out how I survived. Or at least how I think I did. It's still just a theory... but the way Alan said it—*it worked*—the way he looked at me in those final few seconds like I was some sort of miracle straight from Heaven, it has to be it. Nothing else makes sense.

But what was it *exactly* that worked? I still don't even know what he injected me with all those years ago. I'm still just as clueless as those nights when he slid into my room, needle in hand, and watched me sleep. And now that he's gone, I'll never know.

I drown the thought. Memories are too dangerous right now. I need to concentrate, to search for those slight indentations in the blacktop that mean a feeder trap, to spot the cracks that start in the middle of the street and funnel out through the asphalt, going nowhere, before we plunge straight through them.

It's what I focus on, staring at the street like I've downed five Red Bulls and followed them with a Ritalin chaser. It's an act, though—pure bullshit. What I'm *really* doing is trying to keep my attention off the pink-slush snow choking the gutters and the gore spattered all over the sidewalk. The corpses lying there, half-eaten, staring back at me with empty socket eyes and tongueless mouths.

"Dear God," Tank mutters. "Even Afghanistan wasn't this bad."

He's right. It's so much worse than yesterday. *So much worse.* Body parts everywhere. Snatches of blood-soaked clothing and severed limbs. Bodies gnawed beyond recognition, heads turned to skulls, abdomens to entrails. It's pure carnage—like everyone went running for the shelters and fell into an industrial-sized blender instead; one that chewed them up and spit them out all over the street.

And it's quiet.

Piss-your-pants-quiet. No chirping birds. No barking dogs. No helicopters buzzing overhead or jets slicing through the air. No people screaming for us to stop and help them—*Please! Oh, God, please help!*—like they were yesterday. Only the Yamaha and the wind hissing into my ears as we climb out of the city toward the highway, past abandoned cars and gutted semis with their trailers open and emptied.

And ahead of us, buried somewhere in all the whitewash—Tasker and Mac climbing higher, heading for the caves and whatever fresh Hell is lying in wait to greet them when the sun sets. The thought is like a light bursting in my brain—a clarion call rising in my blood. Find your brother, Brynn. Save him.

I gun the throttle and push on.

People appear; those who couldn't escape the storm but survived. Clumped groups of twos and threes wrapped in winter coats and blankets turned to rags. They hobble along painfully. Some barely move at all. Their clothes are covered in frost, their breath scrubbing out in front of them in small, silver bursts.

One of them, a man in a brown trench coat, cradles a girl against his shoulder. Her cheeks are blue with frostbite, her hair a forest of ice. I peg her at seven, maybe eight. She waves at me. A timid gesture I return. *I would help you if I could,* I think as she vanishes around a battered milk truck. *I would give you everything...*

I realize Tank is speaking, yelling over the growl of the ATV. I ease the gas a bit and lean back.

"What's that?"

"I said, are you ever gonna talk to me?"

"About what?"

"About what's bothering you."

"Nothing."

"Uh-huh."

I roll my eyes. "I'm worried about my brother is all. And it's just—" It's out of my mouth before I can stop it. The question bothering me the most. "What are you even doing here, Tank? I mean, with everything going to hell like this? Why did you come for me?"

He pauses, coughs into his arm—something he always does when things turn a little too serious. Ask him a real question, and it's all, *I um, (uh, huh, huh, huh) well, see the thing is (uh, huh, huh).*

"I already told you," he says. "I was worried you'd run off with my pills. I had to—"

"No. Cut the bullshit. What are you *really* doing here? And how the hell did you survive?"

He's quiet for a moment, shifting uncomfortably behind me before he speaks. "I need to look after you."

I don't know why, but his answer pisses me off. "I don't need looking after," I say. It's a lie, of course, but screw telling him that.

"It doesn't matter," he replies. "I gave your dad my word."

"Alan's dead, so you came all this way for nothing."

"Even more reason to be here."

I fall silent and tuck my chin into my jacket as slivers of snow sting my face.

"You don't understand, Brynn. He saved my life. A bunch of guys on the inside had it in for me. Thought I stole some of their bats or some shit."

"Bats?"

"Cigarettes. I stole plenty of crap, had a bit of a rep for it, but never those. Stealing a man's smokes is a good way to get your skull cracked in half. Didn't matter, though. People think what they think. And then one day I took a trashcan to the back of the head in the shower. I had a bunch of soap in my eyes. Had no clue it was coming. Then it was all legs and fists and elbows. I lost a few teeth before I blacked out."

I imagine him lying naked on that cold tile, blood leaking from his mouth and seeping from his ears, trails of pink water swirling down the drain. I shudder.

"When I came to, Alan had three of those bastards slumped against the wall." His arms tense around my waist. "One of them had a shank on him. They were going to kill me, Brynn. Just wanted me to suffer first..." He goes quiet for a moment before continuing. "He didn't just save my life, Brynn. He helped me turn it around. Talked some sense into me. He's the one who noticed how good I was with the tats. Who do you think encouraged me to start my shop?"

"Gee, let me guess."

"He even kicked me some of the seed money. I owe him everything. And as far as how I survived… I owe that to him, too. He texted me. Told me to get to high ground and stay there. I took cover on an apartment roof until I figured out the light thing. Then I hauled ass up here." He shifts forward. "Alan never shut up about you, by the way. It was always, 'you should meet my daughter. You should see her draw.' On and on about how talented you were. How you were going to be this great artist someday. I don't think a day passed without him mentioning you. There's no way I couldn't keep my promise."

"Like I said. I don't need—"

"—looking after. Yeah, yeah, I get it. You're a real badass, B. Either way, you're stuck with me whether you like it or not."

I shrink into my jacket, pissed at the sticky cobweb of emotion Tank's unleashed. I don't have time for this shit—this swamp of feeling churning in my chest like a bad stew. All that matters is getting to Mac and saving him. So who cares why Tank's here, really? Whether it's for me or Alan or by some dumb stroke of luck, he'll help me even the odds against Tasker. And deep down, I don't want him going anywhere. I need him. Right now, he's all I've got.

CHAPTER THIRTY-ONE
PITSTOP

A gob of relief sloshes through my chest when I finally spot the fly shop rising out of the snow like a mirage. "JD's Bait Shop-n-Grill!" An off-white, log-walled building the color of faded sweat. I want to blow straight past it, want to cut north and keep driving until my lips blister and my eyes freeze, but I can't—not with the fuel gauge ticking on empty and my stomach growling for calories despite my nerves. I brake and pull into the parking lot, hop off the ATV.

Tank slides off with me and gives a long stretch. "Why are we stopping?"

"Need to gas up."

"So, we close to these caves, or what?"

"Sort of. The road to Rampart is over there." I wolf down a Snickers and point at the smooth track of snow drifting up into the pines just beyond the parking lot. "We have a few hours of drive time left. Maybe more. I don't remember. I haven't been up there since I was a kid."

"Sounds good. I'll go sniff around inside while you gas up. See if there's anything in there we can use."

My stomach twists. There's no time to play apocalypse ransacker right now. Every second that slips past is a second further from Tasker and Mac, not to mention getting to the shelter before the sun sets. I set the gas canister down and lurch after him.

"Wait. Tank, stop."

He dismisses me with a half-ass wave.

"Seriously," I shout, clomping up the steps after him. "We don't have time for this shit."

"I'll be quick, I promise," he says before rearing back and kicking the red, paint-chipped door with the bottom of his boot. It careens open, and I'm left standing in his wake, staring at the "SORRY, WE'RE CLOSED" sign as it rattles in the window.

———

The place is part convenience store, part fly shop, with fishing vests, rods, and spools of tippet hanging from the wood-paneled walls. Racks of junk food crowd the center, the shelves sagging from years of use, the floors cheaply tiled and coffee stained. Near the back, I spot the so-called "grill," a few red-checkered tables bumped up against a dingy bar supporting several thick plastic bottles of barbecue sauce. One lies on its side in a death throe, its guts crusted all over the counter.

"Here. Take this," Tank says, tossing a loaf of bread my way. It thumps off my chest and I kick it back to him with a scowl.

"What are you doing? We need to go."

He corks an eyebrow at me like it's a stupid question, like I'm an idiot for even asking. "What I'm *doing*, Donovan, is looking for the shit that's going to keep us alive long enough to find that asshole and your brother."

I swing my arm toward the door. "I already have everything we need on the four-wheeler, *Tank*. And there's more at the shelter." At least according to Alan, there is, but I have my doubts. How long can apocalypse food last, anyway? Even if it is non-perishable? A year? A decade? More? And when did he last stock it? Is there enough?

I realize, as usual, I have absolutely no clue.

"Maybe. Maybe not. Your old man had his shit together, and I don't doubt that's the case up there as well, but one thing I learned in the joint is that you always, *always*, got to have a backup plan." He slides behind a row of fly display cases and grabs a grocery sack, starts stuffing it with candy bars and cartons of cigarettes, moves to the liquor shelf, and snags several bottles of Fireball followed by a few bottles of Jack.

I roll my eyes as he dumps the booze in the sack. "And that's your backup plan? Getting trashed?"

"Damn straight." He says it with a wink, like I'm in on this little game of his, like we're about to head to a backwoods kegger with a bunch of high school kids and get sloshed.

"Tank!" I snap. "C'mon. This isn't a joke. We have to go."

He sets the bag down and exhales, raises a hand—one I'm surprised to see is shaking. "Look, I need it, okay? Getting here wasn't easy. I saw a lot of...things. *Did* a lot of things." His eyes cloud over and go distant. "There was this... kid. Real cute. Lots of freckles. Lots of curls. Maybe three or four years old. I stumbled across him and his mom just outside Amarillo. At least I think she was his mom. Her head was too bashed in to tell. It was so... God, there was blood everywhere, Brynn. So much blood. All over the dash." He runs a hand through his hair. "Jesus..."

"Tank..."

He extends a finger. *Hold on.* "When I first get there, I see this car punched right through the asphalt. Like it had been dropped from a plane. And the kid, he's strapped in a car seat, just hanging there in the back, no tears or anything. For a minute, I think he's dead, but then I get closer, and his face lights up like a Christmas tree. This big dumb smile, like he'd given up until he saw me.

"So, I slide toward him real slow like, but the road, it's crumbling right beneath my feet. I can *feel* it disintegrating. But no way I'm leaving this kid there. No *fucking* way. So, I keep edging closer and the road keeps getting worse and worse, and I'm telling myself, 'Keep going, Tank. You got him. You can do this. You can keep him safe,' and I can tell he thinks it too because that smile of his keeps getting bigger and bigger.

"And then, right when I'm about to reach him, the road, it just... dissolves. Just crumbles in front of me like sand, and the kid, he gives me this *look*..." He glances up and blinks, his eyes red-rimmed and wet. "It was like he was disappointed in me somehow. Like he trusted me, and I let him down. He didn't even scream, Brynn. He didn't even have time to open his mouth..." His voice cracks and he drops his head, gives it a shake. "If I'd just moved a little quicker, I could've reached him."

"There's nothing you could have done."

"It's not right. He was just a kid."

He didn't even scream. Vivian did. All the way down. I think of the way she was swallowed up in an instant, the terrible speed of it, sucked away like she never existed at all. It was hard enough watching her go out like that, but a little boy? My heart aches at the thought. I edge forward and place my hand on his arm. "It's not your fault, Tank. You know that, right? At least he didn't slip away alone. That's more than a lot of people can say these days."

He croaks out a laugh, gives me a grudging nod. "Since when are you the optimist?"

"I'm not. I lost my aunt that way. A few days ago."

"Vivian?"

"Yeah." Her face flashes to mind—wrinkles and smoke.

"Damn. I'm sorry."

"Me too."

"What the hell's happening out there, B? Is the world ending? Is this it?"

"I wish I knew."

He looks up, his gaze suddenly intense. "I'm glad I found you. When those things erupted, all I could think about was you. If you were safe. If you were okay. I didn't have any idea, and I didn't like that. I missed you."

"I, yeah...me too." Tank's never much been one for sentimentalism—I'm not even sure we've had a real conversation before this one—so his statement about missing me, and the way he's looking at me right now, like maybe I'm all he has left in the world, has me tongue-tied and stammering.

His brow crinkles, his eyes flat. "I don't want to go back out there."

"Me neither, but we have to." I turn to leave.

"Wait, Brynn." He reaches into his jacket and digs something out, taps it into his hand. Three pills. *Blues. Fucccckkkk.* "I don't know about you, but I need a bump first." He holds his hand out. "Want one?"

I do. Intensely. Insanely. And with a sudden rush of heat that turns my knees to gelatin. I can already imagine it, pressing the pill to my lips, letting it dissolve slow and hot on my tongue, that soft, pillow-high spilling through me like good sex, soaking up all the pain and hurt until it's nothing but a distant cloud on the horizon; a small, dark imprint in the sky you have to squint to see.

Is that so much to ask for? A little relief?

No, it's not.

I step toward him, hand out, my fingers quivering, a sliver of tongue pressed between my teeth. *No! Mac!* It's everything I can do to pull my hand back and jam it in my pocket.

"Put it away. I can't. I'm... off them."

"Really?"

"Yes, now c'mon." I say it quick and then stumble outside before I can change my mind. The smell of pine and snow greets me, and I take a slow, wobbly breath, let it slide out slow through my nose, lean back against the wood planks and close my eyes. *Fucking Tank.*

"Well, heya there. 'Member me?"

The man is seated on the railing a few feet down, rolling a toothpick between his lips. He's dressed head to toe in camo with a gun, one of the big, school shooting kind, propped in his lap, the barrel aimed lazily at my stomach.

Needles of fear lace down my spine. *I know this man.* I've seen him before. The belly. The greasy cheeks and purple pads of flesh hanging beneath his eyes. The salt and pepper hair curling out from under his hat. It hits me. The man from the road. The one with the other guy who'd eyed me like a wolf stumbling across a bloody piece of meat. That lecherous grin and gray tooth. I whip my gaze over the parking lot in search of him, see nothing but mud and snow and trees.

"Brynn, we should..." Tank trails off as he steps outside, his face turning to stone at the sight of the gun. His hand shoots for his jacket.

The man snaps the barrel his way and shakes his head.

"Don't even think about it. Hand it over. Nice and slow. Go too fast and Benny will decorate your chest with a new set of breathing holes." He nods behind him toward the dark wall of pine on the ridge.

Tank hesitates, his hand quivering near his chest. "Bullshit."

"Maybe," the man replies. "That's something you'll have to decide for yourself. But I'll tell you this—the kid's a crack shot. I've seen him take a deer's head off with a three-oh-eight about two hundred yards out, and that's saying something."

Tank looks at the man like he wants to crater his face, and for a moment I think he'll go for whatever is in his jacket, but instead, he slowly retrieves a boxy-looking pistol and hands it over, butt first. The man grabs it with a smile and waves his gun toward the parking lot. "That's a smart move. Now, why don't we all come on down off this porch and have us a little chat. We have some catching up to do."

CHAPTER THIRTY-TWO
MIND GAMES

The man orders us toward the middle of the parking lot, his gaze flicking back to the fly shop every few steps. I scrub my memory for his name—Barry or something. Or was it Kendal? No, that's not right. But I need it. I watched a prime time show on assault once about some wisp of a woman who'd escaped her attacker because she'd said his name. She'd claimed his eyes cleared long enough to let her go. It made sense to me. Men like their victims like they like their porn: malleable. Cowed and compliant. Objects with warm orifices cooked to their liking. It's a fact—assault just isn't as fun when you're human.

The man hocks something yellow from his mouth, looks at me. "Where's the cowboy? And the big guy? They inside?"

Alan. "He's dead." The word comes out stiff. Unnatural. Like it's a lie, and hearing this man, this piece-of-shit, talk about him like he has any right to know his whereabouts sets my blood to boiling.

The man's eyes stretch wide. "*Really*? Now that I didn't expect. Figured you'd be the first to go." He tilts his head, the toothpick darting over his lips like a lizard. "You wouldn't happen to be lying to me now, would you?"

"She's not lying, you dumbfuck," Tank cuts in.

The man swings the barrel his way. "I say shit to you?"

Tank gives him a dead-eyed stare, his eyebrow ring twitching in place.

"You deaf, son?" the man clucks. "I asked you a question. Didn't your momma teach you nothing as a kid? Where I come from, we got us some manners. Somebody asks you a question and you answer." He shrugs. "Simple as that. Now, let's try it again without the smartass shit." His eyes flatten. "Was I talking to you?"

Tank gives the man a look I recognize, his *I'm-about-to-fuck-you-up* look, brow slanted, chin hard, fists clenched. I've seen him make good on it many times, but never with a gun in his face, and never with me as scared about what he might try to do as I am right now.

"Tank," I hiss, glancing his way. "Don't."

"Well, was I?" the man prods.

"No," Tank replies, lips barely moving. I can tell it's all he can do to get the word out.

"Good. Then keep your mouth shut." The man curls a thumb and forefinger between his teeth and unleashes a sharp whistle, the kind of ear-piercing shriek rednecks seem born able to make. "Benny, get your ass out here!"

My knees lock tight as he slinks from behind a tree and jogs toward us, rifle in hand. He moves like a coyote, all loping limbs and awkward angles, looking like he might fall at any moment, which is a lie, a trap, because the truth is he's lethal, and I know it. He ambles next to the man and glances at the fly shop. "There anyone else in there?"

"Won't know till you search it, will we?"

"But I thought we were—"

"I stutter?" The man replies, his chest seeming to inflate two shirt sizes. "I said search it."

"Fine," Benny says. He gives me a side-long glance, his cement eyes hidden behind a cheap pair of aviator sunglasses. I shiver because I know they're pasted on me; I can feel them washing over my skin, running up my legs, and settling on my chest, where they remain. He flashes me a quick grin, his lips chapped, bits of skin hanging off. Repulsive. "Told you I'd see you again."

Then he's gone, hustling for the store, outfitted in gray and white camo like he and the man are some sick hunting tag-team duo and we're the lucky prey. The thought embers through my chest and sets it ablaze—I'm sick of being the prey, I've been the prey for too long now; I'm ready to slit some throats, namely his...*Randall's*. The name is a lightning flash in my brain as I turn toward him.

"Randall."

He raises an eyebrow, surprise lines etching across his forehead. "Well, I'll be damned. You *do* remember me. I'm touched. Especially since we put so much work into tracking you down. It was tough after the road split in half, but we picked up your trail easy enough. Not too many horses around, so thank you for that. Thought you'd lead us to that shelter of yours, but oh no, instead you got yourself into quite the pickle with all them angry little bastards, didn'tcha?"

The feeders. The stallion. *Shit!* I knew we were being followed.

"Please... put the gun down," I say.

"Now why would I do that?"

"You made us an offer. Back on the road."

He spits the toothpick out, looks at me with disgust. "Don't recall doing anything of the sort."

I'm already sick of this stupid game, but I have to play it. "You said you'd trade protection for shelter."

His eyes widen. "Ahh, *that* offer. So there *is* a shelter, is there?"

"Yes," I say grudgingly. *But I'll never show you where it is.*

"Whelp, here's the thing. I'm nothing if not a gentleman. Big fan of the golden rule and all. Like I said, manners. But if someone don't afford me the same level of respect"—he wags a finger at me, clicks his tongue against his teeth—"say, like lying to me, then I'm done with 'em. And, if memory serves correct, you all soundly rejected me. Said you didn't need any help; said you were fine on your own."

I cross my arms to keep them from shaking. "It appears things have changed."

Tank shifts uncomfortably next to me. I don't need to look at him to know what he's thinking: *What are you doing, B?*

The answer: what I have to.

Randall's lips wrinkle into a smile. "Hm. Have they now? Well, that's too bad. It really don't matter at this point, seeing as I can do whatever I want with you now. Think I'll just take that shelter for myself."

I harden. "Like hell, you will."

His nose wrinkles. "Oh, you'll show it to me, all right. One way or 'nother." He says it in a way that makes me think he's looking forward to the challenge. A ripple of fear slides through me at the threat, at what he might do to me if given the chance.

I press him anyway. "Maybe. But I'll make you work for it, and then it'll be too late. The man you call the cowboy took it from us. He killed my dad and left me for dead. He's got a good head start. By the time we get there, he'll be locked inside nice and tight, and you'll never get it open. Even with that big gun of yours." I make sure to drench the word "big" in a *heavy* dose of sarcasm. By the look of it, I might as well have been commenting on the size of his dick.

"Maybe you aren't worth my time, then." He shrugs. "Maybe I should just use this big gun of mine to blow your boyfriend's head off."

"Go to hell, prick," Tank spits back.

With more speed than I would expect from a man his size, Randall whips forward and slams the butt of the gun into Tank's forehead. His eyes roll into his skull and my stomach lurches as he crumples to the snow.

"*NO!*" I say, collapsing to the ground next to him. I pull his head into my lap, his eyelids fluttering. He's out cold. I've never seen him on his back before, and I've seen him in plenty of fights. Once, at a crappy biker bar, he leveled a man twice his size, cracked a full beer bottle across his temple when the man wouldn't stop calling the bartender a bitch. I trace my fingers across his hairline, and they come away smeared in blood.

Randall paces back and forth, shaking his head and staring at Tank, his face beet red. "Your boyfriend must have a huge dick because he just fucked himself. No one talks to me that way! No one! And I'll tell you this. You better get him to fix his goddamn attitude right quick."

I stiffen. I know what this man wants from a woman. What he expects. Fear. Obedience. He wants me to cower like a puppy piss-shamed and beaten. That's what he's used to. Women who wilt. Women who pepper him with cold beers after a hard day at work. Tell him dinner's almost ready, *go relax, hun*. Well, fuck that and fuck him.

I surge upright and stride for him. The gun whips toward my head. "Don't you come any closer."

I lean in and square my forehead against the barrel. "Do it."

The corners of his eyes crease. "Don't think I won't."

"Well go on, then. Blow my head off, asshole. You'd be doing me a favor. We're all dead out here as it is. It's just a matter of time. Sure, you might be able to escape the swarm for a while. A day. A month. Maybe longer. Who knows? But if it's not them, it will be someone with a bigger gun than yours. Or more of them. Or maybe you'll get stuck out here and freeze to death. Or starve. Maybe you'll catch something nasty and need antibiotics, but you won't be able to get any because people will have already scooped them up. Society's fucked, and you know it. So go ahead and pull that trigger, you goddamn hick. See if I care, because without me you're screwed."

His face collapses into a pile of angry folds, his hand tightening on the trigger, and I can almost feel the bullet pierce my skull, can sense it carving through my brain and turning my synapses to glass. But he doesn't shoot. He takes a step back instead and issues a low whistle. "Well, my gawd. Wow. I mean... *Wow,* do you ever got a big pair of balls on you. I like that!" He says it with an amused expression, like I'm a six-year-old puffing out her chest after an early-morning temper tantrum, and it takes every ounce of willpower I have not to leap forward and claw off his face.

He winks at me. "So, boss lady, I'll bite—what is it you want?"

I gesture at the gun. "Quit pointing that at me for starters."

"Don't push your luck."

"Leave her alone, asshole." The voice is limp, and I turn to find Tank struggling to his feet in a drunken wobble, his hand to his forehead, his lips twisted into a snarl.

"I'd think real hard about what you say next."

Before he can reply, Benny bangs through the door and huffs up, cheeks red. "The place is empty. No one's there. I..." He looks at Tank, then Randall. "Hey, what gives?"

"Hero here got out of line. But he's straight now," Randall replies with a glance toward Tank. "Ain't that right?"

Tank glares back at him through a stream of blood, says nothing.

"Aren't you?" Randall repeats. "Because if you ain't, we're gonna—"

"I'm straight."

"Good. That's what I like to hear." He nods to Benny, who's back to eyeing me construction-worker style. I can almost hear him whistling. It makes me sick. "Now, girly here wants to cut us a deal. Isn't that right, sweetheart?"

I clench my teeth. "Yes."

"Well, go on then. What's your deal?"

"The cowboy...his name's Tasker. I want him dead." Finally something I don't have to lie about.

Randall frowns. "I don't see how that benefits us?"

I have to sell this, and I have to sell it right. "Kill him, and we share the shelter."

Benny issues a shrill howl, his chest vibrating, wheezing like he's full of pneumonia, and it takes me a moment to realize it's his laugh. "Well, if that isn't the biggest loada crap I ever heard in my life. You'd never share it with us, bitch. Not in a million years."

He's right. I wouldn't...and there's no point denying it. I spin his way. "Fine. It's yours, then. Do whatever you want with it. Tasker killed my father and took my brother. I want him back, and I want Tasker dead. If you help me do that, I swear I'll show you where the shelter is. You have my word."

Benny smirks. "Like your word means anything."

"It does when you're the ones with the guns."

"She's got a point," Randall says. "And it sounds like this Tasker, whoever he is, is a problem for us, too."

Benny leers at me, his lips so thin they nearly disappear against his teeth. "I don't know…"

"We're wasting time," I say. "Either kill us or let's go. We don't have much sun left to work with."

Randall chuckles and glances at Benny: "Ha! What spunk! I love this girl! You could learn a thing or two from her."

Benny laughs, too, like it's the funniest thing ever, but I catch the quick twitch of his hand and the angry glance my way a second later, the promise buried there. *I'll make you pay for that.*

Randall draws close and presses the gun barrel into my chest. His breath is a sour mix of spit and chew. "We got ourselves a deal. We help you kill this guy and get your brother back, then you show us this shelter of yours, right?"

I nod.

"You do that, and I'll let you go." His eyes tick toward Tank and then shift back to me. "Both of you. No harm, no foul. But if you're lying to me, if you try anything stupid at all, I'll kill your boyfriend first, and then I'll turn you over to Benny here and let him have his way with you. And I can promise you, that is something you do *not* want."

I catch the quick, cruel smile as it slides over Benny's jaw and tremble. But not with fear. With rage. Every fiber of my being coiled tight. They won't let us go. No way. Not when we know where the shelter is. We might come back, so they'll need to die, too.

I square my shoulders and nod. "And if you touch either of us, I'll make sure you never find the place. Ever. No matter what you do to me."

Randall grins at that, a bubble of spit nestled on his lower lip. "Like I said, all balls. Now it's time we stop jabber-jawing and get a move on. We got us a shelter to reach."

CHAPTER THIRTY-THREE
HUNTING

The road winds through the woods in a collection of switchbacks that make the going frustratingly slow. It's all washboards, ruts, and muddy snow as I push the ATV higher, faster. Tank and Randall trail behind in Randall's beat-up, hillbilly dune buggy, the thing huffing out clouds of exhaust as we devour the miles. I'm dying for a sign—*any sign*—of Tasker and Mac. The horses. A hoof print. A strip of clothing. A scrabbled cry for help carved into a tree trunk with a big cartoon arrow: *SOS! Go this way!* There's nothing—just a few broken branches paired with piles of deer scat.

Panic crawls, cold and clear, up my throat.

I force myself to keep looking, my eyes watering against the breeze. Benny sits behind me with his body pressed to mine, his wet swamp breath warming my neck every few seconds with another stale blow of air. He forced me to drive, said he needed to, "keep an eye on me." And he has, along with his hands.

A word sears my brain: *Numb.*

He leans closer and wraps an arm around my waist. His finger-nails are slivered with grime, his meth-head wrist splotched in scabs. I pry his hand free and thrust it back into his lap with a shudder, only for him to cough out that eerie, high-pitched laugh of his as he presses his face closer to my ear. "What? I'm just trying to keep you from falling off."

I clench my teeth: *Numb.*

Clumps of aspen hem us in on either side. They push vertical and scrape the sky with freshly bare branches. They dust the road in leafy, red-orange glitter. Beyond the trees, the jagged cut of the Rockies peeks out, capped in puffy, marshmallow whites like we're in the middle of a Coors commercial, and for a split-second, I'm almost, *almost,* lost in it all before Benny whispers in my ear again.

"Please. Try something. I'm begging you." I catch the dull flash of his sunglasses over my shoulder. A sliver of pasty scalp. He's all ribs and days' old bourbon, pressing into me, suffocating me. He's miles of body odor and stale, reeking sweat.

"Leave me alone," I hiss.

"Oh, c'mon. You can do better than that. Drive us into one of them trees over there. I know you want to."

I say nothing with the vague hope it will shut him up. It doesn't.

"Do it. Let's have some fun."

My stomach quivers at the way he says *fun* like he's already playing out the scenarios in his head—what he'll stick where, which pieces of me he'll cut off and which pieces he'll keep, what body parts he'll turn into souvenirs to share with all his inbred friends.

Numb. Go numbnumbnumbnummbbb.

Something sharp traces down my spine and I clench. A knife. *My knife.* It stops just below my waist, hovers there. "I bet you wanted to stick this in me, didn't'tcha? Well, there's something I'd like to stick in—"

The cramp slices through my abdomen like a rocket. I rip left a second before the feeder hole tears open with a wet sucking groan. The ground sags beneath the tires, swaths of snow and mud evaporating to my right. My pupils dilate, and I frantically thumb the gas as gravity claws at the Yamaha; a slow, fatal tilt that only our momentum overcomes.

We bang back onto solid ground.

Spin.

I can't bring the ATV under control before it overturns and we slam onto the snow. Benny whips somewhere overhead with a surprised screech. A second later, the dune buggy barrels by in a hot spray of exhaust.

I shake my head and attempt to push upright. A gun chatters. Bullets smack the snow near my feet and circle up toward my chest. Flecks of ice spray my face. The echo roars through the silence like an avalanche. Trembling, I raise my hands and stand, stars still spitting through my vision as Randall stamps toward me, the picture of rage—his lips pulled low, his eyebrows stitched together.

"The hell you think you're doing?"

"The cunt broke my nose!" Benny spits. He sounds like he's talking through a pillow, waving the knife at me from behind the ATV blood slicking through his fingers and running down over his chin. "She broke my mudderfucking nose!"

Randall glares at him, then at me. There's violence in his eyes. A promise. He's going to do to me what he did to Tank. He's going to fracture my skull.

"I saved his life," I mutter quietly.

Randall's frown deepens, and he leans in. "Say again?"

"I said, I saved his life!" And it's true. I'm not even sure how I sensed the hole, but I did. The cramp was so...hot. So sudden. *I can walk among them.* The thought comes uninvited, crashes through my head like a tidal wave.

"Leave her alone, you fuck!"

My eyes flick over his shoulder to Tank, who's fighting against the rope Randall used to bind him to the roll bar, yanking like a madman, his forehead swollen and rivered in blood.

I glance back to Randall. "And I almost drove us straight into that hole because your boy was distracting me with his threats."

Randall's brow creases. "Doesn't sound like he *did* anything to you though, does it?"

"No. At least not until he jammed a knife into my back."

Randall's lips quiver, and the rage recedes. It's a look of recognition—one that tells me he's used to Benny pushing things a little too far. He whirls around and stamps over, whips out a hand. "Give me that thing."

"But—"

"No buts. Hand it over."

Benny obeys, looking whipped, looking like the knife is a remote and he's just been busted watching porn.

"You drive this time, idiot," Randall orders, stabbing his finger toward the ATV. "And if she tries anything, I'll gut her friend. Otherwise, keep your dick in your pants and your eyes on the road." He flashes me a wicked look. "For now."

We pick up the tracks an hour later. They're faint at first, little indentations in the snow I think I'm imagining until, no, I see them: horseshoe prints. Two u-shaped sets planted side-by-side. My heart swells at the sight. The snow has mostly filled them in, but they are *there,* stamped into the ground. Randall spots them, too, and surges past us, his eyes hard, focused. *It's hunting time.*

There's no change in Benny, who sits in front of me cardboard stiff. He hasn't tried to touch me once since Randall took the knife, hasn't even come close, and that scares me more than any of his threats. I can practically feel the rage throbbing off him, the hot hate. The only reason I know he's still alive is because I can hear him breathing through his newly ruined nose like he's fighting off a sinus infection, clearing it and spitting copper-colored lobs of phlegm to the side every few minutes. Other than that, it's just the wind snapping past my face and the growl of the engines filtering through the trees.

Rampart Meadows breaks below us an hour later. It's stunning. There's no other word for it. A soft, white lake of snow peppered with iced-over ponds and a river that cuts a wide, bright swath through the valley. And there are feeder holes. Dozens and dozens of them. A honeycomb, thicker on the far side of the meadow near the network of caves I know lie hidden behind all the layers of evergreen and pine. A chill ripples through my blood as we thread our way back into the trees.

When we finally break onto the valley floor, it's to a volley of evening sun that angles off the snow in a way that forces me to squint, the light like glass. For a moment, everything looks pure, like the world is still the same safe place and there isn't a legion of hungry feeders simmering beneath our feet. Then the smell hits, acrid like battery acid, and the illusion shatters. The holes are everywhere. So many of them, I lose count.

How are there so many?

Ahead, Randall brakes and eases to the side of the road, slides out of the driver's seat, and crouches, working his lips like he's got a splinter of bone stuck between his teeth.

"Why'd you stop?" Benny asks, pulling even with him.

"Tracks are fresh here. They're close."

"Then they'll hear us coming. It's too damn quiet."

Randall stands and spits. "Don't matter if they do. What's the cowboy got against us? A pistol or two? And he won't shoot till he thinks we're trouble. We'll take him out before that happens." He glances my way. "He got any binoculars on him? Any way to make us out?"

"No," I lie. I have no clue.

"Good. Then we got nothing to worry about 'cept finding this shelter of yours. And it better be close, understand?" He doesn't need to finish the threat; his eyes tell me what he'll do.

"It is," I say, trying to keep my voice from shaking.

"Let's go," he says as he clambers back into the buggy and rips off down the road, Tank looking back at me through a face full of crusted blood.

Benny hesitates. "We both know this whole shelter act of yours is bullshit."

My ears heat up. I wipe the sweat from my palms on my jeans. "It's there."

"You'd better hope so. You're not going to like what happens if it's not." He glances back with a smile, his gray incisor flashing once more before he turns around and thumbs the throttle.

CHAPTER THIRTY-FOUR
THE CABIN

The road cuts northwest toward the stack of boulders Alan mentioned to Tasker. These giant slate lumps that fringe the far edge of the meadow in a halo of stone and granite. A trace of memory at the sight: a lazy August afternoon, Alan on a tube, floating the river with a six-pack and a fishing pole while me and Mac scampered over the rocks after one another—our laughter hanging above us, high and bright. A memory soured by the grim knowledge that the shelter is still miles away, and if I can't find Mac and escape these assholes before night hits, that's all I'll have left of him. Memories.

Just like Alan.

I shake the thought from my head. I have to handle this shit. *Have to.* All I need is a moment. A sliver of an opportunity to act. But not before they take out Tasker. Or at least distract him enough that I can make a move.

The boulders grow, and with them, my nerves. This is where Alan sent Tasker and Mac. This is where they went. But what if they got here hours ago, despite what Randall says? What if I'm too late and they're miles away and—

Benny stiffens and jams the brakes. We skid to a stop behind the dune buggy, which has halted again, Randall back to staring at the ground with a sour look. He glances at me and his lips curl into a frown. "They've doubled back. I thought you said this guy knew where this shelter was?"

"He does."

"What the hell's this about, then? Why did they turn around?"

"Tasker's never been up here before. He's confused."

Benny leaps off the ATV and jabs his finger at me. "She's lying! She's fucking lying. I told you this shelter of theirs was a bunch of horseshit the minute we stumbled across their sorry asses."

"There *is* a shelter, you dumbass," I snap.

"Hey! Shut the hell up. Both of you," Randall yells before looking at me. "Now there better be a god-dammed shelter, and it better be *real* fucking close, or I'm gonna punch a bullet right through that pretty head of yours. Then I'm going to do the same thing to your shithead friend here and toss you both in one of them holes. In fact," he says, pulling a revolver from the inside of his jacket and planting it against Tank's temple, "maybe I'll go ahead and do it right now. Show you we mean business."

I lunge off the ATV. "Randall, wait—stop!"

He keeps his eyes on Tank. "Why should I?"

"Fuckin' kill him, Uncle Randy! Kill him," Benny screeches, hopping up and down like a grasshopper on speed. "Plug his ass!"

"No!" I protest. "You help us deal with Tasker; we help you. That was the deal!"

"The cowboy's gone. Deal's off."

"He's not gone. He's..." The words fizzle, a shape out of place behind him. A russet streak of color that doesn't belong. I rush forward. "Wait! I know where he is. I know *exactly* where he is!"

"Yeah? How the hell you know that?"

I point over his shoulder toward the curve of road bending back into the trees and the brick-colored lump lying in the snow.

"That's how."

It's the mare. She's lying on her side, legs hinged, and covered in a light dusting of snow, her once creamy auburn coat now matted and roped with mud. Sweat rings cover her shoulder in streaks. A spray of pale pink foam speckles her lips and nostrils. I pray for her flank to rise, to move, but I know it won't. Still, I cage a sliver of hope as I rush to her and palm her cheek. It's stiff. Cold. One dull eye peers up at me through a set of frozen lashes, and all I can think, all I can picture, is Dr. Tsosie as he fled into the night chasing the ghost of his wife to save his horses... *They're all I have left of her.* The grief is immediate and hot. A knife to the ribs.

"Look," Benny blurts to my right. "Footprints."

I gently pull the mare's eyelid shut. "I'm sorry, girl," I whisper, heart heavy. "I'm so sorry."

"Enough," Randall says, jerking me up by the hood and thrusting me toward the prints. "Those your brother's?"

I examine the tracks. They *are* the right size, and I can make out the Adidas logo in spots muddy against the snow. *Mac.*

"Yes," I cough, clutching at the neck of my coat. "They're his."

He yanks me back. "Good. Let's go."

———

The footprints lead us to a cabin. A ramshackle horror, two stories tall, with an attic and a silver tin roof baking through the snow in patches. Rusted red gutters frame the eaves and spill down the water-stained siding. The windows are caked with dust, the logs painted a powder blue and long faded by the weather.

"*This* is the shelter? *This* shithole?" Benny whines, scratching his neck. "You gotta be kidding me." He rolls his gaze to Randall, who's glaring at me from beneath a scatter of branches, his eyes unblinking. Concrete.

I nod, mouth dry.

"She's full of shit, Uncle Randy," Benny says. "I know it. I say we gut her and get the hell out of here before the sun sets."

Randall's gaze remains on me. "You think?"

"Yeah. Can't you tell? Look at her! The bitch is shaking."

Randall glances his way. "Shhh! Not so loud, idiot.

He drops his voice a notch. "All I'm saying is—"

"Just shut up for a second," Randall replies, sliding past Benny and lumbering toward me, pressing so close, all I can see are the broken capillaries crawling across the bridge of his nose and winding through his cheeks. His eyes are cold, emotionless discs, his jaw quivering. "Want to know what I think?"

I don't. All I want to do is run.

"*I* think my nephew might be right. *I* think you've been playing both of us like a couple of fiddles hoping our strings break."

"No. This is it. I swear," I say.

"This is it," Benny mimes, voice high. "My ass."

Randall's eyes bore into me, and I glance back down the road where Tank is lashed to the buggy. I *need* to see him, just a glimpse that lets me know he's still there, still with me, but I can't make out much through all the moss and ice.

Randall draws even closer, his rotten breath spilling over me in droves. "You see, I been lied to all my life. By my momma. My daddy.

Hell, even my bitch of a wife when she was still alive, God rest her soul. And when they lied, guess what they all had in common?" He smacks his lips and waits for my answer. I can't look at him. My attention shifts to his muddy boots and the bramble poking through the slush around his ankles.

"Guess," he prods.

"I don't know."

"They never looked me in the eye."

My gaze snaps up, and I know this is it, that I'm dangling over the edge of a cliff, staring into the abyss, looking at the kind of fall I won't recover from, and if I say the wrong thing, if I stumble even a bit, it's over...for me, for Mac and Tank, all of us.

I slam my hands into his chest and shove him back as hard as I can. "What did you expect? A mansion? A resort? How about a sign blinking down in bright red letters that lets everyone know it's here? Of course, this isn't the shelter. It's *beneath* it. There's a retractable panel in the basement, and if we don't hurry the hell up, Tasker's going to find it before we do. And once he does, there's no getting in."

He nods, slowly at first, his teeth brown, his gums thin, pink strips curling back into his mouth as a smile drifts across his face. "There's my girl. There she is." He motions to Benny. "Go get that dipshit and bring him over here. Tape his mouth first, though—I got a plan."

———

Randall's "plan" is as simple as it is terrifying. One that will end with Tank full of bullets. I reach for his shoulder when he tells me, my heart giving a frightened lurch. "Don't do this," I beg. "Please. I've got a better—"

He backhands me. Hard and fast.

I thump down into the snow with my left ear blaring, blinking once, twice, before Benny materializes above me with a grin. Behind him, Tank makes muffled *mmff! mmff!* sounds, his hair all sharp, platinum points, his eyes wide, his face flushed, duct tape circling his mouth as he strains against Randall to reach me.

Benny loops an arm around my neck and rips me to my feet so hard my teeth clatter. "Told ya it wasn't gonna be long, bitch." He cinches his elbow tighter as Randall ticks off orders to Tank—these hissed snippet words I can barely hear.

"—gonna do this, or she's gonna get cut...a bullet in her head... swear I will." He smashes a fist into Tank's gut, and he crumples to the ground.

"Nooo," I groan.

Randall spins on me, a vein throbbing across his forehead. My vision flickers.

"Give her here."

Benny shoves me into his arms, and Randall seizes my wrist and twists it painfully behind my back. A flare of heat cuts through my shoulder. A blowtorch of pain. "Go 'round back and wait for the shots," Randall tells him. "Once you hear the Cowboy start firing back, you're good."

Benny twitches like a freshly lit firecracker, then pulls a black revolver from his waistband and slips into the woods, becomes a shadow, and then fades to nothing at all.

"You don't have to do this, Randall," I manage to choke out through clenched teeth. "I'll get you in, I promise."

"Shut up," he barks.

I wriggle forward. "Tank, stop!"

Randall hikes my wrist higher, and something in my back pops. A cry works up my throat. Tank pauses at the tree line, his shoulders heaving with each breath as he turns and glances back at me. I can barely stand to hold his gaze, to look at him like this. Captive. Subdued. Broken.

"Well, go on then," Randall drolls. "Git. And make sure it looks real." He grabs my hair and jerks. "Or you know what will happen."

Still, Tank stares at me, the empty Glock duct taped to his hands, the barrel aimed at the snow. Randall shifts and presses something hard to my temple. His pistol. "You need me to say it again?"

Tank gives a slight shake of the head, his eyes baleful. Red rimmed. "Then go."

He does, and my heart carves through my chest. One look at the gun in Tank's hand and Tasker will kill him. Randall chuckles and nudges me toward the trunk of a blue spruce, holds me there.

"Once the Cowboy is busy shooting your boyfriend, Benny'll mosey right on in and pop him from behind. Now, all we need is some popcorn."

Tank eases into the open with a cautious glance. I look away—I cannot, *will not* watch this. Randall grips my chin and forces it up. "*Ohhh* no. You're gonna watch. Every second of it."

"I won't open the shelter," I spit. "You'll never get the codes from me, you—"

He crushes my cheek into the tree and grinds the bark into my flesh. "Listen here, you foul-mouthed cunt. I've had enough of your shit. You ain't in charge. You never was." He grabs my hair and yanks my head higher toward a blood-streaked sky. "You see that? We got us a good half hour or so before the dinner bell rings, and I intend to be locked away safe and sound by then. So, you're gonna do everything I say, or I'll scalp that brother of yours forehead to neck and force you to eat it. Understand?"

Blood thrashes against my eardrums. Tears cloud my eyes. I blink, nod.

"Good." He raises the gun toward the cabin as Tank limps into the yard and nears the porch. "Just a little closer. Then the fireworks can start."

My eyes click left to sodden branches and needles. Right to dead air. Down: the toe of Randall's boot.

Smash it!

No, his boots are steel toed. All around it twigs and brush. Useless. A flash of silver draws my focus higher. To his waist and the hilt of a knife.

My knife.

I torque down with all my weight and lunge for it. My cheek shreds as it burns across the bark, my fingers open and desperate. For a horrible moment, I can't reach it, can't escape his grip, but then his knees buckle and my hand closes around the hilt. I pull the knife free and plunge it into his thigh with a sharp strike, twist it, and hit bone.

"TANK, RUN!"

A wretched howl erupts from Randall's mouth as the gun explodes near my ear. I slither from his grip and pull the knife with me, wet, gummy sounds crawling up his throat as he topples to the ground.

I burst for the woods, my left ear deaf and shrieking with concussive force.

"You bitch!"

The gun barks again, once, twice: *CRACK! CRACK!* Bullets strike a tree to my left. Splinters sting my face, my cheek.

"Get back here!" Randall's voice is wild, crazy.

My pulse ignites, my breath coming in quick, aching gasps. Blood coats my lips. Branches claw at my arms, at my face and hair. If he catches me, I'm dead.

I windmill through the trees, knocking aside pine boughs and the branches of brittle oaks. Snow rains over my head in clumps. Ice showers my neck and back...and the ringing won't stop; it's disorienting—loud enough that I can't tell if he's right behind me or still lying where I left him.

My foot slips on a patch of wet, uneven earth, and I slam down with an angry dagger of pain. The—*I've really fucked up this time*—kind of pain. Black spots arc through my vision, and I can't breathe. But I *have* to breathe, *have* to move.

The cabin. I need to get to the cabin.

I clutch my ribs and force myself upright and into a crippled jog. Randall bellows behind me maniacally, but already his voice is fading, falling farther behind with every step. Or is it? The ringing in my ear is too deafening to know—this whooshing cotton blare that leaves me dizzy and disoriented.

I risk a glance toward the quickly darkening sky. There's no time to make it up the river to the shelter before the feeders emerge, no time for the happy ending I knew was never really ours to begin with. Only time to kill Tasker and say goodbye to Mac before the feeders take him. It's my last thought before the world erupts in gunfire.

CHAPTER THIRTY-FIVE
BAIT

Randall's assault rifle chatters from the tree line. Bullets snap through the branches. Throaty *Pock! Pock! Pock!'s* that smack the front of the cabin and force my head lower as I stumble through the thicket. Glass shatters. Wood splinters. Metal pings off metal. Another window bursts. Gunfire closer now, snapping back at Randall from somewhere inside. *Tasker.* It *has* to be.

I dash through a copse of aspen and into the backyard, skid to a stop. There's a rustle to my left. A shrill neigh. The *stallion!* Lashed to a post near a decrepit utility shed. He's gaunt-looking, severe, his ribs scraping his coat like he's been ridden for a week straight instead of two days. But *alive.*

He whips his mane and lurches away from all the noise, the whites of his eyes flaring with pure panic. I whisper to him and tell him to calm down, and he stills for a moment, chuffing at me with a soft blow of his nostrils.

Another volley of gunfire. *Get inside, Brynn!*

Knife in hand, I edge toward the back porch, about to rush for it when a sudden bolt of pain tears through my abdomen. The cramp is hot molten agony ripping through my quads, flooding my calves.

I double over and a string of saliva bubbles off my lip. My entire world narrows to this moment, every molecule of my being vibrating because I...

Can't. Fucking. Move.

Motion ripples through the kitchen window. I glance up to sharp cheekbones and thin hair—a face behind the glass. *Shit!* I topple over and force myself into a crawl, work my way behind a pile of old plastic chairs, and pray Benny didn't see me. He can't see me. *Not yet.* I think of Mac lying in a pond of blood, his body riddled with bullet holes, his face lifeless and slack, lips blue. It's what will happen if Benny finds out what I did to Randall. My mouth goes sticky at the thought. I tighten my grip on the knife.

Please don't see me. *Please...*

There's a rattle on the porch. The *thwack!* Of a screen door, and I know, I just *know,* I'm screwed, that he *has* seen me, but I can't force myself to look up, can only draw closer to the ground and will myself to be one with it, to blend into the snow and simply disappear. Cold ices against my forehead and floods my cheek. My teeth grind together as I work through yet another wave of cramps.

Footsteps clomp down the steps and crunch toward me. "Well, well, well. You're just full of surprises aren't cha? You gonna keep up the hide-and-seek act, you dumb bitch? You know I can see you, right?"

I stand, trembling, as clumps of snow fall from my hair and coat. *Keep it together,* I tell myself. *Think.* Smile lines crease his cheeks like dirty, half-open umbrellas. He raises his aviators, his eyes glittering over his swollen, broken nose. The way he looks at me—lecherous and wanting—sends spiders racing over my skin; it's like he's a tiger and I'm a wet bucket of meat.

I stiffen as a bullet ricochets on the other side of the house. His smile broadens. "Don't worry about the gunfight. My uncle will keep your boy entertained for a while. Long enough for us to finish what we started on the road, anyway." He wags his revolver—the one he has aimed at my chest. "Now tell me, naughty girl, how'd you get away from Randy?" His eyes trail down my arm as he says it, his pupils hardening at the bloodstained knife dangling in my hand. They flick back up—now two blazing dark coals. "Oh, you bitch. You clever, nasty little bitch. Drop it."

"No." *Keep coming, asshole.*

He takes another step and cocks his head. "You're about as dumb as they come. If you'd just played by the rules, none of this shit would've happened. We might even have been inclined to let you loose at the end. But no...you had to go and complicate things. Make them difficult. Now the gloves are off. Us tying up your boyfriend and slapping you around a little bit? That was nothing. Just you wait and see what I'm going to do to you now." His left hand drops to his belt, to his groin. He gives it a tug. I'm shaking so hard, I feel like I'll crumble and come apart. But I have to press him, have to draw him closer. It's my only chance; what I know and what he doesn't.

I glance at his crotch with a laugh. "Pff, I doubt that thing even works."

His eyes go feral. *Ding! Ding! Ding!*

"Oh, it works all right," he growls, "and I'll show you just how well."

Push that button. Keep him moving. Just a little more now. "On little boys, maybe."

His mouth twists into a snarl, his cracked lips thinning. "You slut," he spits, stomping toward me. "You little whor—" His right leg punches through the snow and his eyes shoot wide.

"Goodbye, Benny," I say with a wave.

"No!"

He lunges at me, his arm windmilling for my ankle, snaking for my boot. His fingers sink into the snow and drag back, carving little trenches through the powder as the hole consumes him. A last flash of oily skin and he's gone. The feeder trap unleashes a hot blow of rot that forces me back a step where I stand breathless, heart thudding, curling and uncurling my fingers as I stare down into empty nothingness.

Go. Move.

I race around the hole and dash up the rickety steps and lurch for the screen door, which is busted, splintered where Benny kicked it in. I blow past it and slip into the kitchen. The smell hits me first: a miasma of spoiled food and stale air. The dank reek of earth and mold. Curdled milk. There are dishes everywhere, cluttering the sink and the counter, infesting what little free space lies between a jumble of cereal boxes and empty cans on the table. Wallpaper chokes the room in a swirl of chrysanthemums and daisies, twisting higher toward a gluey strip of crown molding.

Gunfire rattles above me as I make my way into the living room. Heavy footsteps send spirals of dust shivering from the ceiling. Angry voices. A painful yelp. Then pleading. Begging. Another throaty cry and the roar of a shotgun.

Mac.

I take the stairs two at a time, everything a blur as I round the landing and surge down a dimly lit hall, blow into the room at the end of it, my knife up and ready—aching to plant itself in the middle of Tasker's chest.

There's a blow to the back of my head.

Then nothing.

———

I blink. Everything comes back in a blurry lurch. Gray-black smudges of color blink in and out. Smeary like a Monet painting. Someone is yelling. Snips of words fill my ears.

"—it at? Where's it—"

A jab to my ribs, and I suck in a ragged breath. Another jab and I roll away with a web of pain surging up my side. *No more. Please, no more.* A dull hammer pounds against the back of my head, thumping in time with my pulse. Nausea churns through my gut and threatens to geyser from my mouth.

"Where is it?" the man repeats, his voice husky and raw. *Tasker.*

I pop my jaw and sit up, try to focus. He's crouched in front of me, mantis-like, arms slung over his knees, wearing the same cracked, black leather vest he had on last night. No cowboy hat though, his face drawn and haggard, his eyes red from lack of sleep, his features pinched. *Fucker.*

Warmth drips down my neck, and my hand shoots to the back of my head. My palm comes away drenched in blood. *Oh, God.* It's smeared all over my jacket, my jeans, this dark vermilion sheen that makes it look like I've been stabbed about forty-seven times. A thought spears through my brain: *He's killed me. I'm dead. I'm—*

"You're fine, Brynn. *Fine.* It's not yours, it's his," Tasker says with a quick nod behind me. I turn and nearly puke at the bits of skull and brain spattered over the floor, the shiny remains of a man's head. A pelt of gray hair is pasted over half his face, the other half gone, blown away. Beside him, a shotgun stands propped against the wall.

Tasker smooths his mustache. "Bastard must've been hiding up in the attic or something. I knew someone was here. Couldn't find him, though." He waves at the shotgun. "He tried to spray me with that thing, but I turned it on him before he could. Just managed to spot him coming down the hall. Then in you come like Rambo with that knife of yours. I had no idea it was you."

I whip my gaze over the room. It's empty, the walls pocked with bullet holes, the floor covered in drywall dust and plaster. Shards of glass speckle the floor, and there's a long swipe of blood painted beneath the windowsill. A mattress is shoved next to the closet along with a pile of blankets. There's nothing else. No *one* else.

The air around me explodes. Bullets punch through the wall and pound into the far side of the room. I flop down and cover my ears. Tasker scrambles to the window and unloads a few rounds of his own, cannon shots from his .357 that are even louder, and then circles back.

"Bastard's gotta be out of bullets soon," he says out of breath.

"Where's Mac?" I ask, frantic.

Tasker frowns. "He heard you scream. Or at least thought he did. I told him it was impossible. That there was no way."

My eyes narrow. *I bet you did.*

"But he wouldn't listen," Tasker continues, oblivious. "Said it was you. That you needed help. He was gone before I could stop him."

Christ. I steal a quick glance through the shattered window. The light has turned to ash, all the sharp edges dulled to a buttery smear. Not long now. Maybe twenty minutes. Maybe less. I push up. Tasker places a hand on my shoulder and shoves me back down. "You're not going anywhere. Not until you tell me where the shelter is."

I catch the shadow of motion behind him a half-second too late. There's a dull thud and Tasker's eyes roll toward the ceiling. He wavers in place for a moment, then folds in on himself and topples to the carpet. I skitter backward and press against the wall. *Randall!* He must have snuck in while we were—

"Hey, hey. Calm down. It's me." It takes a second before I recognize the hair and eyes, the gun in his hands, jutting from a ball of tape.

"Tank!" I say, scrambling for him. "God, I thought you were dead. I thought…"

"No. No, I'm okay thanks to you." He nods behind me. "That him? Tasker?"

"Yeah."

"And your brother?"

"Outside. Looking for me."

"Shit. What do we—" his eyes flick toward the corpse. "What the hell?"

"It's the guy who lived here. Forget him. Here, give me your hands."

He does, and I sink my teeth into the tape and rip a piece free. "The horse I told you about is out back. The stallion. You need to go get him." I spit the tape out and tear off the rest. "Meet us out back. I'll get Mac and we'll go."

He shakes his head. "Hell no. Not with those psycho hicks outside. Not to mention this close to dark. We'll get torn up."

"I'm not leaving Mac. And the feeders won't touch me."

"What are you talking about? Of course, they will."

"Alan injected me with something as a kid. Some serum. Micro-dosed me for years. I think it's why I survived last night. Why they went after Alan and not me." I grab his coat and shove him toward the hall. "It's why I'm alive, Tank."

He stares at me blank-faced, finally opens his mouth. "Doesn't matter. Those two are still out there."

"No. Benny's dead. I lured him into a feeder trap. Randall's all that's left, but I stabbed him in the leg. He won't be able to catch me."

His eyebrows arch. "Damn, Donovan. Remind me never to get on your bad side." He squeezes my hand and sighs. "Fine. We get your brother, but we do it together. Then the three of us bunk down here for the night."

"We can't. There's no light. No power. They'll swarm the house. I have another idea."

"Of course you do. What is it?"

"We reach the shelter tonight."

"Uh-huh. And just how are we going to do that?"

"The horse."

He glares at me. "That horse will never make it that far. You said so yourself."

He's right. I did... and he won't. But I have one last desperate gamble to play. One final card up my sleeve that may or may not get us all killed. There's just one thing I have to do first.

CHAPTER THIRTY-SIX
A DISH SERVED COLD

Tasker.

Groaning and rubbing the back of his head, hand sweeping through those dense straw curls.

Tasker.

The man I trusted with my life. With Mac's. The man who was there for me when Alan wasn't. The man who loved my mother.

Tasker.

Mac's father. The man who betrayed Alan. The man I'm going to kill.

I raise his .357 and level it at his chest, slide my finger over the trigger, and pause as his eyes flicker. He moans and tilts his head up, focuses on me, on his gun. In my hands. His eyes clear. "Ah, shit."

"Sit up," I order.

He does, pushing himself against the hallway wall where Tank and I dragged him to escape Randall's gunfire. He fingers the back of his scalp and winces. "I don't suppose we can talk about this?"

I shake my head. Several bullets thud into the room, the sound dulled by all the drywall. Tank nudges me. "We gotta go."

Tasker holds up a hand. "Wait. Just wait a sec."

"You screwed me, Tasker," I reply. "How could you do that? To me? To *Alan?*" I think of him writhing on the couch, on the floor. The feeders devouring him. How his face jerked as they tore into him. My eyes constrict. "He was your best friend. He would have done anything for you."

"You know why," he mutters.

I want to punch a hole through his heart and watch him suffer. I want to gut him with my knife. But I can't. As much as I hate him for taking Alan from me, for stealing Mac and putting him in danger, he's still family. A shitty, abusive, back-stabbing sort of family, but family just the same. So, I'll give him the same chance he gave Alan.

His eyes remain on the gun. "Wait, wait. Now just hang on a moment and—"

I pull the trigger. I'm not one for guns, a clumsy shot at best, but I'm close enough that it doesn't matter. The .357 recoils and the bullet punches straight through his quad. He buckles forward with a cry.

I turn to leave.

"Brynn... damn it. Hold on, will you?" He tears off his vest and ties it around his thigh with a hiss. "I didn't want things to turn out like this. With you. With..." He snorts out something between a laugh and a cough and tries again. "I—look, just promise me you'll find Mac, okay? Keep him safe. Tell him I..." He blinks, looks away. "Tell him I tried."

I say nothing, suddenly ashamed of what I've done. I should feel better about this, should feel vindicated, but I don't—all I feel is *empty.*

Tank nudges me again as a fresh round of bullets tear through the wall. "Brynn..."

"Goodbye, Tasker," I mumble.

He winks at me, and I can't help but think I've made a mistake, that I've somehow screwed up. And maybe I have. But I don't have time to think about it or the luxury to care. I turn and rush down the stairs without looking back.

———

Outside it's nearly dark, the sky laced with orange vapor trails of light. The last bleeding edge of the day peeks over the mountains—hulking, dark giants eating the sun. And it's cold, getting colder, only a few minutes to find Mac before night closes in and the feeders emerge.

Tank heads for the horse, but not before I death-grip his arm and pull him back. "Search the shed. We need light. As much as you can get, okay? Look for anything we can use. Gas. Propane. Whatever."

He gives me a hard look. "You better know what you're doing."

"I do."

"Be careful, Donovan."

I nod, and we split up, me jogging for the woods, Tank running toward the shed and the stallion. It's a bad plan. He has no clue how to control a horse, much less ride one. If he pulls it off, it will be a miracle, and that's what I'm down to at this point: miracles.

The .357 feels heavy in my hand as I bolt into a strand of pine, my brain a scattershot of frenzied thoughts. I can't hunt for Mac quietly, hoping to stumble across him like I'm on some Sunday morning Easter egg hunt. I'm not that lucky. There's really only one option, and if Randall hears me, he hears me.

I throw my head back and scream: "Mac! Mac, where are you?"

I wait for the gunfire. For the bullets to howl overhead, but there's none. Just silence and a maze of darkening limbs. I weave through the trees and circle the cabin. He can't have gone far. I call his name again. It's a desperate mother cry—the kind of shriek you hear in department stores when a toddler goes missing. High going higher. Wobbly and unhinged. About to crack. Still no response. Just the thunderous echo of my voice and a slight breeze tickling the pine needles.

"Maaaaaaac!"

Blood hammers my ears. Panic surges and claws at my chest, my throat. I've got to find him. I've *got* to. I catch a flash of pale blue through the branches across the backyard and stop. Was it his jersey? I'm seeing things. Still, I scramble back and squint. Yes, a slice of his jersey beneath a coat! And his face! I blow out of the trees at a full sprint, swerve around an ancient swing set and charge for the far side of the lawn. Charge for *him*.

He looks at me frog-eyed, hands crisscrossing his chest as he waves me back. He snaps his gaze right and mouths something. It's a warning. Him telling me to—

A bullet snaps past overhead and pounds into the house. *Thwack!*

Another pings off metal.

I slip and nearly fall but somehow manage to keep my balance, to keep my feet *moving*. Then it's a flurry of steel, bullets spraying everywhere. Hissing into the snow. Whirring through the air.

A trail of heat singes my bicep and spins me around. Tasker's gun flies from my hand. I crash to the ground and roll. *Cover... find cover!* The thought is the only thing that keeps me alive. I spot a pile of firewood and leap for it as a pair of bullets rake the snow where I was a moment earlier. *PUFF! PUFF!* Wedge back against it and curl into a ball.

My first thought: *I'm hit.*

My second: *Jesus, does it hurt.*

I slide a hand over my mouth to keep from crying out.

"Gotcha!" Randall's voice spikes from the tree line, sounding like he just hit the target at the county fair.

The sting is fierce as I finger the sleeve of my jacket and gingerly roll it up. There's blood...but not much. A trickle. A flesh wound. The gun barks again, and several bullets thunk into the pile of wood, the sound like eggs cracking, only louder.

Then nothing.

Only the wind and the beat of my pulse.

The ragged scrape of my breath.

A rustle bleeds from the edge of the yard, and I know he's stepped from cover. "All right, listen up! I'll cut you a deal. You get us in that shelter of yours, and all's forgiven. I swear."

There's movement to my left—Mac creeping through the trees toward me. I shake my head and gesture for him to go back. He slides a finger over his lips and jabs at the porch. I look, see nothing but chairs and boxes of junk, and glance back at him, desperate. He shakes his head and points higher. This time I spot the shadow darkening the window, and I know what I need to do.

"Hey, you hear me, girl?" Randall bellows. "Look at the sky. Time's up! You're getting us in that shelter right now, understand? Right this minute, or I let Benny loose on your brother."

"Benny's dead," I holler back, struggling to keep the pain from my voice.

"Bullshit." He falls silent, and I can sense the doubt brewing there, the question forming somewhere behind those cruel eyes of his. Then he's roaring, all panicked anger as he hollers, "Benny!

Benny, quit playing around and get out here!"

"Yell all you want, but he can't hear you anymore," I shout. "I lured him into a feeder trap. Watched him scream all the way down."

There's a moment of quiet—that empty, dead space between lightning and thunder—and then he's rumbling through the snow toward me, his gait awkward, his breathing rough. "You're fucking dead!"

I hold my breath at the sight of his boot, his camouflaged leg as it swings around the edge of the woodpile. Then the gun. His eyes. Cold—so much hatred there, so much rage, and for a moment, I think he'll get a shot off, that he'll turn me into a headless corpse when the shotgun roars. Randall's arm vanishes in a shower of meat and bone. He collapses like an accordion, transfixed, his eyes on me the entire way down.

Through the window I catch Tasker staring down pale-faced. He nods at me once before toppling in a lazy lean to the left. A hand brushes my shoulder, and I twist around to Mac grasping at my coat and wrenching me up. I'm shaking so hard, I can barely move. "C'mon! C'mon!" he urges, glancing around the yard. "We have to go!"

I nod dumbly and stand. My pulse gushes somewhere behind my ears. Randall coughs behind me. A sick, wet cough that bubbles up his throat, over and over, louder and louder, until I realize he's not coughing at all. He's laughing.

At me.

I glance back at him, and he picks his head up off the snow with a grim smile, pieces of his arm scattered behind him in a crimson, V-shaped spray. "You're too late," he chokes out, still laughing. "Too... fucking late."

CHAPTER THIRTY-SEVEN
ERUPTION

I spin a slow, terrified circle. He's right. Randall is *right*. Jesus. I've never seen so many mounds before. They heave and jerk all around us, that brittle popcorn sound crackling away like we're standing in the middle of a movie theater lobby. A dry *POP! POP! POP!* that makes my blood run cold.

Mac grabs me and points at the porch steps, eyes wide. "Look."

I follow his gaze and spot the fountain of black bodies bubbling beneath the porch, working through the slats. And not just there. *Everywhere.* They drill in and out of the ground, hesitating and whirling away with deadly-beautiful grace. They surface and tunnel back into the earth like it's made of water, the motion a timer; the same behavior I saw on the road with Alan right before the light washed away. We have minutes left. No, seconds.

Mac pulls close and I slip an arm around him. "What do we do?" he asks, looking at me like I have an answer, which I don't.

There's no way out.

No. Way. Out.

Nowayoutnowayout...

A rattle rises near the house, and the thump of—"

"Brynn, over here!"

—hooves? Yes, *hooves! Tank!*

Mac stiffens. "Who's that?"

"A friend," I say and tug him forward. "C'mon!" Then we're both running in an awkward, crazy dash, swerving around mound after mound as we burst for the horse. Tank rounds the corner, the stallion side-stepping, swaying unsteadily, but moving... *moving*.

My heart leaps. There's still a chance.

The ground surges in front of us, closer to the horse, and Tank whips to the side, nearly falling before righting himself. A moment later he snaps the reins, guides the stallion around the mound, and pulls close. I shove Mac forward, desperate to get him off the ground. "Get on! Get on!"

Tank thrusts a hand down to help, but Mac bats it away and spins on me. "No way! Are you crazy? There's not room for all of us up there. You'll be killed!"

Cracks rip through the snow. A mound heaves a few feet off. Icy jolts of fear sting my limbs. I grab his coat and shove him back toward the stallion. "Mac, I won't. You have to trust me on this. They won't hurt me."

He shakes his head and grips my wrists, his mouth twisting down at the corners. "What are you talking about? You'll—"

"MAC! Just get on!"

With a final, wild look, he scampers up behind Tank. The stallion stamps a mad circle and thrashes his mane. I dart forward and take the reins from Tank and force the horse's eyes to mine, brush my palm over his cheek and beg him to, "Calm down, boy. Just trust me one more time, okay? Just once more. Can you do that?"

He brays like he understands, and I lead him away from the yard and toward the road as fast as my wooden legs will move, which isn't nearly fast enough. When I reach it, there's a sharp series of snaps—a thousand knuckles popping, popping, popping—and I know they're here.

———

The cave is right where I remember it. A hundred yards past the boulders, nestled in a tall thread of pine next to the river. I stare at it, a sliver of fear coating my spine, and just like that, I'm a kid again with Alan crouched next to me and pointing at the bats wheeling into the purple-bruise sky in search of insects. He thought it was beautiful, the way they moved, their fluttery, fluid motions. I thought they looked like bits of ash vomited from a giant mouth, and that if I got too close, a stony tongue might flick out and slurp me inside.

The cave is less than a mile, Bear. Can you believe that? It goes right through to the lake. People do it all the time. C'mon, let's go in. Just a little ways, okay? Alan's breath is warm against my cheek as he says it, his arm suddenly slung around my shoulders and scooping me close. I can smell him, all salt and skin. I can *feel* him so huge and strong. A sharp ache carves through my chest at the memory. *There's nothing to be afraid of. It's only the dark. Here, let me show you.*

The dark before it was truly scary...

"Another way, huh?" Tank hisses down at me from the horse. "Have you lost your freaking mind, Donovan? No way am I going in there."

He's right. It's suicidal, but it's the only choice we have left. We'll never last the night out here.

Feeders flow from the cave in a river of serrated armor. Angular bodies that swarm through the moonlight with frightening speed. Several tilt vertical and quarter their heads as if sniffing the air and, for a moment, I'm certain they'll smell me...or Mac and Tank, but they don't. Instead, they flow around us toward the woods and plunge into the soil to tunnel beneath our feet. It's agony being this close to them, has my legs seizing like mad, and I'm not the only one.

The stallion snorts and stamps, fights the reins, and lurches back a step. I lurch with him, struggling to bring him under control. He's breathing fast...too fast, like me, and he's shaking, already coated in a thin film of sweat despite the chill. If I force him any closer, he'll bolt. Or collapse like the mare. And if that happens, Mac and Tank are screwed. More than screwed. Dead.

"Uh, uh. No way," Mac echoes, his voice barely a whisper—steeped in fear. "We'll be killed in there." He glances at me, bug-eyed. "Even Dad would think this is crazy, Brynn. There has to be another option. We should climb a tree or something. Find some higher ground."

"No," I reply. "They'd tear it apart trying to reach you."

"So this," Mac says, gesturing wildly at the cave, "is *safer?*"

"Yes."

"Like hell," Tank grumbles.

"Like hell is right." I jab a finger at the snow. "Most of them are already out of the tunnels. I can feel it." It's true. The cramps turning my calves to concrete have eased and the stream of feeders leaking from the cave is already drying up.

"Listen, Mac," I continue, "what Dad would want is for us to be together. To be safe in the shelter. And we would have been if I'd just *listened* to him. I didn't, and it screwed everything up." I stare at him, then at Tank. "So, I'm asking you, both of you, to trust me like I should have trusted him. We'll get through this. I promise."

Tank shakes his head, his hair glowing like bleach in the moonlight. "Yeah, I'm not buying that. If we go in there, we're done, and you know it. They'll eat us for breakfast."

"No, they won't," I say nodding to the three torches protruding from the saddlebag. "Not with those."

"Those will give us thirty minutes. *If that,*" Tank spits back.

"It will be enough," I say, grabbing one. It's crudely fashioned, with rough strips of cloth dipped in the kerosene Tank found in the shed knotted around the end. The fumes singe my nose. "It's less than a mile."

"How do you know?" Tank asks.

"Because Alan told me."

He slides a hand over his face and moans. "God. How'd I know you were going to say that? *How?* I should have stayed in Austin."

"But you didn't, did you?" I clap his leg and smile. "Now light them."

CHAPTER THIRTY-EIGHT
THE CAVE

My soul aches as I watch the stallion disappear into the gloam. I don't want to leave him, want to pull him through the mountain and save him like he saved us, but I can't. He'd never follow, and I'd never forgive myself if something bad happened to him. Which it would. He's better off here, in the meadow, where he can graze until someone finds him. Or kills him.

Cold beads of sweat seep from my neck.

What if I've ruined him? What if I've ruined all of us?

The thought chases me into the cave, worthless because we're already ruined, *have* been ruined since the moment I OD'd on the interstate nearly a week ago. All the decisions I've made since then have been nothing more than a few drowning last gasps for air.

The torches are bright. Brighter than I thought they'd be. Enough light to cast a hot glow over the rocks and make them shine like rows of fractured teeth as we pass. Enough light to keep the feeders away for now. Another lie I'm only too happy to tell myself in order to keep my feet shuffling deeper into the cave.

I take the lead and push forward at a steady pace. A fine layer of black grit crunches beneath my shoes, a substance I recognize as ancient bat guano. I search for the culprits hanging above us, hidden somewhere in all the stalactite-peppered limestone, and find none. They're gone, of course—they've long since fled to a warmer climate to hibernate. That, or the feeders got them.

Just like they'll get you.

No. I squeeze my eyes shut for a nanosecond, open them and focus. The cave is otherworldly—like we've been transported to some alien planet with no way out and, for all I know, there isn't one. For all I know, Alan was lying about all of it to get me to wander around inside with him for a few minutes before heading back to camp. *People go through here all the time...*

Something brushes my shoulder and I jerk away, but it's only Tank's hand. "I'll lead. You take the back."

"No."

"Yes. You can feel those bastards. They can't sneak up on you like they can us. You keep Mac and me back there and they're liable to pick us off one at a time. At least with you in the rear, we'll have a chance."

It's a good point, so I step aside and let them pass. So far, there have only been a few small feeders hanging just outside the torchlight, their drills buzzing in odd increments like they're talking to each other, their pitches and tones higher than I'm used to—these warbling shrieks that make me want to jam my fingers into my ears until they fade. But I can't, and they won't, so I try my best to ignore them and continue on.

The rock slants. We dive further.

Deeper.

The passage narrows and forces us to duck in spots. It's damp down here. Thick with must and cold. A wet, penetrating cold slices through my coat and ripples across my skin in the form of gooseflesh. I shiver and try to guess how much time has passed. Ten minutes? Twenty? Longer? I have no clue. Every second down here feels like an eternity; an endless nightmare that's even worse than the endless nightmare outside the cave—something I didn't think possible.

And all around us sounds.

Legs clacking. Rocks shifting. Drills spitting. Shapes bolting away everywhere I swing my torch, *everywhere* I look. There are more of them now. And larger. They crawl over the walls and grip the stalactites, press in on us until I'm struggling to hold it together, to keep the dread from surging up my throat. To stay calm.

If there was another way—*Any. Way.*—I would have taken it. But there wasn't, and if I don't keep my cool, if I don't act like I know what I'm doing, we might as well blow out the torches, hold hands, and sing Kumbaya until the little shits rip us apart. And there's something worse than the vague dread pressing down on me with all the weight of a semi-truck. A truth I don't want to admit: Mac's flame is dimming, and mine isn't far behind.

A clatter rises, and a black shell blurs past my foot toward Mac's. "Get it off me! Get it off!" He spins a wild circle, eyes frantic, lips peeled back from his teeth. Bits of flame rain down from his torch and hiss off the stone as he swings it at his shoes, the fire crackling blue and nearly going out.

I lunge for his shoulder and dig my fingers into his collarbone. "Mac, stop! You keep screaming like this, and you'll bring more. It's gone." I sweep my flame in a circle. Dozens of feeders weave away through the limestone columns and rock outcroppings—a nest of cockroaches with the lights flipped on. They freeze just outside the glow and shiver back again. Hang there and wait.

"It bit me!" Mac says, hitching up his jeans to reveal a nasty gash curling over his ankle.

Tank whirls around, his eyes glimmering orange with firelight. "Hey! We've got bigger problems. Look."

I glance past him, and a cold swell of panic blooms in my chest. Staring back at us are three fissures carved through the rock. One is massive, cutting nearly to the roof of the cave—a yawning sinister laceration I want no part of. The others are smaller, the last nearly half my size, with dark water stains leaching down the limestone in the form of milk-colored crusts.

"Which way?" Tank asks.

"I... I don't know," I reply. "Alan never said anything about the cave splitting like this."

"Just *pick* one," Mac says, playing his torch over the rock, his eyes wavering like pinballs. "Hurry. We can't stop. We *can't*. They'll get us."

"Kid's right. We gotta go," Tank says.

I stride past him. "Hang on. Give me a minute"

"What are you *doing?*" Mac hisses.

"Finding the way," I say over my shoulder. "Just keep the light on them. Both of you."

I lay my hand against the stone near the first fissure. A dull ache swims through my veins. A queasy-hot repulsion: *Nope. Dead End.* I glance at the smaller opening next to it and know there's no way in hell I'm crawling in there. Hard pass. I move to the last opening and trace my fingertips along its edge and feel... *nothing.*

Nothing at all...

"This way," I order.

"You sure?" Mac asks.

"No," I reply. "But it's all we've got."

———————

We press on. The walls tighten again and force us back into single file. I stick to the rear. Mac limps in front of me like a shadow, featureless and indistinct—a child's sketch of a skeleton as he ducks and works his way into a tight gap. I turn sideways to follow and suddenly can't get a breath. It's gone, sucked away by the weight of the rock—this great wall of stone pressing against my chest. Bits of light streak my vision. The air is stale, like no human has ever breathed it before, and all I want is to glimpse the moon and the stars, to lose myself in the unending velvet curve of a night sky. I need light. *Real* light. Not this kerosene-soaked excuse flickering in my hand. This smoking, orange flicker.

I need air. Water.

A bubble of panic: I made a mistake. I took us through the wrong passage.

I've killed us.

No. Not yet, I haven't. I think of Alan, of him lying there on the couch. Dying. Dying *for me.* His voice blows through my brain like a warm rush of wind: *Say it, Brynn. Tell me you won't give up.* The last promise I'll ever make him. One I won't break.

I wiggle from the space an inch at a time until I'm free, a distant crackle vibrating through the rock as I do, this strange shudder that feels like the cave is digesting a meal. Several feeders skitter back as I play the flame in a circle, hovering just beyond the fringe of light, their heads blooming like some terrible bouquet of flowers as they pulsate open and shut.

A thought pricks to life at the sight: *Why aren't they attacking us? They should be attacking us.* This is the place to do it—a place where we can't move, can't run, or defend ourselves. The thought pricks at me as I turn and catch up to Mac. There are feeders everywhere, behind us and in front. I can hear them, sense them. See them scattering away from Tank's torch light—the only one that's still burning bright. They could easily overwhelm us if they wanted to.

So why haven't they?

A smell singes my nostrils—sulfur and vinegar. Nitric acid. It's so strong I can *taste* it. I spit it from my mouth only for it to rush back in with the next breath. Rotten eggs.

"*Whoaaa...*"

Tank's voice filters through the cave full of awe. The passage widens in front of him into a gaping rictus. A jet-black scar torn through the rock darker than the depth of space. A long dark serration that beckons us forward with all the warmth of a skull's mouth hungry to swallow us whole.

Tank clambers over a pile of fallen debris and enters the chamber first. Mac and I follow, sweeping our torches in a broad circle. The cavern is...*big. Massive.* Devouring the torchlight wherever it spills. Stalactites hang overhead like giant stone icicles. Pyramids of glossy black stone rise from the floor, stacked chest high. They're eerie-beautiful as they reflect our flames in a thousand points of light at once—these little flickers of orange and gold radiance that make it look like we're standing in the middle of a cloud of fireflies.

A clack resonates from the far edge of the cavern and my back cramps. Another rattle and my biceps follow. Something's...off. And the reek, it's so strong here, so abrasive, it feels like it will eat straight through my nasal membranes.

Mac spits to the side as if reading my mind. "Ugh. What *is* that smell?"

"It's terrible, is what it is," Tank responds, plugging his nose as he plays his torch over the chamber. He gags and glances at me. "I don't like this. This feels bad."

It does. My skin is crawling, my legs quivering again, filling with that strange, creeping dread. That now familiar heat that lets me know that something is about to go really, really wrong.

There's a crackle nearby. Mac jumps and swings his torch. It whispers blue and smokes out. "Shit!" He smacks the wood like it's a flashlight, like the batteries are dead and it will leap back to life at any moment. "*No, no, no, no.*"

I move to re-light it with mine and stop as a series of bone-on-bone snaps echo off the walls. Pinpricks crawl across my neck, naked terror boiling in my spine. I suddenly know why the feeders haven't tried to attack us, why they ushered us down here in the first place: the perfectly round, glassy piles of stone stacked throughout the chamber aren't rocks. They're feeder eggs. And we're their food.

CHAPTER THIRTY-NINE
FOOD

"What's happening?" Mac screeches as we press together.

Snap! Snap!

I swing my torch and the flame rays over the nearest pile. An egg clacks to the stone and wobbles toward us, something sharp piercing the shell.

SNAP! SNAP! SNAP!

"Brynn," Tank hisses over his shoulder. "What do we do?"

My mouth glues shut. There are too many of them; eggs everywhere I look. We'll never make it, no matter how fast we run. Even with Tank's flame still crackling greedily at the wood, it's not enough light to protect all of us, to protect... it rips through my head thunderbolt: I don't need protecting.

I'm the answer. I have to protect *them.*

I turn and thrust my torch into Mac's hands. "Here, take this. Hold it low. Keep them away as long as you can."

He stares at me, face white and trembling.

"Mac! Take it!

He does, and I dive into my coat pocket and retrieve the knife. The blade nicks my thumb as I pull it out. It's sharp. Crazy sharp.

Good. It needs to be for this to work.

All around us the flare of drills rise, the sound of knuckles popping and cracking. I shrug off my coat and yank up my sleeve. Tank spins my way and spots the knife, looks up, eyes wild. "What are you *doing*?"

I meet his gaze. "What I have to."

I've toyed with suicide. I've researched it—cloudy two a.m. fantasies planted in front of a computer screen scrolling through dreary blog posts. Pills, of course, pills. By the handful. By the gallon. Shotguns are popular. Razors too, but it can't be some pathetic slash across the wrist. Some thinly veiled cry for help. No, if you want a lot of blood, if you *really* mean business, you cut vertical.

I clench my teeth and press the blade to my skin.

And slice.

Blood spits over my arm in a warm gush. The pain is electric. Paralyzing. I clutch my arm and crumple into Mac, who catches me, his voice shooting hot in my ear—"Holy shit, Brynn! Holy shit! Why'd you do that? Why?"—as I crouch and smear my blood all over his jeans, his shoes. Above the right one, the feeder gash is already webbing through his skin, the veins turning black at the fringes. "Brynn, stop it!" he says, pulling his leg away as something hard scrabbles over my ankle. Tank swings at it with his torch, and I move to him while he's distracted and drown his black Gore-Tex pants in my blood, smear it over his shins and boots, my arm screaming with each swipe, tears spilling from my eyes.

He grabs my shoulders and yanks me up: "Have you lost your goddamn mind? You can't do this!"

"I have to! Don't you get it? This is the only way you survive. Whatever's in my blood, they *don't* attack it." I wipe more on his waist, his jacket. He snatches my hand and squeezes.

"Jesus. Enough, already! Let's go."

We fly across the floor, our torches bathing the egg piles in a wicked orange light. *Burst spider sacks.* It's all I can think as hatchlings push through their shells, through their membranes, and emerge writhing and wet. Except they're so much bigger than spiders... and there are so many more of them.

They spill to the rock like a wave of black death, consuming the floor, the walls, the entire chamber now a hideous roil of motion. One that avoids our feet.

It's working... somehow my plan is *working!*

I clutch my arm to my chest and shudder at the pain, at the wet squish of blood swamping my sweater. Snaps of light cloud my vision. The cavern fades in and out. I slow and stumble. Fingers clutch me, keep me upright. I blink and see Mac's hand flying over my forearm, tying his coat around the wound, cinching it with a knot.

"Press hard. Like this." He grabs my hand and shoves it to the coat, squeezes. "Now, come on!"

Then we're running again. Lurching. Jerking left. Cutting right. Tearing between boulders and sharp towers of rock. More feeder piles. Mac's torch winks out and Tank's is all that remains—a solitary beacon of light in an ocean of black.

Bobbing and weaving.

Guiding us on.

Through the haze, the far wall of the cavern appears. Shadows leap across it and spill toward an opening—a fissure that climbs to the ceiling. *A way out.* I risk a glance over my shoulder: feeders are everywhere—an oil slick of them boiling down the piles. Buzzing. Shrieking. Drills firing. My stomach twists at the sight.

"Don't look back!" Mac shouts as we pour from the chamber

and into a tunnel. I wobble-run after him, everything slowing, reality turning to syrup as I fight to remain conscious, to put one foot in front of the next.

I *have* to stay awake. I have to *keep moving.*

Ahead of us, Tank roars and swings his torch at a slew of feeders leaking over the wall. He sends one reeling into a limestone column, and we're through, veering left into yet another series of passages, crunching over bits of white rock, climbing through piles of stone the color of chalk.

Bone.

Bonnnnneees.

A slope of them bathed in pale moonlight.

I gawk at it, and the world rotates. *Press down. Keep the pressure.*

It's like someone else is speaking, telling me what to do. I obey the voice and my arm becomes a sizzling skillet of pain—enough to bring me back. My eyes snap wide. Moonlight again. Draped over a graveyard of rib cages and skulls. Mixing with thigh bones and verte-brae scattered over a field of scree. A bone forest. A graveyard of food for the nest.

Tank sweeps his torch my way. "They're coming. Let's go!"

We scramble upward—up, up, up—my legs going numb. Stupid. They wheel beneath me in awkward angles, they stutter and trip, no longer able to obey my brain. Yet still I climb, stumbling over jaw-bones and crashing through rock. Scaling boulders and working up the slope until, with a last gasp of energy, I fall.

Pain and weight. Concussive force against my skull.

Reality spins and waxes over. My heart thunders fast in my chest. Blood seeps through the coat. I've lost so much of it. *Too much...*

A voice pierces my ears. Words I don't understand.

"Leave me," I slur into the dirt.

"No!" *Mac.* He works his hands around my waist and heaves. It's not enough. I'm too heavy. Another set of arms circle my waist and I'm somehow up again, leaning on Tank. On Mac. Moving forward. Stumbling on.

My legs burn. My lungs. Then air so cold it clears the fog permeating my head long enough to make out the corpse of a long-dead lake. An empty dry scab etched into a sprawling meadow. All around it, massive shadows cut skyward toward a sparkling bright sky, a brilliant mist of white strung overhead like a handful of powdered sugar. *Stars.* I stop and stare. They're so beautiful, *the* most beautiful thing I've ever seen.

Tank slaps my cheek. "Hey. Stay with us! Focus, Donovan! Where's the shelter?"

Yes. The shelter. What Alan told me on the curb...*look for the pump house.*

It's there—a smudge of a wood shack clad in panels of corrugated iron across the meadow, the rear of the structure buried in the sloping incline.

"T-there. It's..."

My head tilts forward and bounces off my chest.

———

Water.

Water everywhere. Fresh and inviting. A cool, clear blue plane waiting for...something.

Waiting for... me.

Yes.

Why?

Because you're on fire. You're burning up.

I am. My nerves are frying, turning to wisps of smoke, my skin blackening. I *need* water...but it's suddenly so far away. Too far to reach.

But it's not...

How?

Let go. Just. Let. Go.

I want to. So very badly. But no, not yet. There's something else I have to do first.

There's nothing to do. Rest now.

There is. I... I can't. I—

Wake up. You have to—

———

"Brynn, wake up!" A voice leaching through the ether, familiar and gruff. *Tank.* "Shit. She's still out. Let's get her inside."

"I can't get the door open. It's locked!" Mac this time.

"Over there! Break the window!" Tank cries.

Glass shatters and my eyelids flutter open. The world is upside down, everything spinning. Snow. Earth. Sky. Stars. Ground. My arm sloshes somewhere above my head in an agonizing throb, blood dribbling past my wrist. I'm *hanging.* Slung across Tank's shoulder, his jacket scraping my face. "P-put me down," I manage. It's barely a gurgle. One he doesn't hear.

"Get it open, Mac!"

"I'm trying, okay? Shit. This glass is so sharp. It's—oh, man..."

I hear it first: that familiar skitter. Then the smell hits—a tide of sour milk swimming in bacteria. I tilt my head up and blink. Feeders. More than I've ever seen. An *army* of them. A dark wave glinting in the moonlight, crackling like a thousand splintered bones.

"Oh my... God," Tank, mutters.

Something clicks. A lock.

"Got it," Mac shouts.

Tank spins and we're inside. My arm is a scalding haze of pain, my body knotted and cold as Tank lowers me to the ground and gives my chin a gentle shake. "Brynn. Brynn, hey, can you hear me?"

I swallow and squint up at him. "Yeah." The crackling grows louder. Closer.

Mac appears, holding Tank's torch, his hair wild. "She okay? Is she... is she dead?"

"No," Tank says, "not yet. But if we don't get her—"

"I'm fine," I whisper, my mouth dry. Sticky.

"My ass you are." His jaw tightens. "Brynn, is this it? Is this the shelter?"

A drill ignites. Another. Hundreds. Thousands. Tank glances toward the door and then back to me, his lips twisting into a grimace. "If this isn't it, we gotta go. Right now, before they surround us."

I lift my head. It's tough to tell with the torch flickering like a child's night light, spattering the room in leaping shadows. Sheets of tin rise from a concrete slab, tacked to a naked wood frame, everything brittle looking, as though the entire structure would come apart in a stiff breeze. There's some sort of irrigation pump on the wall, spitting a tangle of pipes into the ground, and a gas can lying next to it, caked in rust. Further back, in the corner, a fuse box is mounted to a sheet of plywood. There's nothing else.

"I—I don't know," I manage to choke out.

Mac crouches and cups my cheek. "Think, Brynn. *Think*. What did Dad say?"

"He said to look for... for a..." A panel. *The fuse box.* "Here. H-help me up."

Tank loops a hand through my armpit and pulls me to my feet. The world tilts and splinters, my legs unable to hold my weight as he barks orders at Mac. "Get over to that door and keep an eye on them. Let me know when they're close."

He nods as Tank drags me, woozy and spinning, toward the back of the shed. We reach the fuse box, and he pulls the cover open to a keypad—one he jabs at furiously with no result. "Dammit! Powers out."

"They're coming!" Mac cries.

"There," I say, pointing to a lever next to the box. "Try that."

Tank flips it and the keypad flickers green, a single word glowing in the center: CODE. Beneath it, a digital keypad with eight digits.

"Quick. What is it?" Tank sputters.

Black spots flood my vision. My head droops. I know the answer, but I can't seem to dig it from the wet cotton of my brain. "Alan said it was...it was..."

"Brynn! C'mon!"

Mac's birthday! I spit it out: "Eleven, nine, two-thousand-eight!"

Tank punches it in and the keypad buzzes. "Dammit! I can't see for shit in here."

"We're out of time, guys," Mac yells. "They're here!"

The world explodes into sound as he says it—drills rising outside like tornado sirens, high-pitched and screeching. They puncture tin and fracture cement. They swell through the air until I can feel them vibrating my bones. The shed won't survive this. We won't—

A smell cuts through the thought—the sharp scent of gasoline. I glance back to see Mac sloshing it all over the walls, the door. *Shit*. I know what he's about to do.

I hammer Tank with my elbow. "Again. Try again!"

He punches the code into the keyboard with a trembling finger and this time the keypad flashes and retracts upward. Behind it, another screen blares to life, this one with bright red letters that blink: IMAGE PLEASE.

"Take this, assholes," Mac screams behind me. There's a hot whoosh and a blaze of light as a curtain of flame consumes the door, and then the wall. The heat is immediate—we have minutes left before we all burn.

"Shit! What image?" Tank says. "How do we make this thing work?"

I flash to Alan. What he told me: *The tattoo—it's the key, Brynn. The only way in.* I go for my sleeve... and stop, stare stupidly at the coat there, knotted around my ruined arm.

"Brynn! What image?"

"It's a scanner. But we can't use it. I... I messed up, I—"

He shakes me. "Stop! Just tell me how it works."

"The first tattoo you gave me. The swallow. It's the key!"

"So, use it, already!"

"I *can't*," I say, raising my arm. "I cut through it in the cave!"

"Oh, no," Mac mutters. "We're dead..."

"Wait," Tank says, his eyes suddenly glittering through the smoke. He hands me off to Mac and tugs up the sleeve of his jacket, shoves his arm in front of my face. "*This* tattoo?"

My mouth goes dry. "Yes... but how?"

"Alan said it had to be perfect, made me ink it on myself first."

He turns and slams it against the screen. A light sensor flashes over his arm and rises back up again. Nothing happens. A vein snaps across his forehead. "We have to get out of here."

"We—" I cough the smoke from my throat. "We can't. They'll kill you out there. Try it again."

"No. There's no"—he covers his lips and hacks—"no time."

Mac pulls his shirt over his mouth and shields his eyes. The flames are roaring now, spreading above us, currents of heat boiling down. Outside, the drills scream.

"We have to—"

A sharp *CLICK!* echoes through the room. I whip my head toward the sound as a vertical seam of light splits the far wall and widens to reveal a door! Camouflaged by tin. Impossible to see until now. Sliding open...

My vision melts. The room spins, smoke soaking into my lungs as I crumple to the floor.

"Brynn, get up!" Tank roars.

I shake my head and slur out words that don't make sense. My tongue has gone fat, useless.

Pressure on my wrist, a hand gripping mine, another grabbing the other, and then I'm sliding over the floor, staring up through thick coils of smoke. Sheets of flame roll over the ceiling, liquid and alive. A rafter cracks, sparks singing my lips, my forehead, my vision smearing to a bubbling, orange-gray sheen. The door was a lie. A dream. Everything was. Voices call down and beg me to hold on. Tongues scream at me using words I can't understand.

And I don't care to anymore.

There is no shelter. There never was.

I don't care, I don't care, I don't care...

CHAPTER FORTY
SHELTER

**Opiate Withdrawal Timeline:
Phase 3**

Length:	Up to two months (but let's be honest, you'll never really feel like yourself again).
Symptoms:	Mood swings. Anxiety. Insomnia and depression. Fatigue. Cravings, cravings, cravings.
Summary:	One day at a time. It's all you've got.

Pain.

Endless, ungodly pain.

My entire existence.

All I know. All I am.

Pain.

———

At times there are voices. Whispers in my ear that cut through the agony. A murmur here. A sigh there. They want to help me, to bring me back to... somewhere... to some*place*. A place that matters.

To them. Not to me.

It used to, but not now. Now, it's too far away, and I'm too tired, and I just want to disappear. It would be the best thing, really, for me to disappear. For everyone. *The best thing...*

———

Light. Sound. A frantic gulp of air. My eyelids twitch. My arm throbs. It's stuck, hands gripping it—holding it down. And I'm freezing. So cold. My heartbeat feels all wrong. (*Ba-bum, ba-ba-bum, bum... bum.*) I try to move and can't. There's a buzzing near my ear. *Feeders!* They're all over me, crawling up my legs, plunging into my chest. A drill revs and surges for my neck.

"Keep her still!" a voice commands. "Hold her down if you have to!"

The hands shift to my shoulders. Weight presses down on my ribs. Words: "*Hey, hey.* I'm right here, Brynn. You're going to be okay."

A lie. The voice is tight, panicked.

I gasp for air. In. Out. Out. In.

Air that doesn't come. And then I'm suffocating—shrieking and crying, thrashing, the taste of blood in my mouth, spit coating my lips, until a sting pierces my arm. Then the blackness closes in again. That heavy crushing dark where all I feel is nothing. And that's just fine by me.

———

Fog. A cloud of chemicals eating my flesh. I want to escape it, *need* to escape, would do anything to, but I...

Can't.

Fucking.

Move.

My legs are carved from stone, my arms, sticks tacked to my shoulders. I'm a chalk outline sketched onto the sidewalk. A smiling, cement smudge waiting for rain to wash me away.

Faces appear. Lips that slice into cruel grins as they pass. Others offer curt nods. One a tip of his cap. I try to call out to him, to scream for help—*Please, God. Please someone help me!*—but when I do, I find my tongue is gone. In its place is a snake, one that sinks its fangs into my gums and fills my mouth with its bitter poison.

———

Fingertips brush my forehead, a soft voice rushing into my ear.

"Sweet girl, I've missed you so much."

The tone stirs something tender in my chest. Something painful.

"Can you wake up for me?" the voice asks. It sounds like wind chimes; like a warm, summer sprinkle kissing fresh leaves.

No. Let me go.

"We need to talk. Just for a minute. Then you can go, I promise."

My eyelids rise to a slice of lush green countryside, trees and grass folding in all around me. A patchwork of primrose and lilac bloom in delicate shades of pink and purple, a woman sitting among them, her hair the same color as Mac's, her eyes like sea foam.

I *know* her. How do I know her?

"M-mom?"

"Hi, baby," she says, reaching out and trailing a finger over my cheek. "So beautiful." She smiles, and I flood with warmth, which is good because I'm cold—so very cold—and being close to her like this, just seeing her again, is like feeling the sun kiss my skin after a lifetime of winter.

I realize I'm crying, tears cutting down my cheeks in streams. "I've missed you so much," I say, reaching for her. "Where have you been?"

She pulls me close and cups me to her chest. "With you, Brynn. *Always* with you."

"I... what I did that night..." The tears come harder. "I'm so sorry, Momma. I didn't mean for that to happen. If I hadn't grabbed the gun..."

The tears come harder, and she presses a finger to my lips. "It's not your fault. It was *never* your fault."

I take her hand and pull it to my heart. "I want to stay here. Please let me stay here with you."

She shakes her head. "You can't, baby. Not yet. You're still needed."

"I don't care."

"I'm so proud of you, Brynn," she says with a kiss on the forehead. "So proud..."

"Please, no!" I try to keep her there, to hold onto her, but she's already fading, blurring away.

———

My eyes click open.

Tank crystallizes above me, his face a mash of concern—jaw clenched, eyes in a squint, a single vertical crease baked into the bridge of his nose. "Welcome back," he says, leaning closer. "How are you feeling?"

"Like shit," I groan. I'm shivering, my skin a sheet of ice despite all the blankets piled on top of me.

"You lost a lot of blood. If Mac hadn't wrapped your arm like he did, I don't think you would have made it."

"Where am I?"

His lips curl into a half-smile. "The shelter. You did it, Brynn. You got us here."

The *shelter*. I sit up. Pain rips down my arm and Tank gently guides me back to the bed. "Whoa, take it easy there, killer. I spent way too much time patching you up for you to undo it so quickly."

I don't want to take it easy. I want to leap out of bed and see what Alan built. I want to sprint through the place and scream that we made it. *We actually made it!* Instead, my head lolls to the side, feeling light, feeling like it's full of helium as I glance at my arm, which is bandaged from wrist to elbow in thick strips of gauze. I look back to Tank, astonished. "Where'd you get all this?"

He waves an arm toward the door. "This place has everything. Your dad stocked it with all kinds of stuff. Antibiotics, sutures, painkillers, you name it. Speaking of." He grabs a container and shakes loose a few pills, presses them into my hand along with a bottle of water. "Take these."

"What are they?"

"The good stuff. But not *too* good, if you know what I mean. Just some ibuprofen."

I nod and pop them in my mouth and take a drink. My throat feels like the surface of the sun. I can practically hear the water sizzling off my tongue and turning to steam with each sip.

He grabs the bottle. "Okay, okay, that's enough. You're going to make yourself sick."

"More," I order. "*Please.*"

"Later. First, you need to rest."

My pulse quickens. "Where's Mac? Is he—"

Tank slides his hand over mine. "He's fine, Brynn. He's sleeping. Like you should be. Now rest. You're safe here."

I lean back and close my eyes.

I'm safe...

———

My arm is throbbing like crazy when I wake again (along with the rest of my body), but luckily there's a fresh bottle of water and several Advil waiting for me on the side table. I gulp them down and prop myself gingerly against the wall. In the corner, Mac is snoring in a chair with what looks to be a leather journal spread over his lap. His cheeks are sharper than I remember, chiseled to points, his knuckles scabbed over in spots. There's a vicious-looking cut snaking down his arm that I guess is from our scramble through the cave. And his hair—the way it curls over his brow, his nose pinched beneath it at the tip; I don't know how I ever missed it. He's Tasker through and through. It was so obvious. All this time.

Tasker.

I flash back to him tipping over after he shot Randall. The way he looked at me through the window before he crumpled as if to say, *There, we're even.* But we're not even. We'll never be even after what he did to Alan. Still, I can't hate him like I did when he abandoned me at the shop. Not after he saved my life—a life I've filled with too much hate as it is. Too much anger and rage. It's time to try something else.

Mac yawns and opens his eyes, catches me looking at him. He pops to his feet and rushes over. "Hey, you're awake."

"Yeah," I mutter. My voice is still shot, barely a whisper.

"How you feeling?"

"Why does everyone keep asking me that?"

His eyes flick down to my bandaged arm. "Why do you think, dummy?"

"It worked, didn't it?"

"I guess, but it was so stupid, Brynn! Tank said he didn't know if you'd make it. You lost so much blood. I thought…" His voice cracks and he shakes his head. "I thought you were dead for sure."

"I would have been if it weren't for you."

"That's not true. You're too tough to kill."

"No," I say, "you saved me. You slowed the bleeding with that coat." I grin up at him. "The fire was a bit much, though."

"Yeah, maybe…" He trails off for a moment and his eyes brighten. "You'll never believe this." He leans over and hitches up the cuff of his jeans. "Your blood…it stopped whatever was going on with my leg. It healed it."

I gawk at the skin. It looks so much better. A soft, pale pink instead of the gray I remember from the cave, the dark web of veins gone—nearly healed. "How?" I ask.

"No clue. But it did." He grins. "Wait until you see this place, Brynn. You're not going to believe it."

"So, show me."

"When you're better. You look awful."

"Gee, thanks," I say, trying to push myself out of the bed. I make it a foot before the room tilts and I crash back to the pillow, out of breath. "Okay, maybe you've got a point."

He laughs and pulls the chair close, sits. "I usually do."

"Quit while you're ahead."

His eyes crinkle. "Nope. You're stuck with me whether you like it or not."

I smile and take his hand. "I think I can deal with that."

———

Better takes weeks. I have no energy. It turns out blood really helps with that, and I gave more than I had to spare. My arm itches and burns. Tank cleans the wound and changes the bandages every day. He checks the sutures for infection and tells me what to watch out for—red skin, yellow discharge—his old army medic training in action. I hate being his patient, hate how weak I feel, hate the stitches even more. I want to rip them out and scratch through the skin until my arm stops itching. I try, but Tank yells at me to knock it off, that the cut will take longer to heal if I keep picking at them, so I escape to sleep instead, and when I can't do that, I lay still and suffer.

And suffer and suffer.

———

My room is small, spartan even, about the size of a college dorm. The walls are beige, the ceiling white. There's my bed, a recliner, and a small trash can in the corner tucked beneath an air vent with a fan kicking off and on every thirty minutes or so. I make a game out of it and try to guess how much time has passed since I last woke up. That's the extent of my entertainment—sleeping and guessing at the time. Without windows, it's impossible to tell.

When I'm lucid enough, I rely on Mac and Tank to keep me from completely losing my shit. They do a pretty good job of it. They bring me water and food. Mostly dehydrated stuff. Ramen. Soup. Mac and cheese. Various beans paired with crackers, everything bland and boring. I try to eat, but it's difficult—my appetite is gone.

Tank tells me something new about the shelter every day. He's like a show-and-tell kindergartener in the way he waves his arms and shakes his head in wonder as he speaks: *Your dad dug a water well. That's why the water tastes so much better than the shit down in Austin. It's fresh filtered. And there's this command center where me and Mac watch the feeders creep around at night. Alan mounted a bunch of exterior cameras. They don't even try to get in here anymore, Brynn. They did at first, but I think it messed up a few of their drills, the little fuckers. Like tore them apart. Whatever shit Alan put in these walls... that hematite or whatever you said it was... it really did the trick. And you should see the generator. It's huge. We can stay down here for years!*

I want to tell him that's kind of the point, but I keep my mouth shut. Hope is in scarce supply, and there's no reason to rain on his excitement, or Mac's, who, at some point, decided to take on the role of stepmom. He dotes on me day and night, reminds me to drink enough water and to eat when I don't feel like it. He walks me to the bathroom after I graduate from the bedpan and supports me on the toilet so I don't topple off. It's beyond humiliating.

In between trips, we share stories about Alan, Mac laughing and shaking his head, me smiling and playing along like I want to talk about him. I don't. Not really. He's already everywhere I look. In the closet stuffed with his clothes. On the shelf layered in disaster planning books and field survival guides. In the stupid pictures he hung on the walls: lots of sugar-sand beaches I'll never go to with blue tropical water I'll never feel. The entire shelter is a reminder—it's like we're living inside of him. Except it's his corpse because he's dead, and nothing I do will ever bring him back.

———

I grow stronger.

Mac and Tank give me my first official tour of the place, and it *is* impressive. There's a great room with floors frosted in warm, coffee-colored tile, a sofa, and a couple of recliners. A giant TV is mounted on the wall next to a dartboard. Beneath it, there's a cabinet containing every board game imaginable: Monopoly, Clue, Sorry, Checkers, Scrabble. A foosball table is perched in the corner, a trunk sitting nearby full of old movies. I guess Alan thought the end of the world would be pretty boring, and so far he's right.

Tank shows me the kitchen. It's stocked with plates, cookware, utensils—the works. Next to it is an industrial-sized pantry crammed with all kinds of food—cans of soup, chili, and stew. Cartons filled with rice, dried fruit and beans, grains, and powdered milk. There are so many bottles of jam and honey on the shelves that I lose count. Boxes line the floor, stuffed with bags of vacuum-sealed jerky, fish, MREs, all neatly labeled, all packed with care. I barely have time to take it all in before Tank pulls me back into the kitchen.

"Watch this," he says, reaching down to open a compartment in the floor—more boxes full of supplies. A container holding various cooking oils. "These are everywhere. There's all kinds of crap hidden around here. And in the ceiling, too. Guns. Ammo. Clothes. Bedding. Medications. You name it, Alan stocked it."

And he did. Everything is here but him.

CHAPTER FORTY-ONE
A FRESH START

One afternoon, several months in, I sneak into the Command Center and settle in behind the large wooden desk in the center of the room. There are several monitors perched upon it, displaying the shelter's perimeter: the dried husk of Carter Lake, the mountains, an old access road overgrown with weeds. A dusting of snow with stalks of dead grass thrusting through the crust, ruffled by the breeze. A nice enough day, but it might as well be blizzarding for all I care. Why spend time looking at what you can't have? The outside world doesn't belong to us anymore, to the humans. It belongs to the feeders. I tell Tank and Mac that every time they ask me to join them on their little excursions outside.

They don't ask anymore.

I'm watching them now on the monitors as they carry a scorched plank from the pump house and dump it into the pit they dug, soon to be buried with the rest of the structure's remains. The shelter door never worked right after the fire. It charred the scanner and fried all the wiring—useless now. Thank God Alan built an access hatch in the rear of the shelter, or we'd be buried, too. Tank says they'll plant grass and shrubs to conceal what's left of the entrance, which isn't much. He's been adamant about that. *No one can ever know we're here, Brynn. Ever.*

He's right, of course. We'd be overrun in a day if word got out about this place...if there's anyone left out there to overrun us.

I turn my attention to the envelope sitting on the desk. The real reason I'm in here: Alan's note. Mac left it for me to read when I was ready. He found it in one of Alan's journals along with instructions about the shelter. All the day-to-day stuff. Operations, emergency procedures, maintenance, that sort of thing, none of which I'm interested in. Only the letter.

I'm not ready, will never *be* ready, to read it. It's all that's left of him. A final conversation. One last goodbye. After that, he's gone for good, nothing left to discover, no piece of him still out there waiting for me to uncover. But I can't wait any longer. I have to know what he said. I have to read it. I owe him that much.

I owe him everything.

With a shaky hand, I peel back the envelope and slide the letter free. An age-worn photo tumbles out and my throat thickens. It's an old picture of us—me sitting on his lap at a company Christmas party, wearing a red silk dress, smiling up at him like he's Santa Claus himself. I flip it over to an inscription: *This one was my favorite. It carried me through...*

I slide it aside—*that's not fair, Alan. Too soon*—wipe my eyes and begin to read.

> *Brynn,*
>
> *I hope you aren't reading this, but if you are, I didn't make it. I'm sorry for that, but it means you did, and that's a good thing. Maybe I finally did something right for once. Lord*

knows I've done enough wrong over the years, made a lot of mistakes. A lot of them with you and your brother. Your mom.

First off, I need you to know something. Losing your mother is the single biggest regret of my life. Not a moment goes by that I don't think about what it cost me. What it cost you and Mac. Sorry isn't a big enough word to describe that kind of pain, and it never will be. If I could turn back time, I would. I'd do it all so differently, but I can't, so that's all that I've got for you, I'm afraid. Apologies.

I heard somewhere that the two most important days of your life are the day you're born and the day you find out why. Well, I found out my why the moment I held you in my arms for the first time. Those eyes, that smile—I'd never felt something so close to God as that day, and I swore I'd do anything, ANYTHING, to protect you, no matter the cost. So when the feeders took my leg, nothing else mattered but figuring out a way to keep you safe.

It's why I was gone so much. I didn't know what I was up against. I had to find other people who believed, who knew what to do. And I did, Brynn. I found them. Some had lost legs and arms like me, others so much more. It made me paranoid. It kept me on the road too long, away from you kids and your mom. But the thing is, I couldn't stop digging. Even if I'd wanted to, I couldn't have stopped. Hell, I even tracked a lead to some Indian reservation near the Grand Canyon. Some rumor about an old Havasupai medicine man who'd been said to have actually captured a couple of these things. The place was near impossible to reach, but I damn well did it. I found him, and sure as shit, he had one.

It had been so long since I'd last seen a feeder, I almost thought I'd imagined the whole thing, that it had all been some sort of hallucination. His name was Running Bear, and he knew more about these things than anyone I'd ever met. He's the one who got it in my head that they came from the oil. That they were planted long ago to protect the earth from our greed. That people woke them.

When I left, he gave me this concoction made from their venom, just enough for one person. It's all he could spare. Only one he said, or it wouldn't work. Told me to micro-dose you with it, said that if I did it long enough, you'd be inoculated. So, I did. I gave you little doses for months until it was gone. Your mother caught me in the end. I'd never seen her so mad. Told me she'd divorce me if it ever happened again. I begged her not to and said I'd get my act together, which I never did. I'm not sure why she stayed with me—I never could give it up.

But how could I? After all I'd seen? After all that had happened to me? I could feel them stirring in the earth, getting closer and closer to waking up. Could feel it in what was left of my leg. There were these cramps. It's hard to explain, but I knew we were living on borrowed time. So, I built this place. Spent every nickel I ever made on it. All I wanted was to keep you safe, wanted to make sure we had somewhere to ride this out together—as a family.

That's it. All of it. The whole truth. I hope someday you'll forgive me, Brynn, and even if you don't that you'll find a way to live. To love. Find happiness in this crazy world if you can. Look after your brother and know I'll always be watching over you two. Always.

Love you, Bear.

Dad

I set the letter down and push back from the desk, my back rigid, my hands shaking. Again, the thought: *He was right. He was always right.* And then I'm crying, sobbing with my head buried in my arms, tears drizzling into my lap, crying so hard I don't hear Mac and Tank slip back down the ladder and into the shelter until Mac knocks on the door.

"Hey, everything all right in there?"

"Go away." My voice is ragged. Ruined.

He ignores me and comes in anyway, a hand sliding over my shoulder. "He left me one, too."

I swallow, take a long, shivery breath. "That's good."

"He loved us."

"I know."

"He was a great dad, wasn't he?"

I nod. The best, and I know what I have to do.

———

"No way," Tank blurts out when I tell him my plan. "Hell no. Are you crazy, Brynn? After all we did to get here?"

"I have to," I say. "It's what he would have wanted." I glance at Mac and immediately regret it. His face is three shades whiter than ten seconds ago. He stares at me with his jaw undone. Hanging open.

"Dad wanted us all here, safe." He waves at the shelter, his eyebrows leaping toward his hairline. "Which we *are*."

"For now," I mutter.

"For as long as we want," Tank adds.

I shake my head. "Nothing's forever." Alan. Vivian. Almost losing Mac. It's a truth I know all too well.

Mac pops to his feet with his hands in his hair. "What's wrong with you, Brynn? Why do you have to make everything so hard?" He stops, exhales loudly. "Look, I know you got really messed up getting us here. We all know that. It's why me and Tank have let you mope around for months on end without doing any of the work."

"Hey, that's not fair," I snap back. "I help out... some." I don't. Not really.

He and Tank exchange glances. Mac rolls his eyes, looks back at me. "I miss Dad, too. Just as much as you. Maybe even more, and he's not even my real dad."

"Mac, that's not true."

His face crumples. "Yes, it is, but whatever. The point is, we've all been through a lot, okay? All of us. Maybe not as much as you. But that doesn't mean you get to take off in search of some guy who may or may not even be alive to find some cure that may or may not even exist. It's insane!"

Tank nods. "Kid's right, Donovan. You know he is. I'm sorry, but you're not leaving."

I glare at him. "It's not up to you."

"Goddammit, Brynn. I always knew you were a bit sideways, and I've always loved you for it, but this is a whole new level of crazy. You want to leave"—he spreads his arms, shakes his hands—"when we've got all *this?*"

"It's a death wish," Mac adds. "She's always had one." He stares at me with such heat in his eyes, I wonder if I'll catch fire. He's right, though. I'll probably die out there. Probably become dinner for some cannibalistic tribe. But how do I tell him I can't sentence him to a life underground in this prison? Because that's what it is: a beautiful prison. Down here, he'll never really live, never get to chase girls around town or drink beers with his dumb friends at college parties. Down here, he'll never become the engineer he's always dreamed of being or learn how to play guitar. He'll never get the chance to fall in love or have kids of his own he can worry about someday. Down here, he might as well already be dead.

And how can I do that to him when I have the key? When I *am* the key.

"You're not leaving, and that's that," Mac finishes, crossing his arms.

"You done?" I ask, popping an eyebrow.

He stares back at me stone-faced.

"Well, are you?"

"You're impossible," he mutters and flops onto the couch. He gives me a sarcastic turn of his wrist. "Well, go on, then. Tell us what you're gonna do because I know you're gonna do it anyway."

"I will if you two will shut up for a second." I dig my fingernails into my palm. I don't want to tell them any of this, but they have to know, or they'll never understand. They'll never let me go. "The thing is," I stammer. "I've been doing a lot of thinking, and there's one thing I can't get past."

"Yeah? What's that?" Mac asks.

"That I'm a shitty person. And I have been for a long time."

"At least it's a solid start," Tank mumbles with a grin.

I roll my eyes at him and continue. "Ever since Mom died, all I've done is run away. From Alan. From the past. From anything hard, really. I mean, I abandoned you, Mac. I left you with Vivian when you needed me the most. I should have stayed."

"It wasn't *that* bad," he says with a shrug. A lie.

"Yes, it was, and I knew it was messed up of me to do it. But I did it anyway." I look at Tank. "And I was a shitty employee. I barely showed up, and when I did, I was wasted."

Tank shrugs. "Well, I mean, you were okay sometimes..."

"No, I wasn't. I skimmed cash from the register whenever you weren't around, not to mention all the pills."

"Wait. You *what?*" He says it with a look like I just spilled hot coffee in his lap.

"You heard me. I stole from you. I never understood why you didn't fire me until I learned about the whole Alan thing. I mean, all I cared about was scoring enough cash to get my next fix. That's all I really wanted. To escape. From what I did to Mom, to Dad. To you, Mac. I couldn't handle it. I hated myself." My gaze drifts lower, to my thumb, which is busy spinning circles on my wrist. "I still do. I think that's why I started taking the pills to begin with. They gave me a way out... a way not to *feel* anymore." My voice cracks on the last word.

Mac's voice softens and he moves to stand. "Brynn..."

"No, hang on," I say, motioning him back to the couch. "You need to hear this. I've been selfish and now suddenly here I am with this ability to walk around with those..."—I wave toward the walls—"...with those *things* out there like I'm one of them, and it's all because of what Alan did to protect me. To protect all of us. I mean, my blood healed your leg, Mac. It freaking *healed* it, didn't it?"

He stares at me, opens his mouth to say something, and shuts it.

"Alan found a way *out.* Not just for this place. Not just for us. For *all* of us. For everyone who's still struggling to survive out there. If I don't try to help them, then what kind of person does that make me?"

"They aren't your problem," Tank says.

"So, what—we should just hide down here forever? Just bury our heads in the sand while the rest of the world gets ripped to shreds?" I push to my feet. "Don't you understand? I *can't* do that again. I can't keep running away. If I do, you might as well round up every pill in this place because that's what it's going to take for me to stay." I thump back onto the chair and stare at them. I'm leaving whether they like it or not. I just hope they'll have my back when I do.

Tank blows out a long, slow sigh, eyes Mac. "Well shit, man. She makes a decent point. What do you think?"

Mac says nothing, just leans forward and holds my gaze for a long moment, his eyes turning pink at the edges. Finally, he speaks. "If you leave, you have to promise me something."

"Name it. Anything."

"That you'll come back."

———

I wait for warmer weather. I take my time. There's no need to rush. Unlike the panic job at the shop, this time the only life on the line is my own. Tank teaches me to shoot a Sig Sauer P226 taken from Alan's weapons stash. It's a wicked-looking gun, which I like, and not very heavy, which I like even more. He shows me how to hold it, how to steady my breathing when I pull the trigger. *Pull it slow. Don't jerk or flinch.* I grow pretty decent at it, enough so to put someone down if I have to. Tank tells me it's the gun the Seals carry, which is good enough for me.

We spend the evenings playing board games and joking around. Mac laughs, but his eyes don't mirror his lips; there's no smile baked into his gaze. I catch him staring at me at times like he thinks I'm already as good as dead out there. It breaks my heart to know he's probably right.

There are questions. How long will it take me to reach the reservation? How long it will take to get back? What do I plan to do when I run out of food? Water? Questions I shrug off. Questions I can't answer. There's advice: Don't travel during the day. Travel at night. It's safer. People are more dangerous to you than the feeders now. Know your surroundings. Know who to trust (families with children and women) and who to avoid (men, mostly).

As the weeks pass, part of me argues to stay, that what I'm doing is reckless, but deep down I know that if I do, I'm condemning Mac and Tank to a life in the shelter, which isn't really a life at all. Not when there's a chance I can find the man who changed my blood. If I can, I might be able to do for them what he did for me—allow them to go outside freely and without fear. And if I can't, there's got to be someone else out there who can.

On the day of my departure, Mac whips up a heavy breakfast of chocolate chip pancakes along with mugs of fresh coffee and biscuits. He puts on a brave face and refills my plate until I can't eat another bite. I know he's breaking inside, because I am, too. Afterward, I struggle to keep from crying as we climb the ladder to the hatch. If I start, I won't stop.

Outside, the morning is chilly but not winter cold—a temperature I can handle—and the cool breeze is wonderful after months of sterilized air.

"You still sure about this, Donovan?" Tank asks.

"No. Not really," I reply, trying not to look at him as I sift through my pack.

Mac jams his hands in his pockets. "Then stay."

I turn, stare at him. "You know I can't."

He nods, mouth tight. "I know."

"Come here," I say, pulling him into a hug. His shoulders have broadened, his arms now cut with actual muscle. He's getting stronger, becoming a man, and deep down, I know he doesn't need me nearly as much as he thinks he does. "I'll be back, okay?" I whisper in his ear.

We separate and he brushes his thumb over my cheek. "You better be, or I'll have to track you down and kick your ass."

"I will. I promise. Once I find a cure."

"You know you're crazy, right?"

I smile. "Yeah. What's new?"

He grins. "But I'm proud of you, sis. Mom would have been, too."

The comment is almost enough to undo me as I turn toward Tank. "Watch out for him, will you, Tank?"

He wraps his arms around me and presses his forehead to mine. "You know I will. And... it's Leo."

"What?" I ask.

"My real name."

"Your name is... *Leo*?" I struggle not to laugh. I'd always envisioned him as a Jack or a Mike. Maybe a Chris. Something tough. Leo is just so... not him.

"Oh, shut up," he says and presses his mouth to mine. His hands clutch at my hair, my cheeks. His lips are warm, and when he pulls away, his eyes shine with tears. I've never seen him cry before. Ever. I wipe one away and trace a finger over his jaw.

"Oh, good God, you two." Mac moans behind me. "Will you get on with it, already? It's too early for this shit."

We all laugh at that, and for a moment things feel normal, light, like the world hasn't completely fallen apart around us. After another round of hugs, I shoulder my pack and turn toward the road. We've mapped it out. West over the mountains and then south until I hit the canyons.

"Six months, Donovan. No longer," Tank says. "Or we come after you."

I nod. Six months. A year. A lifetime. Whatever it takes. I made a promise to Alan that I wouldn't give up. Even when things seem darkest.

And I won't.

WAIT, BEFORE YOU GO ...

Want to know what happens after Brynn leaves the shelter? Want to see what she faces next—when survival is no longer the only battle? Want the first chapter of the sequel to *What Waits Below*—before anyone else gets it?

Get your exclusive sneak peek right now! Just scan the QR code below or click here to get instant access.

I love connecting with my readers. When you sign up for my newsletter, you'll get early access to bonus content, insider news, book updates, and behind-the-scenes stories—never spam, just the good stuff.

One last favor: reviews keep authors alive. If you enjoyed *What Waits Below*, please post a quick review on Amazon, Goodreads, The StoryGraph, or your favorite review site. It makes a huge difference.

Thank you for reading—I wouldn't be able to do this without you.

ACKNOWLEDGEMENTS

Six years. That's how long it took for me to publish this book. Two years were spent drafting the thing. Then another polishing and rewriting it. Countless five a.m. mornings, draining cups of coffee to turn this manuscript into a living, breathing book.

Which I somehow did.

I chased a traditional publishing deal, submitted it to agents, and then, after I had one, to publishers. I came oh so close with several of them—almost making it—but didn't quite cross the finish line. Dejected, I decided to set it aside.

I wrote another novel. And another. I penned a gob of short stories and released a short story collection. By then, publishing *What Waits Below* seemed like a distant dream, and by all accounts, one I should have given up on long ago. But I couldn't. The characters wouldn't let me. They kept stomping around, banging on the inside of my skull, demanding to be let out. They had their own lives to live, and how could I deny them that right?

Listen, writing a book is a magical thing. It grows and develops and comes to life, word by word, page by page, year by year, until it beats with a heart of its own. It speaks to you and whispers in your dreams. It unfurls like a flower in bloom, bearing plot points and character motivations. You laugh as you write, and at times you cry. You live and die with your characters, and they become, in some ways, as real as your closest friends...as your family. It's not unlike raising a child. You want them to succeed, to thrive and achieve their dreams, and your heart breaks when they don't.

As you can probably guess, this book is special to me. I've given it all I've got, and it's time I release it into the wild.

First, and most importantly, thank you to my wife, Jennifer, for always supporting this crazy dream of mine—to write—and for allowing me the space and time to do so in our jam-packed lives. Thank you to my three wonderful girls, Harper, Riley, and Addie, for your constant inspiration and love. You three mean everything to me. Thank you to my parents, Neal and Becky, my wonderful in-laws, Mark and Jan, and to my sisters, Nicole and Elise. I wouldn't be where I am without your support. Thank you to C.P. Dunphey, and the many, *many,* hours you spent on the phone with me, discussing Brynn, Alan, Mac, and Tasker's journeys. They are who they are because of you. Thank you to Laura Pritchett for nurturing my budding writing career, and for helping believe that I could *actually* write in the first place.

Launching a book is no easy feat, which is why I also need to thank the following authors who took time out of their busy days to read and blurb this book: Clay McCleod Chapman, Andrew F. Sullivan, Chris O'Halloran, Carson Winter, C.B. Jones, and Beau Johnson know that your support means more to me than you know. I owe you one.

And of course, thank you, dear reader, for picking up *What Waits Below* and giving it a shot in the first place. Without you, none of this crazy writing stuff would matter.

Until next time,

—Caleb

ABOUT THE AUTHOR

Caleb Stephens is an award-winning thriller author based in Denver, Colorado. He's the author of the psychological thrillers *You'll Never Know*, *If You Lie*, and *The Girls in the Cabin*, and a two-time Colorado Book Award finalist. When he's not writing, Caleb enjoys spending time with his wife, kids, and his furry son, Bodhi—easily the most spoiled member of the family.

To learn more about his work and grab a free story, check out his website www.calebstephensauthor.com, and follow him on TikTok and Instagram @calebstephensauthor.

Read a thrilling excerpt from Caleb Stephens' psychological thriller *You'll Never Know*.

CHAPTER 1

GRANT

"I think we're lost," I say.

"We're fine," Avery replies with a wink, her hand resting loose on the wheel of our white Jeep Cherokee as it rumbles up the rugged road. The Uncompahgre National Forest presses in around us, shadows flickering over the hood, the mountains rising ahead, looking ominous and indifferent.

"How did you hear about this hike again?" I ask.

"I found it on Reddit," Avery says.

My eyebrows rise. "Reddit? Seriously?"

She shrugs. "What? It had a thousand upvotes."

I laugh. I can't help it. My wife is easygoing like that. To her, every moment is a cause for adventure—which I love, but right now I want her to pull over. I need to check the map. The road has split three times already, and I lost cell service miles back.

"Are you sure about that?" I ask. "Reddit also thinks birds aren't real."

"That's not true," she says with a grin. It's a weapon she uses against me frequently. Anytime we have a disagreement, all she has to do is smile: fight over.

"It is, I swear. Look it up."

She returns her gaze to the road. "The thread did say the trail's a little hard to find."

"I'd say it's more than a little hard to find. Here, let me see if I can figure out where we are." I retrieve my phone and try, knowing full well I won't be able to get a signal. The forest is growing thicker by the minute, the trees crowding in on either side of the road like silent sentinels, attempting to block out the sky. "Actually, can you pull over for a second? We might need to turn around."

"No, we don't. We're good. Look." She points, and I spot the gutted remains of the structure ahead. It's the landmark Avery told me to be on the lookout for when we first pulled off the highway—a cabin ravaged by a long-ago fire. It means we only have another quarter mile to go. Still, I can't help but feel a twinge of dread at seeing a building that looks like a blackened skeleton half swallowed by the trees sitting out here in the middle of nowhere.

Avery pops an eyebrow. "Okay, you can admit it now."

"Admit what?" I ask, pretending not to know what she's talking about.

"You know exactly what."

"Fine," I say with an exaggerated huff. "You were right."

"And?"

"And I was wrong. We're not lost. Better?"

Her smile widens. "Much."

A few minutes later, we break from the trees and into a clearing that takes my breath away. The horizon is drenched in a spectacular wave of color. Mountains spring up around us everywhere I look, all of them dressed in vivid suits of blue and green. The peaks climb toward the sky in a dizzying array of granite crags and vertical pitches that are so beautiful they almost look artificial. Living in Durango, I'm used to gorgeous scenery, but nothing like this. The view is stunning. For a moment, it feels like we've been transported to Switzerland.

"Wow," I mutter, hypnotized. "This is amazing."

"So beautiful," Avery echoes as we reach the lot.

She pulls off the road and parks near a sign indicating the trail-head. I'm about to get out and take it all in when she reaches over and lays a hand on my knee. "Wait a second. I have something for you." She slides a small box from the pocket in the door and hands it to me. It's a present, fully wrapped and topped with a white bow.

"Did I forget an anniversary?" I ask, surprised. "What's this all about?"

She laughs. "Open it and find out."

I do exactly that, expecting to see a book or new wallet, but instead find myself staring at a framed photo. At first, I don't understand what I'm looking at. It's nothing but a black canvas with a white blob in the center that—

Oh my god.

The image takes shape and the world outside the car turns to a smear of color. None of it exists—the sky, the mountains, the trees— all of it is gone in an instant. The only thing that matters is what I'm clutching in my palms. The picture isn't of a blob but rather of a head rounding down into a face with a small bump of a nose. Lower, I can just make out a belly sprouting two little legs and an arm caught in what looks like a wave. Because it *is* a wave—I'm looking at a hand growing five little fingers.

"Is this real?" I whisper in awe.

Avery doesn't reply. I look up to find her crying, tears spilling over her cheeks in silent streams. She nods. "Look at the bottom corner."

When I do, I see the baby's stats—a length of nearly six centimeters and an estimated age of twelve weeks. The name Avery Wilson is stamped above them, along with a date. The ultrasound was taken two days ago.

I try to speak, but I can't. I'm unable to push the words past the lump in my throat.

"It's real, Grant," she says. "I'm pregnant."

"But ... how?" It's the only question I can think to ask because Avery can't get pregnant. What I'm looking at is impossible.

"Honestly, I don't know," she says. "My gynecologist thinks it's a miracle."

I continue to stare at the photo in a daze. A father. I'm going to be *a father*.

Me, Grant Wilson.

I'm going to be responsible for shaping a new life.

"Hey, breathe."

Avery's fingertips graze my cheek, and I realize I'm shaking. Words pour from my mouth in a jumbled mush of sound. "I don't ... I thought ... I mean ... wait, how long have you ..."

"Known?" The corners of her lips kick up into a pair of dimples. "A while. A little over two months."

I gawk at her. "And you're just telling me this *now?*"

"I wanted to make sure it was going to stick first." A sliver of fear flashes across her face and her lips firm. "It still might not. We're not out of the woods, yet."

"I still can't believe this," I say, rubbing my forehead. It must have happened in Napa. I relive the vacation in a flash of heat. Our honeymoon. A bougie, sun-splashed week full of luxury and four-star cuisine. And sex. Lots and lots of sex.

A laugh bubbles up her throat, and she wipes her eyes. "Oh,

you'd better believe it. We're going to have a family."

"I'm going to be a dad," I mumble in a daze.

"Yes, you are," she says, laying her head on my shoulder. "Get ready."

When I don't move, she takes hold of my chin and pulls my face toward hers. "Hey, it's going to be fine. We're in this together. You're going to be a great father."

"You really think so?" I manage.

"Yes. Now, come on. I want to get this hike in while I still can."

She gets out, and I follow, the summer sun warming my skin the second I step outside. A gentle breeze ruffles my hair and drifts over my skin.

I'm going to be a father.

"Hey," Avery says, wagging a bottle of sunscreen at me from the other side of the car. "Can you help me with this?"

"Of course." I make my way over to her and she presses the bottle into my palm as she pulls her auburn hair over her shoulder. Besides her smile, her hair was the first thing I noticed when I bumped into her nearly a year ago. Hair so red it stole my breath. As did her eyes. They're this beautiful shade of light green I immediately lost myself in. One look, and I knew I was in trouble.

"Make sure you get my neck," she says.

I don't. I spin her around instead. She starts to protest, but I lean in and kiss her. Her lips soften, and we remain there, lost in each other for a blissful moment, until she places a hand on my chest and pushes me back with a grin. "Save your energy for the hike. There will be plenty of time for that later."

"Fine," I groan, but I don't step back. Instead, I reach up and brush my thumb over her cheek.

Her nose crinkles as she looks at me. "What?"

"I can't wait to do this with you."

"Well, let's go, then," she says, eyeing the trail.

"No." I lower my palm to her stomach and hold it there. *This.*

She slides her fingers over mine. "Me too." With a final squeeze, she snatches the bottle of sunscreen and raises it. "Now put this on."

"Yes, ma'am," I say with a chuckle.

After I'm done, we circle to the back of the Jeep. Avery pops the hatch and swings it up. Lying inside is a backpack stuffed with several bottles of water, two bags of trail mix, and a pair of long-sleeved shirts for both of us in case any clouds blow in.

"Here." She tucks the car keys into the backpack and hands it to me. "This is yours to carry."

"Of course," I say, shouldering it. "So how many miles is this hike, anyway? Wait, are you even okay to hike? What did the doctor say about exercise?"

She rolls her eyes. "I'm pregnant. Women do it all the time. I'll be fine."

"I know. It's just—"

The sound of an engine cuts me off. We turn together in time to see a black van with tinted windows roll out of the trees. I groan. I knew this was coming; a place like this is far too beautiful to keep to ourselves. Still, I'd dared to hope.

"Let's get going," Avery says. "Maybe we can beat them up the trail."

I don't move. I simply stand there, staring at the van as it barrels toward us. It's paint-chipped and covered in rust, the shocks squealing as the tires bounce up and down. The sound is at odds with the peace of this place. And the vehicle is going fast. Too fast. A slash of annoyance cuts through me when it rips to a stop a few feet away, covering us in a thick plume of dust and exhaust.

I cover my mouth and cough. "What the hell?"

Avery takes my hand and tugs. "Seriously, let's go."

But I still don't move. For some reason, I can't stop staring at the idling vehicle with its battered, black body and dark windows. It's ugly and doesn't look like the kind of car a typical hiker would drive. Something about it feels wrong.

Avery pulls harder. "Grant ..."

"Okay, yeah, this is getting weird." I'm about to turn and follow her, when the passenger side door bangs open, and a man steps out. He's big and dressed all in black. Black shoes, black pants, black shirt, black gloves. A black ski mask.

And in his hand, pointing at us, is a black gun.

CHAPTER 2

My blood turns to ice. My existence becomes a series of micro-sensations: the gooseflesh rippling over my arms, every hair rising. The acrid smell of exhaust invading my nostrils and pooling at the root of my tongue. Avery's hand squeezing mine, my palm going slick with sweat.

The rattle and cough of the engine.

The waves of dread stitching up my spine.

Time as it slows and turns to syrup.

Questions rip through my head like bullets: What the fuck is happening? Who is this guy? And what does he want from us? Why is he standing *here* of all places, in the middle of this gorgeous natural oasis, holding a gun?

I don't have time to consider the answers before he says, "Get in the van."

"*What?*" I reply, stunned.

Through the mask, the man's eyes turn to slits. Blue eyes. Eyes that feel like icepicks as they narrow on me. "Are you deaf?" he asks. "I said, get in the van."

I glance at Avery in disbelief. Her eyes are blinking open and shut like she's taking little pictures, trying to work out what's happening one image at a time, her face pale.

"Why?" I ask, turning my attention back to the man.

He laughs but there's no humor in the sound, only menace. "How about we all sit down and I'll fill you in over a cup of coffee. Are you kidding me? Get in the fucking van or I'll shoot you both!"

A voice like speaker static hisses from the back of my mind: *Don't do it, Grant. Do it, and you're both dead.* Not that we have a choice. If we don't do what he says, he'll kill us. I'm positive he isn't bluffing. There's no good outcome here.

"Okay," I say, guiding Avery closer to me. "Just take it easy. We'll do what you say."

"Not you," he says, his gaze shifting from me to Avery. "Her."

Her. The word smashes through my skull like a cannonball. *He means Avery. This man intends to take my wife.*

I step in front of Avery and slowly raise my hands. "That's not happening."

"It's not up to you."

"She's not going anywhere without me."

"Grant..." Avery whispers behind me, but I don't turn around. I keep my focus centered on the man.

"You're not taking her," I say.

He tilts his head and regards me, his eyes narrowing to two blue flames. His grip on the gun firms, and he steps forward and levels it at my head.

My eyes screw shut a second before he fires.

My ears explode. The sound that follows is like a power drill burning through my skull. A high, piercing shriek. One I shouldn't be able to hear because I should be dead. But I'm not.

I'm alive.

How am I still alive?

Because it was a warning shot. He must have moved the gun before he pulled the trigger.

My eyelids click open, and I try to make sense of what's happening. The man is standing right in front of me now, barking words I can't hear through the ringing in my ears. His voice is a muffled throb. It's like he's standing above me, yelling down through ten feet of water.

I shake my head and try to clear the cobwebs. Pop my jaw. "I can't hear you," I say.

It does nothing. His eyes are two electric pools of anger. His entire body is a snarl. I vaguely register Avery's fingertips brushing my arm from behind. I can't let this man take her.

"Don't do this," I plead. "You can have our car. My wallet. Whatever you want, it's yours."

He shakes his head, his gaze coming to rest on Avery.

"No," I say. "*No.* Please listen to me. I can get you money if that's what you want. I just need—"

Before I know what's happening, he slams the butt of the revolver straight into my temple.

My head snaps toward my shoulder.

White lights wheel through my vision.

Sparks firework and hiss in my brain.

My knees buckle, and I crash down. My teeth clack together when I hit the ground, the taste of warm metal flooding my mouth. The tang of iron and copper. Flecks whirl through my vision, and I know I'm seconds away from passing out. But then I hear the scream and the world comes rushing back.

"Grant!"

Avery's scream.

I wince and roll over, see the man dragging her toward the van.

No, no, no, no ...

I plant one hand on the ground and force myself to my knees. Reality flickers in and out in waves. A sticky warmth covers my cheek. Blood. It doesn't matter. Not the fire raging in my temple or the nausea greasing my gut. Not the way I sway like a tree when I take to my feet and nearly topple over. The only thing that matters is saving Avery.

I lurch forward. I will kill this man. I will turn whatever face lies beneath his mask to pulp. I don't care if he shoots me. He's not taking my wife.

But then my vision clears, and I stop. He's no longer pointing the gun at me. He's pointing it at Avery, the barrel planted squarely against the side of her head.

My rage snuffs out in an instant. I raise my palms in a silent plea. Because I know that this man, whoever he is, is capable of violence. He's already proven it. I have no doubt he'll pull the trigger if I take another step.

"Take me," I beg.

The man doesn't say anything. He just stares at me with two ice-colored eyes that look like shards of glass ready to cut. And then he speaks: "Don't follow us. Don't contact the police. Go back to your Airbnb and you'll receive further instructions. If you go any-where else, or you tell anyone about what happened here"—his eyes tick toward Avery—"we'll kill her. You have one hour. Don't make us wait."

We. Us. Because someone else is driving. I didn't even register that fact until now. All of my logic washed away the second this man stepped out of the van holding death in his hand. I peer past him and try to see who's behind the wheel but all I can make out is the vague outline of someone else.

"Toss your phone into the van," the man orders.

With shaking fingers, I pull it from my pocket and lob it through the open door. The gun swings from Avery's temple and comes to rest on me before arcing right. He fires twice: *Crack! Crack!* One of the tires on the Jeep explodes.

When I look back to Avery, she's pressing a hand to her belly.

Oh god, the baby.

The thought is like a switchblade planted between my eyes—a bright splinter of pure panic. Because whoever these people are, they aren't just taking my wife.

They're also taking my child.

My eyes lock with Avery's. Tears stream down her cheeks. Her face is bone white. She says something I can't hear over the roar of the engine as the man pulls her inside. But I recognize the words. I see them in the way her mouth widens and the tip of her tongue lightly taps her upper row of her teeth. I feel them in the shape of her lips when they round into a soft O a second before the door slams shut.

I love you.

And then she's gone.